A CONVENIENT RISK

Sara R. Turnquist

To Tina —
Happy Reading!

Psalm 139:1-6

A Convenient Risk

by Sara R. Turnquist

For my husband, my biggest fan.

CHAPTER ONE

Beginnings and Endings

AMANDA STARED AT the blood on her hands. Her husband's blood. She was numb. Cried out. She shoved the door open with her hip and stepped into the fading day. Her focus was on the water pump across the yard. The few steps stretched out before her. Holding her hands away from her body, she moved toward it, not caring that she stirred the dust of the dry earth beneath her feet.

The pump's handle was solid and cold. She yanked her hand back. Jed's blood now stained the metal. It couldn't be helped. Grasping the handle once more, she pulled it up then pressed down. Her long blonde hair fell into her face. Amanda fought the urge to push it to the side. Again and again she pumped, until water began to flow from the spout. Thrusting her hands underneath, she rubbed at the dark red covering her skin.

Once all traces were gone, she tugged at her apron, wrapping her hands in the thin fabric. When she looked at them again, they shook. And she could still see the deep crimson upon them.

She blinked. The red vanished.

Spinning on the balls of her feet, she turned back toward the house. The clicking of her shoes alerted her that she was once again inside.

And the smell.

"Where were you?" A gruff voice greeted her.

She jerked in that direction.

The tall frame of the doctor filled the doorway to her bedroom. His scowl accused her.

"I needed some fresh air."

He shook his head. Had she disappointed him? "You were needed in here."

She nodded, lowering her gaze to the floor as she stepped toward him.

He held up his hands. "There's no point now. He's passed."

"What?" It wasn't possible.

The doctor moved past her, his shoulder grazing hers. "It was only a matter of time."

Amanda's heart stopped. Cold surrounded and pervaded her being. Her breath rushed out of her. Would she be able to draw in another?

In time, it did come, but with it came the tears. There were more. After all.

Brandon Miller pushed the paddock's gate closed and secured it. Gazing out across the moving cattle, he frowned. Would his efforts be enough? He doubted it. All the wishing in the world would not pay the bank.

He shoved away from the fence and turned toward the homestead. Time for lunch.

As he slipped into the house he spotted his uncle hobbling across the room. Rushing to the older man, Branson put an arm under the man's bad side. "Uncle Owen, you should have called Cook to help you."

"She's busy getting things ready for you and the boys. I couldn't bother her. 'Sides, I get around just fine."

Brandon shook his head. The man leaned even more on his nephew. His body was worn. Too many years abusing it. If he took another fall...

Best not to think about it.

They reached the dining table at last, and Brandon shifted his uncle's weight into one of the chairs.

Uncle Owen let out a sigh. Surely the man could not deny that it was becoming more difficult for him to get around the house.

The front door opened, and Brandon's ranch hands trailed in—dirty and dusty as ever. They were a misfit group indeed.

"Whatever Cook's got stewin' smells mighty good," Cutie, the smallest of the men, said as he turned his chair around backward and straddled it.

Brandon furrowed his brow. Cook wouldn't like that one bit.

Cutie glanced the other way.

Slim, who was tall and well built, not at all slim, cocked his head at Brandon. "Any idea when the new cattle are coming in?"

Brandon ran a hand through his thick brown hair. How was he going to answer? He had neither the money nor the means to procure additional cattle. Though his ranch desperately needed more for the auction if they were to make enough to sustain this place. Perhaps he should tell the men there had been some sort of delay.

He opened his mouth to speak, but Cook came into the room and all eyes fell on her.

"Now, I don't want to hear any more gums flappin'," Cook's voice boomed as she bustled around the men, first setting the dishes of food down and then grabbing for napkins and placing them in the men's laps. "Y'all best be eatin' up!"

Brandon smiled at the woman. How did she always know?

"Not this second!" She slapped Dan's hand when he reached for the serving fork. "You know how we do things. Grace first."

Dan glared at her but withdrew his hand.

Brandon gave the men a once over and then bowed his head, returning thanks for the food.

Only then did Cook nod and return to the kitchen.

Brandon couldn't help but notice that Uncle Owen watched after her until she disappeared through the doorway, leaving nothing but the clatter of pots and pans. Their dinner music.

Slim met Brandon's eyes. "So, boss, about those cows—"

"I hear chatter in there," Cook called.

Brandon looked down and shoved a bite of beef into his mouth. It was clear who ran this ranch.

❧ ⁘⁘⁘ ❧

Cold. The air whipping her hair chilled her face, but it couldn't touch her heart. That was already lost. Was this all she would ever feel? Perhaps that's what she deserved.

A small hand pulled at her skirt. Samuel. She couldn't forget him. He deserved better. More than what life had dealt him. Leaning down, she swept him into her arms and held him to her chest. If only there were some semblance of warmth there for him. It couldn't be helped.

"Don't cry, Mama." His tiny voice broke through the silence. Small hands framed her face. "Pa's in heaven, right?"

Nodding at her son with his simple faith, she set her forehead on his, closing her eyes so he couldn't see her tears.

Movement to her left gave her pause. But she dare not look. Probably another well-meaning friend come to comfort her. A face among many.

"They need to start." It was Reverend Mason.

Men with their shovels clanging fell into step behind him. Why now? Could she just have a few more minutes before time continued? Before the inevitable swept her along?

"Ma'am?" The preacher's voice was kind, but insistent.

Didn't he know her world was falling apart? That nothing would ever be the same? That she had lost the only one who ever knew…who ever understood…

A hand fell upon her arm, and she did not try to resist as the reverend tugged at her, pulling her away from the graveside.

She snuggled Samuel closer to her chest, placing a hand behind his head and pressing his little face into the crook of her neck. He didn't need to see. No, she couldn't let him see as the two men scooped dirt onto his father's casket.

"Mama, you're hurting me," came the muffled little voice.

She loosened her grip. And guilt slammed into her—she had caused enough pain, enough grief. No more. And certainly not for Samuel. He was everything.

"The next few days will be hard, Mrs. Haynes. Don't expect anything different. You will have to find a new normal. Life as you knew it is gone."

Amanda nodded numbly as she pressed a kiss to the side of Samuel's head. New normal. What did that mean? What was normal? Her husband had been ill for near three months. She had watched him waste away. And her child watched his father suffer until death released him.

Shouldn't they welcome a new normal? But Amanda would give anything to have Jed back. Not to hear his voice, or feel his arms one more time, but to know that everything was going to be all right. Was that selfish? Because right now, the future looked grim. How was she to care for Samuel? For herself? For the ranch?

The preacher stopped in front of Amanda's cart. They stood in silence for several moments.

"If you need anything, let me know. The church is of little means, but we may be able to help some."

Her eyes met his then. What could they do? The good church-going people of Wharton City barely managed to pay the reverend and keep the doors open. Help her? No. Amanda refused to lay herself on the mercy of the church. She would find a way.

"Thank you, Reverend, for your kind offer. We will manage."

Then he gave her a long look, his mouth a thin line. Who cared if he believed her? He lowered his voice. "Your parents, are they still back east?"

Her eyebrow shot up. What exactly was he getting at? That she should return to her parents' home? He didn't know what he was saying.

Holding her chin high, she maneuvered Samuel to her right hip so she could look the preacher square in the face. "Yes, sir, they are."

"Perhaps they would enjoy a visit—"

"I appreciate your kindnesses toward me and my son, Reverend Mason. If you'll excuse me, I have much to attend to at home."

The reverend's mouth fell open and shut, his eyes wide.

Amanda lifted Samuel into the cart and then, grabbing the bench firmly, pulled herself up.

Then, with a fire in her belly, she jerked the reins and prodded the horse forward.

***

Brandon perused the aisles of the General Store. He already had his purchases in hand, but there was no rush to return to the ranch. More questions, more doubts from his ranch hands awaited him.

Why couldn't they just trust him? Why couldn't he find the right answers? Just today, he'd had a run in with Mr. George C. Perkins. The banker was as slimy as they came. But Brandon needed to remain in his good graces.

His ranch would be forfeit if he didn't find some way to infuse it with added income. But where would such a salvation come from?

He moved closer to the front of the store. The clerk and the customer at the counter were talking. Perhaps he should wait before approaching with his wares. Still, he could not help but overhear...

"...I just can't imagine what the poor thing is going to do," the customer feigned Christianly consideration after someone.

Brandon suspected her real concern was a piece of gossip. But whom did they speak of? Had someone in the community fallen ill?

"Doesn't she have kin back east?" The clerk had stopped working altogether.

"Yes. But her parents are poor. Not much help there. Why, she'd have to find a way to make money. That little woman would end up supporting that son of hers and her parents, too," the woman prattled on.

Supporting? Now he was curious. Brandon wasn't one to listen to idle gossip, but he found himself intrigued. He picked a can up off the shelf and pretended to read the label.

"It's a shame. That ole' husband of hers wasn't the best, but at least he did give her something." Brandon wasn't looking, but the higher pitch of the customer's voice gave her away.

Ah. They must be talking about Amanda Haynes. He had heard Jed had passed away. Sick with tuberculosis these last couple months. Terrible shame.

"A name and a home." It was the lower tone of the clerk.

"And food on the table."

"She worked near as hard as he on that ranch. I bet she's the only reason it kept running."

That's right. Jed had a ranch. Not a large one, budding really. But it had cattle. And that was just what Brandon needed. Some cattle.

"Well, one thing's for sure, she can't run it by herself." That higher pitch was starting to unnerve him.

"Who knows what'll happen to her?"

"She'll have to take the first offer that comes along. She is mighty pretty."

"That is the truth."

Offer? Offer for what? Marriage? They were talking about a proposal. Well now, that would be one way to secure that cattle. Then they could both get what they want: he would offer security for her and her son, and he would get the cattle he needed for his ranch. Was it too perfect?

"Mr. Miller?"

Brandon jerked his head toward the sound. Had he spoken out loud?

The clerk and the customer, a tall woman with dark hair, were both staring at him.

"Yes?" He straightened.

"Can I help you with anything?"

"No, thank you." He held up the can. "I'm just looking at this…" Glancing at the label, he noted that it was infant food. Brandon quickly put it behind his back. "I'm checking out what you have over here. Can't say I've noticed this shelf before." His face warmed.

The clerk quirked a brow. "All right. If you need anything, let me know." She turned back to the customer, but continued to give him sideways glances.

Brandon put the infant food back on the shelf and rubbed his palms, now sweating, on his trouser legs. Then he took several deep breaths. Was this plan sane? Or was he crazy?

Glancing at the clerk, he noticed her looking in his direction, but her voice was lowered to the point he could no longer hear her conversation.

He needed to get out of there. Then he would be able to think.

Taking his wares to the counter, he paid, mumbling simple pleasantries along the way. Relief washed over him when he stepped into the sunlight. He had to make a plan. And soon.

* * *

Amanda heaved a sigh as she picked up the bucket of water. Why did she have to fill it so full? Because she loathed making multiple trips. So, she walked back toward the house, leaning to one side, her shoulder nearly pulling out of its socket as she carried her load.

She climbed the porch steps with much effort and breathed in relief when she reached the door. Pressing on it with her body, she was startled when it didn't give way under her weight. Water sloshed onto her dress hem and shoes.

After releasing one hand's hold on the bucket, she worked the latch.

Nothing.

What?

Samuel.

Had he locked the door? Again?

Slamming her palm against the rough wood, she called out. "Samuel, let Mama in."

A giggle sounded from the other side.

She groaned. "Samuel, this is not a time to play games. Mama needs to get in the house."

More laughing.

The water's weight became more than her arm could bear, forcing her to set it down.

"Mama wants you to open the door right now, young man." Amanda tried not to let her anger into her voice, but it came through in her raised volume.

Banging both of her flat hands on the door, and then shaking on the latch, she began to lose her tightly held control. "Samuel Isaac Haynes, do you hear me?"

"Is there a problem, ma'am?" a voice behind her spoke.

She spun toward the sound. A dark-haired man sat on a caramel colored horse. Had she see him before? He had a dark, scruffy beard that had probably only been growing for a couple days. His equally dark eyes seemed to look through her. Ah, yes, he was another rancher. What was his name? Something Miller...

"Ma'am?"

She realized she had failed to answer him.

Taking a step away from the door, she squared her shoulders. "I am perfectly well. I seem to be...temporarily locked out of my home. But it's nothing to concern yourself with, Mr. Miller."

His eyebrows raised for just a moment. Surprise? At her comment? Or surprise that she knew his name? It didn't matter. "What can I help you with, sir?"

He remained silent for a moment, and then looked down at his hands on the pommel of his saddle. "I was...ah...hoping I could speak with you."

Her eyes held his. She crossed her arms in front of herself. "As you are."

His face colored, and he nodded. "Yes, that I am." He licked his lips and looked from side to side. "Perhaps this is not the best time." Dark eyes shot to the locked door.

Amanda's temper flared. "I can assure you, Mr. Miller, I am quite well. And whatever your business is, I am certain now is as good a time as any."

Mr. Miller's face became slack, and his eyes widened. It was several seconds before he seemed to gather his wits. Then he spoke. "The thing is that I have a, um, proposal...that is, a proposition for you."

Amanda's brows furrowed. "Proposal?" A marriage offer so soon?

Her husband was not yet one week in the ground. He couldn't be serious.

Mr. Miller continued to shift and fidget in his saddle. "Yes. I, ah, know about…that is, I understand that your situation is, well, you have no means to care for yourself and your son…"

Fire ignited in her belly. Couldn't care for herself and her son? Of course she could! She would do anything…everything…her shoulders fell. Of course he was right. Her hands were tied. There was no real work for a woman in her position. How would she support herself and Samuel?

That very question had kept her awake every night since Jed's condition turned serious. But that didn't mean she had to take any offer that came her way. Did it?

Amanda eyed Mr. Miller. He seemed a pleasant enough fellow. She searched her memory. What did she know of him? Not much. Although she had never been much of a busy body, keeping mostly to the ranch and the home. All she truly knew was his surname.

"Mrs. Haynes?"

Shaking her head, she refocused on him. "I'm sorry, what?" Had he continued talking?

"I said that I could take care of you and your son, offer you the kind of stability you need. A home, food, whatever you need to be comfortable."

Her eyes narrowed. "Why would you do this?" What was he after? She watched his eyes closely. Was that a leer? Or just an insecurity?

He cleared his throat. "I am in a position of needing to expand my ranch. If possible, I would like to take on your late husband's herd."

Relief washed over her. He didn't have designs on her. They would each bring something to the table. A deal.

Would he want her to also share his bed?

"Would I have my own room?"

The man blinked as if that had not occurred to him. Had it not? "Yes, ma'am." There it was again, the reddening of his face.

She released her arms and let them fall by her sides, eyeing the ground. Should she take this offer? Was there likely to be another? Or one so gracious?

Interlacing her fingers at hip level, she met his eyes again, opening her mouth to speak.

But he spoke before she could. "I'll give you some time to think about it."

She closed her mouth and nodded. That would be best. Not a quick decision. "Thank you, Mr. Miller."

"I'll call again tomorrow afternoon." He pointed behind her. "But I think you're other problem may be solved."

She spun around.

Samuel stood in the doorway, door opened just enough for his face to fit through. How much had he heard?

Amanda jerked her foot back to stop the door.

Samuel ducked back inside and pushed on the door, but it wouldn't budge with her foot in the way.

"Good luck," Mr. Miller called, tipping his hat.

Amanda smiled and nodded before turning back toward her son and forcing the door wider. "Samuel James, you are in big trouble!"

As Samuel ran further into the house, Amanda couldn't help but glance over her shoulder at the retreating figure on horseback.

The truth was that his offer was fair. Probably the best she could hope for. If she received another offer of marriage, it would likely include a different understanding. Concessions she wasn't sure she would be willing to make. But, in her situation, she might have to.

Perhaps Mr. Miller would have a deal after all.

⁕⁕⁕

Brandon fidgeted with the cuffs of his best Sunday jacket. Moisture beaded on his forehead. Was it warm in here? He shot a glance at the preacher. The man seemed fairly comfortable in his jacket.

Perhaps it was something else then. He gazed at the ceiling and took some deep breaths. Was he truly that nervous? Why? It wasn't as if this was a real marriage. Though it was the only one he would ever have.

He never had such silly notions as love. That was a grand idea, but did those marriages ever work out? His parents had been matched for better reasons and they seemed well suited for one another. Surely that was wisdom enough to seek a more logical process for choosing one's life partner.

And what he knew of Amanda Haynes, though little, did not put him off. She was pleasant enough to gaze upon. Everyone that spoke of her told of what a good wife she was. The only criticism Cook ever heard tell of was that she kept to herself. He could find no fault in that. It may even be a trait that earned her admiration in his eyes.

A hand landed on his shoulder.

He turned.

Reverend Mason looked at him. "I'm certain she will be here any moment."

Brandon nodded. How long had it been? Was she late? He glanced at Uncle Owen and Cook, seated in the first pew.

Uncle Owen gave him a nod and a smile.

Was he doing the right thing? No doubt he did the prudent thing. For this poor widow and for his own ranch. But did he preclude her from finding love again? That is, if she put such stock in these things.

The door to the small church opened, breaking his thoughts.

Amanda stepped in, holding her son's hand, straggling behind. As she walked down the aisle toward him, her eyes remained glued to the floor. But his were on her. Would he remember how she looked this day?

She wore a cream-colored blouse trimmed in lace fabric. Her skirt was smooth and pink. Perhaps her best church outfit. Had he expected a white dress? No, that would not have been appropriate for a woman who had…well, who had already been married.

Her long, blonde hair had been pulled back and up in an attractive style with curls piled on top. She had even adorned the right side with flowers, which matched the bouquet she carried.

The boy did not seem truly aware or pleased at the circumstances. He scowled as his mother pulled him along. As she neared the front of the church, she set him on the front pew opposite Uncle Owen and Cook. She spoke some words to him in hushed tones. He whined in protest, but soon quieted. Then she pressed a kiss to his hair, and he leaned back, folding his arms across his chest.

What was Brandon going to do about the boy? He hadn't considered how the youngster would feel about a new man in his mother's life. And so soon after his father's death. But nothing could be done about it at this point. Sometimes very adult decisions had to be made regardless.

Amanda turned and faced Brandon, smoothing a hand down her skirt. Then her eyes were on his.

And his breath caught.

She was quite a sight, up close. Her cheeks were flushed and eyes bright from the slight exertion. That only served to highlight her features.

"Sorry I'm late." Her words came out in a breath.

Brandon opened his mouth to speak, but no words came out. So, he closed his mouth and simply nodded.

"If everyone is ready, we can begin." The preacher stepped closer.

Amanda nodded, licking her lips and grasping her flowers. Did he see a slight tremble in the delicate buds?

"Yes, Reverend," he said, swallowing against a dry mouth. He shifted to face Reverend Mason and sensed Amanda do the same.

The preacher spoke words about the institution of marriage, but Brandon had a difficult time listening. He found himself stealing glances at Amanda. What was she thinking? Did she have second thoughts? Regrets?

Still, they moved through the ceremony, responding in turn when they were asked.

Amanda spoke the words that would bind her to Brandon without hesitation. Should it surprise him? It did.

"Now it is time for the presentation of the ring." Reverend Mason turned toward Brandon. "Do you have the ring?"

Brandon reached in his pocket and produced the circlet of gold.

"Will you take the ring and place it on your bride's finger and repeat after me?"

Brandon spoke the words after the preacher as he took Amanda's smaller hand in his underneath the bouquet. Sliding the ring on her finger, which seemed impossibly smaller than his, he was surprised when he encountered resistance.

Her other wedding band.

His eyes shot to hers.

Hazel eyes widened and slid closed.

Reverend Mason, having paused, spoke in that moment. "Is there a problem?"

Brandon slid his wedding band off her finger.

Amanda pulled her hand out from under the bouquet.

The preacher's brows shot up. "I see." He eyed Brandon.

As did Amanda.

Everyone seemed to be waiting on him with baited breath. What was he to do? Was it his place to remove Jed's wedding band? Surely that was something she needed to do. But everyone looked at him as if he should act.

So, he reached for her hand once more.

Her eyes flitted between his and the wedding band on her finger.

He gently grasped it and pulled. It wouldn't come. Twisting a little, he felt it budge. From there, it took little work to get Jed's wedding band off.

His face warmed. Why did he have to do that? It just wasn't right. To remove another man's claim on his wife. She should have been the one to do it.

But he held fast as he slid his wedding band onto her finger.

Reverend Mason let out a sigh and continued, instructing Amanda to place her hand in Brandon's.

He held out an open hand to her, but he now held Jed's wedding band.

As her fingers reached for his, they hovered for just a moment over her former band. Perhaps no one else would have noticed. But Brandon did. And why shouldn't she? It had been on her finger for years. She must be loath to part with it, perhaps one of the last pieces of her husband she had left.

Still, she pressed her fingers over his as instructed.

Brandon closed his hand around hers. And he continued to watch her face, but her eyes shifted toward the preacher soon after. Was she afraid? Embarrassed? He had not meant to offend her.

But soon after he turned his attention toward the preacher as well for the remainder of the simple ceremony. It wasn't long before Reverend Mason spoke the final words and declared them husband and wife.

"You may now kiss your bride."

Brandon looked at Amanda.

She didn't meet his eyes. Her gaze caught on his chest.

Why had he not thought about this particular part of the ceremony? The woman seemed so scared, so vulnerable. She needn't be.

He leaned forward, tilting his head down and pressed a kiss to the side of her face before pulling back.

When she met his gaze, her eyes were wide. Did she wonder at his simple contact? He wanted nothing more from her than what they had discussed. If she feared differently, then she was mistaken.

All he wanted…needed was that cattle. He needed it desperately. Now it was his. And that was all that mattered. Wasn't it?

CHAPTER TWO

New Life

AMANDA AWOKE TO another day. What would it bring? It had been late the previous day when she and Samuel had finally moved into Brandon's home. Not that he saw to it. He had been too concerned with Jed's cattle. When he said he was only interested in the herd, he had spoken truthfully. Shouldn't she be grateful?

Part of her wondered, though. Should she have protected Jed's legacy better? Been more selective about her partner?

But she hadn't a choice. Not truly. There were not likely to be many offers forthcoming. Not with a child. And Brandon seemed decent enough. At least he didn't expect marital favors from her to boot.

Cook and Slim had seen to her and Samuel's things. They had been nice to her. Though she insisted she could manage, Cook would not let her lift a finger to move in. Which caused Amanda to wonder, with that woman to run the house, what was left for Amanda to do?

Sitting up in the bed, she stretched. How was she to make a life in this strange place? A fine window had been carved out in one wall of the bedroom. She moved over to it and drew the curtain to the side. Through it, she could see the barn and a portion of the herd grazing. A fair prospect.

Moving through her morning routine, she became stuck on what to wear. Was it inappropriate to continue to wear mourning attire? She still wanted to honor Jed's memory, but didn't want to offend Brandon. Then again, he hadn't seemed to care much about what she did.

Black it was.

After donning her dress, she stepped into the hall, straining her ears. Pots and pans clanged in the kitchen further away. But that was the only evidence of life beyond her small quarters. Taking another step across the space, she knocked on Samuel's door.

A muffled groan greeted her. She smiled in spite of herself. At least this remained the same: Samuel liked his sleep.

"Samuel, it's Mama."

She pushed the door open and slipped into his room.

Her small man lay bundled in his sheet and quilt, still snoozing.

Crouching by his bed, she laid a hand on his back and shook him. "Time to wake up, my sleepy head." Leaning forward, she pressed a kiss to his mussed hair.

He groaned and stirred.

She sang a bright little tune to help him welcome the day.

Samuel turned his face toward her and smiled.

"There's my sweet boy." She rubbed the hair at the top of his head and swept errant strands from his forehead.

He opened his eyes and looked up at her as she continued to caress his face.

"Mama?"

"Mmm hmm?"

"When are we going home?"

She sighed. Why did he have to make this harder? "This is our home now."

He groaned again and turned away from her.

She laid her hands on his back. "Come on, sweetheart. We talked about this. Mr. Miller is going to take care of us."

"I thought you were going to take care of us."

A dagger pierced her heart. It couldn't have hurt more if it had been real.

"You know I wanted to." Her voice broke. "But I…" She couldn't finish that sentence. How could she tell him that she wasn't capable? That a woman in her position only had two choices? Get married or go crawling back home to her parents? And the latter was not an option she was willing to entertain.

Samuel flipped around to face her. "Don't be sad, Mama. I'm sorry." He raised up in the bed and leaned toward her.

She swept him into her arms and held him fast. He was everything to her. How could she not keep him safe from the harsh realities of the world? From her own ineptitude?

Kissing the side of his face, she struggled to contain her emotion. "What do you say we help get breakfast going?"

He nodded against her shoulder.

Amanda rubbed his back as he pulled away from her. She watched as he walked toward his trunk. And her heart continued to ache. For him. For herself. For the loss of their place in the world.

*   *   *

The smells of breakfast cooking stirred Brandon from sleep. He jerked awake. How had he lingered so long? Now in a seated position, he wondered where he was. Glancing around the room, he remembered. Uncle Owen's room.

But he was alone.

How had the older man risen, dressed, and hunkered out without waking his nephew? Brandon had never been the heaviest sleeper. But a late night rustling Jed's cattle had worn on him.

Rubbing his eyes and yawning, he rose and then stretched long, releasing any lingering sleep from his muscles.

A shriek sounded from the other side of the wall causing his head to jerk in that direction. The voice gave way to laughter, and his body calmed. These were uncommon sounds indeed.

The house was always still as death when he rose. And he cherished his early morning walk of the grounds before returning to a house alive with Cook's meal preparations.

What had her in such fits this morning? Uncle Owen? Brandon had his suspicions about the two of them.

After dressing in a hurry, he then moved in the direction of the kitchen. The sight that greeted him gave him pause.

Cook stood in the middle of the room watching Amanda Haynes work. The young widow rolled out something that appeared to be dough.

Uncle Owen sat nearby in a dining room chair. Had Cook allowed him to bring one in? The young boy sat above Uncle Owen on a counter.

He looked down on the older man working a knife against a block of wood. Whittling? Uncle Owen? The man hadn't picked up a knife in months! Said his hands were too stiff.

"Then you just roll the dough as usual and cut out the biscuits," Amanda said, her back to Brandon.

"Well, I declare!" Cook slapped her leg. "I never would have thought."

"It makes them nice and fluffy." Amanda turned to look at Cook, and Brandon saw her in profile. A hair fell in her face, and she moved her hand to sweep it back, brushing flour across her forehead. It only heightened the beauty of her features.

Brandon shifted his weight, and a floorboard creaked.

All eyes turned on him.

Amanda handed the rolling pin to Cook and clasped her hands in front of her hips, ducking her head as if she had done something wrong.

Cook offered him a wide grin. "Good morning, lazy bones. Nice of you to join us."

Uncle Owen laughed and turned his attention back to his whittling.

"I…suppose I was tired." Brandon stepped farther into the room.

"I suppose you were," Cook said, winking at Amanda and grabbing for the biscuit cutter. She then pressed it into the sheet of dough.

Amanda took a step away from Cook and over to the nearby table that bore a stack of pans. She placed a hand on the surface, running her fingers along the wood. "If you will point me toward the plates, I can set the table."

"You've done enough. Please, sit. Take a load off." Cook looked between her and Brandon.

"Yes," Brandon chimed in. "Please, sit." He took a step toward her, hand stretched out in the direction of the dining room.

As he drew closer, she moved away, as if repelled by his presence. Tossing a glance at Samuel, she then turned and walked where Brandon had indicated.

Once they stepped through the swinging door, they were alone.

Her eyes wandered over the empty chairs. Was she unsure whether or not she should sit? Should he sit first?

Brandon reached for the chair closest to the door and, pulling it out, settled into it. Then he met Amanda's eyes.

Her brow quirked.

He indicated the seat across the table.

She moved toward it and situated herself there, somewhat hesitantly.

Now that they were seated, Brandon realized how awkward it was for them to be sitting, with no food, and nothing to talk about.

He splayed his hands on the table, suddenly interested in the pattern of the wood.

Her chair creaked as she shifted, smoothing over her skirt.

Only then did he notice she was dressed head to toe in black. Why? Their marriage had brought an end to her mourning. Should he be bothered that his wife still mourned her first husband? Because he couldn't find it in his heart to fault her. The man was buried not two weeks ago. No one could expect her to be rid of him.

Her eyes met his. Had he been staring? He must have been.

"I'll get us some coffee." He stood, nearly toppling his chair he rose so abruptly.

"I can get that…" Amanda started, rising as well and coming around the table.

They came to the door at the same time, hands touching when they reached to push it open.

Brandon drew back at the contact.

As did Amanda. She clasped her hand with the other, staring at the door.

And he once again found himself watching her.

"I'm sorry. I just—" he started.

"No, I thought I—" she said at the same time.

Her eyes slowly came up to meet his.

He let out a sigh. "I don't want you to be uneasy around me."

She remained silent for a few moments, eyes falling to the floor.

"This is your home now, too. I want you to feel comfortable. But I don't want you to think you have to treat me any sort of way."

Amanda's eyes rose to meet his again.

"Aaah…" He shrugged, looking at the floor. "I'm not saying the right thing here." He turned to walk away.

She put a hand on his forearm.

He froze at the contact, eyes on her small hand, then on her face.

"No, Mr. Miller, you're doing just fine. I just…I don't know how to say 'thank you.' You don't know how much your kindness means to me."

He nodded.

She offered him a small smile, which he returned. "How about I get us that coffee?"

"All right." She let her hand fall from his arm. Then she stepped back toward the table.

He held up a hand to the door, but paused. "And it's 'Brandon'."

She turned. "Pardon?"

"As opposed to 'Mr. Miller.' Everyone here calls me 'Brandon'."

"Brandon." She nodded.

He flashed her one of his more charming smiles, showing his teeth.

This may be the beginning of a perfectly amiable relationship.

Grass crunched beneath her feet. Amanda gazed across the pasture at the movement of the herd. A beautiful sight. How she longed to get her hands dirty again! But she had not found a way to make herself useful yet.

Could she don a pair of work gloves, grab a rope, and work alongside the ranch hands as she had at home? Jed never had a problem with it. In fact, he had appreciated her hard work.

More than once, when she'd been injured, he had even said he missed her working alongside him. Yes, she had been wanted. Needed. And it was wonderful.

Not here. All Brandon wanted was Jed's cattle.

Drawing her attention back to the other side of the fence, she watched the movement of the red-brown and white animals as they brushed against each other, seeking out the best grass.

But she continued to walk. Could she even distinguish Jed's cattle from Brandon's? Had he branded them yet? If his desire to attain them had been any indication, then he had done so that very night.

A figure approached, riding a painted horse, moving along the fence line. As he came closer, she noted the shorter stature of the man—Cutie. He tipped his hat as he drew near.

She waved, hoping he would keep on riding by.

"G'day, Mrs. Miller."

Why did they have to call her that? Some misplaced form of respect? She never knew if she should insist they call her 'Amanda.' Perhaps she should ask Brandon.

"Good day!"

Cutie pulled on the reins, bringing the horse to a halt.

She held a hand over her eyes. "What can I do for you?"

He shrugged. "I was about to ask you the same thing."

"I'm just out for a walk. Enjoying the sights and sounds."

"Probably not the smells." He smiled as his horse shifted beneath him.

She returned his smile. "I'm used to it."

He raised an eyebrow.

Amanda looked down the fence line from whence he had come. "Checking for damage?"

His gaze followed hers. "There was a storm last night. Gotta make sure no tree limbs fell on any of the posts."

"A storm?" Her question was not one of surprise. A light sleeper, she had been up from the moment the first gust of wind blew past the house.

"Yeah. It didn't wake you?"

She shook her head and chose not to share her sleeping habits with this young man she didn't know all that well.

"It sure did bother old Daisy."

The dog. Amanda had only once chanced upon the hound dog that lived in the barn. A pleasant enough creature, it had no objections to Amanda, so she had none for the aging animal.

"She howled most of the night. Kept us up."

"I'm sorry to hear that."

Cutie nodded and watched Amanda's face for a few more moments. His stare became a little more intense than Amanda was comfortable with.

"I think I'll head toward the creek. This way?" Amanda pointed down the gently sloped hill.

"Yes, ma'am. Keep walking toward that tree line a piece. It's just past it."

"Thank you, Cutie." She offered him another smile and then turned in that direction.

He made a clicking sound with his tongue and then there were only hoof beats.

Moments later, she looked over her shoulder. He was nearly out of sight. She put a hand on her stomach and let out a sigh. Should she feel more comfortable around these men? Something still made her feel uneasy. Like she wasn't quite welcome.

Crack! A sickening snap off to her right drew her attention. From somewhere within the herd came the cry of a wounded animal.

Amanda leaned on the fence and scanned for what she feared may have happened. But the cows would not move out of the way. There was only one thing that sound could be—an injured calf, perhaps its leg broken from being stepped on.

Looking in the direction Cutie had gone, she hoped against hope that she could wave him down. It was no use. He had disappeared from sight.

What should she do? She couldn't leave the animal to suffer. The barn was too far away. Could she carry the calf herself? She would have to. Besides, she had done plenty of ranch work alongside Jed and his ranch hands. Including much work with the calves. Surely, she could carry the smaller animal.

Jumping onto the fence near the post, she scaled the wooden beams as gracefully as she could. Yet she was thankful she did so without an audience. And then she was in the pasture. But she was not alarmed. She had been in with the herd many times.

Moving slowly so as not to startle any of the larger animals, she maneuvered between them toward the unearthly screeches. Moments later, she saw the injured youngling. It lay on the ground, its leg at an odd angle. Amanda's stomach turned, but she fought the wave of nausea that threatened to overcome her.

Amanda knelt next to the poor creature. It was much bigger than she had anticipated. How old was this calf? There was no way she could carry it. Looking up, she searched for Brandon or one of his ranch hands. That was a mistake. The cattle loomed over her, all around. She almost fell back from the intensity of their glares.

A loud huffing sounded from several feet away over her left shoulder. She turned. And found herself staring into the eyes of an angry bull.

⌘

One of the things Brandon loved about ranching was the routine of it all. The chores were the same each day. All the cows and horses needed the same things as they did the day before. There was just enough variety to keep things interesting. Brandon was not someone who liked drastic changes.

And this marriage had brought a drastic change. A beautiful woman and a small boy now lived in his home. If that wasn't enough, she seemed to show up everywhere he turned. It just wasn't suiting him. In fact, it was downright distracting.

Brandon finished putting out his horse's food, stepped out of the mare's way, and secured the stall door. He reached in and gave his horse a pat on the neck and rubbed Candy's soft muzzle.

"Good girl. Eat now."

He grasped a pile of rope in disarray from nearby and strode out of the barn.

Cutie rode up, stirring a cloud of dust.

"How does the perimeter look?" Brandon glanced down the fence line, imagining he could see all the way to its edges.

"I checked everything but the west side, Boss. Gonna go out there next."

Brandon nodded and continued looping the rope.

"What the…?"

He jerked his head around.

Cutie's horse bucked and pulled.

"Cutie?" Brandon hung his rope on the closest fencepost and moved toward the horse.

"I think something is wrong with one of Patch's shoes." Cutie pulled at the reins, but the animal would not still.

Brandon held out his arms to halt the animal, but the horse continued to shift and stir. At last, he was able to grab the bit and hold Patch while Cutie slid off.

"Take her inside and check it out. The fence inspection can wait."

Cutie nodded, taking the horse's bit and leading her into the barn.

Brandon watched them go. They'd had about all the bad luck they could stand for a while.

A breeze blew over him, carrying with it a strange sound. Like a screech. Brandon inclined his head in that direction.

What was it? An injured cow? He scanned the pasture for any sign of Slim or Dan. Both were supposed to be watching over the herd. Neither was in sight. Should he wait for them to catch it or check it out himself?

⁎⁎⁎

The bull continued to eye Amanda. She rose to her feet with slow movements. Was it her imagination or did the bull tilt its head?

Should she run? Glancing the fence line out of the corner of her eye, she noted the distance that fell between her and her destination. She would never make it.

The large animal nodded its head, up and down, up and down, its horns rather prominently displayed. And the warmth drained from Amanda's body.

Then the bull looked past her. Somewhere into the distance. Why?

Straining her ears, she heard it—hoof beats—slowing as they approached. Dare she turn to see who was brave enough to come to her rescue?

"Do not move," a calm voice said.

Brandon! Relief poured through her. He would know what to do, wouldn't he?

The calf continued to screech. And though it tugged at her heart, she could do nothing to help the injured animal.

Brandon was near. She could sense it. And he continued to inch his horse forward. The thumping of the horse's hooves on the grass allowed her to track the mare's location.

The bull flicked his tail back and forth, but kept watching her.

Warmth now emanated from the horse's body as Brandon pulled up next to her.

Brandon spoke, his words coming as if chosen with care. "I'm going to take off my shirt…"

What? What was he doing? Why would he take off his shirt? Her heart raced. Still, she had no choice but to trust him.

In her periphery, she saw movement as Brandon unbuttoned his shirt and slid it off.

"Raise your right arm to me. I'm going to lift you onto the horse and then I need you to hold on to me. Tight."

Licking her lips, she nodded. Would she be able to do this? Then she closed her eyes. She had to.

"Are you ready?" His voice was calm. Too calm.

Amanda opened her eyes. "Yes." Would she survive this? With a shaky hand, she raised her arm closest to him.

The bull snorted.

A strong arm grasped her, catching her upper arm and dragging her onto the horse. As soon as she was solidly on the animal, she grabbed ahold of Brandon as tightly as she could.

They took off. The bull pawed at the ground, making all manner of grunting noises, but as if by some miracle, he ran off to the left. All of this happened as if time had slowed.

The horse continued to push forward. And as they neared the edge of the fence, Brandon urged the horse to go even faster. Were they going to break through? What would happen to the cattle with the fence destroyed?

But as they approached the fence, the horse leapt. Amanda gripped Brandon impossibly tighter. Jolted when the horse landed, her teeth chattered.

Only then did Brandon slow the horse. He then placed a hand on her upper arm and pushed.

She released him.

He sucked in a deep breath and expelled it.

Had she been holding him too tightly? Her face warmed.

He took hold of her shoulders. "Are you all right?"

She nodded, and though their faces were but a breath apart, she was not quite able to meet his eyes, fighting tears in her own. Only then she found herself staring at his bare chest. Jerking her head away, she averted her gaze.

"Do you realize what could have happened?" His voice rose.

She nodded, still not able to meet his eyes. The force of his emotion hit her. Was he so concerned after her?

"I would have had to shoot that bull."

What? Eyes wide, she tilted her face up to look at him.

"That bull is worth half my herd."

So he was only worried about the cattle. Not her. His precious cattle.

"I was just trying to save the calf—"

"You should never have gone over the fence." There was no forgiveness in his voice. "These are matters for me and my ranch hands. You are not capable—"

There was that fire again. In the pit of her stomach. "I assure you, Mr. Miller, I am quite capable. I was simply unaware that it was breeding season."

His eyes were hard, but she refused to give an inch.

"Just promise me that in the future, you will leave these things to the men. You are not one of my ranch hands."

What could she say? Clearly, she was not welcome on the ranch either. Cook took care of the house, and Brandon took care of the ranch. And she…she was an unwelcome guest in his home.

She swallowed against a lump in her throat. *Don't cry. Not now.* "As you wish."

Her hands became rather warm. She looked down. They were

balancing her by resting on his legs. Jerking them back to herself, she almost toppled over.

Brandon grabbed for her shoulders. His tone softened when he spoke again. "You've just been through quite an ordeal. I shouldn't have yelled like that. I'm sorry."

Yelled? He hadn't yelled. Not truly. Spoken firmly, yes. But not yelled. Not like Jed when…

"Let me get you back to the house." He reached his arms around her to grasp the reins again. With his arms surrounding her, she had no choice, but to lean against his bare chest.

"Wait!" She put a hand against him. Then pulled back from the contact with his skin.

Their eyes met.

She broke away first.

He seemed confused.

"What's going to happen to the calf?"

"I'll send Dan or Slim after it. But I need to get you settled first."

Then, without further discussion, he whipped the reins, and the horse moved forward, as she pressed her back against him. Maybe he did care. If only a little.

And then she wondered what he had done with his shirt. She had a vague memory of something flying overhead as he lifted her. Had he thrown his shirt? Had that served as a distraction for their getaway? Was that the miracle?

As they neared the house, she began to wonder what the others might think with Brandon shirtless and she a mused mess. Would they think she and Brandon had…? That the bull story was made up?

She prayed they believed. What would it mean for the others to think that of her? That she might have moved on? What would Samuel think if such talk reached his ears?

CHAPTER THREE

Trouble

BRANDON PAUSED AND let out a long breath. His horse shifted underneath him. Overseeing the herd during the day was not his favorite job, nor was it one he dreaded.

He did enjoy being among the herd. His herd. As his chest expanded, warmed by that thought, his gaze drifted across the pasture. This field held the cattle that had once belonged to Jed. No longer. All that Jed had now belonged to Brandon. Including his headstrong wife.

What was he to do with the woman? What was the chance of her risking her life again?

He raised his face heavenward and sent up a silent prayer of gratitude that he and Amanda had both survived the events of the other day. Beyond that, he did not know what he ought to say.

His thoughts were a jumbled mess. He could not grasp anything clearly. So, he sat in silence and let the Holy Spirit pray for him. That brought him some peace.

When he thought of Amanda, the bull loomed before him and fear welled within him, threatening to choke him. The same fear he felt the day before when he had come upon the scene. He had been terrified for her.

Should he have grabbed for his gun and shot the bull? That might have wounded the animal. And a wounded animal was even more dangerous. No, he had done the right thing. Only, his anger had then gotten the best of him. And his pride.

Lord, forgive me, my pride! Was it so wrong to be thusly overcome? Rubbing a hand across his forehead, he attempted to wipe the images from his memory. It was no use. The growing tension in him, the relief as he held her securely in his arms, the warmth that spread through him at her nearness…the way she clung to him and looked at him that day. He had almost lost his resolve.

All of it rushed through him anew. And he experienced every emotion as if time slowed.

Oh, God.

What was he going to do? He could not allow this to continue. She must stay out of harm's way. How was he to accomplish this? There must be limitations, boundaries.

What if he could prevent these things from happening in the future? If she would only stay away from certain places. He had already forbidden her from the pasturelands, going over the fence. But would that be enough?

So many things in the barn could be problematic. The horses, the tools, the hayloft… It would just be best if she didn't venture into the barn.

Yes, that would work. Perhaps he could even consign her to the homestead. He pictured it in his mind, and the plan seemed well laid out. All that remained was delivering the edict.

⁓෴ℰ ℰ෴⁓

Amanda leaned against the front porch post and smiled. Samuel had taken a liking to that old dog after all. He and Daisy chased each other in the large side yard between the house and barn. Picking up a stick, he then shook it toward the animal. Daisy jumped, gaining more height than Amanda would have given her credit for.

At least Samuel had adjusted well. Between Uncle Owen and Cook, they had made sure the boy felt welcomed and included. Uncle Owen taught Samuel to whittle, which Amanda remained skeptical about, and Cook had made him cookies every day since their arrival.

Amanda gazed off toward the horizon. The setting sun split the sky with an array of colors soothing her worn nerves. She had nearly recovered from her near-miss two days past. Scanning the pastures, she noted that the cattle had not missed a beat. They had not a care for the happenings of one woman. No, they just kept on grazing.

Samuel's laughter drew her attention back to the yard, but as her eyes drifted over the pastureland, she noted the pond in the distance. Odd that it should catch her attention. Why did it?

Narrowing her gaze, she focused on the pleasant little water source and the cattle munching nearby. Jed had a similar pond on his land, however he did not allow the cattle to remain in that particular pasture long before rotating them to another field. What had he said about standing water? She couldn't remember. But there had been some reason he didn't let them graze there for prolonged periods.

Shifting her focus back to Samuel, she smiled again as he and Daisy ran around the yard. Her heart warmed. Indeed, Samuel had adjusted well to his new life here. Perhaps she would in time.

A loud snort to her right gave her pause. She turned her head in time to see Brandon approaching on his caramel-colored horse.

He pulled on the reins as he neared the porch. His eyes met hers, and he tipped his hat.

They had not been alone since her rescue. And he had barely spoken two words to her at breakfast that morning.

"Good day." A smile tugged at the corner of his mouth, yet his lips maintained their neutrality.

She moved around the post so it wasn't blocking her and tipped her head. "Afternoon."

His head inclined toward Samuel and the old dog. "I see Daisy has made a new friend."

"Yes, I believe she has." Why did things have to be so awkward?

A silence fell between them.

Brandon shifted in his saddle. Why didn't he dismount?

"Are you well?" He looked at her again. "I mean, after the other day…with the bull."

Her face warmed. "Yes." And she was, except for a few bruises on the area he had grabbed to pull her to safety. She crossed her arms, rubbing a hand along her upper arm where the marks remained covered by a light sleeve.

"Good."

Silence again.

Awkward silence.

"I wanted to apologize—" he started.

At the same time, she said, "I never said thank you for—"

They both paused.

She offered him a timid smile and then looked at the ground, suddenly rather interested in the wooden boards that made up the porch. Would this tension dissipate as they became accustomed to each other?

"Please," Brandon said, breaking into her thoughts. "Ladies first."

Amanda met his gaze again. "I never said thank you for what you did." The last word was broken. He deserved her gratitude, but once again, she found herself leaning on someone. She had been useless.

Brandon nodded, but did not smile. He then looked off into the distance. Was he uncomfortable with her words? Should she not have said anything?

Then his brown eyes were on her again. "I wanted to apologize for my behavior."

Her eyes widened. His behavior? What could he mean?

"I reacted badly and chose my words even more poorly."

In her mind's eye, she replayed the incident. She could not find fault in his words. He only spoke the truth of it. His bull was worth half his herd, and her thoughtlessness could have cost him the prize animal.

"Amanda?"

She raised her head to meet his eyes, only then realizing she had been staring at the boards of the porch again. "Yes?"

"Will you accept my apology?" His brown eyes were warm and soft in that moment. He seemed sincere. Regardless of her belief in the necessity of it, he meant it.

"Of course."

He nodded. His whole body seemed to relax. "Thank you."

She smiled and forced herself to uncross her arms.

Brandon then pulled the reins to the right, turning the horse. "I'll get back to the cattle then."

"Mr. Miller," she called, holding out a hand as if that would halt him.

He did pause, turning the horse back toward the porch, maneuvering the animal closer to her.

She caught herself. Should she say something about the pond? It was none of her business. Truly, she shouldn't get involved. But these were Jed's cattle, too, and she had a duty to see that they were well cared for. Yes, it was best she speak up.

"I just wondered… How long have the cattle been in the pasture with the pond?"

Brandon looked over at the field in question and then back at Amanda, eyebrow quirked. "A few days."

"And will you rotate them soon?"

He shook his head, jaw tightening.

That should have been sign enough for her to go no further, but still she pressed on.

"I understand that it's not good for cattle to graze near standing water for any length of time. Perhaps you should consider rotating them soon."

His shoulders stiffened. "And where, pray tell, does this advice come from? This great ranching advice?"

Amanda's face heated. "I used to help out around the ranch. It's just something my late husband said."

"Did he happen to say why?"

Her face warmed several more degrees in the moments she remained silent. "No. But he was quite adamant of its import."

Brandon's eyes bored into her. With his muscles tensing, he sat tall and rigid on his horse, presenting a more intimidating picture. "I can assure you that I have a rotation pattern I follow. It has served me well. If you must know, I had to split the herd for breeding season now that I have two bulls."

Now that you have Jed's bull.

"So I cannot rotate the land as frequently as I would like. But I will maintain a close eye on the cattle to ensure that no harm comes to them, and we will watch to make sure the land is not overgrazed, as is our duty as ranchers. For this is our livelihood."

How dare he push her to the side! As if she were as useless as he imagined her to be. One way or another, he would learn her value.

She shot back, "I mean no disrespect. But I also know that not every rancher can know every trick. Least of all a rancher who is fairly new to the practice. It was simply my intent to help educate you."

Amanda spun, moving toward the door.

"Mrs. Miller!"

Whirling at the sound of the name she refused to take ownership of, she glared at him.

His eyes flashed, and his jaw clenched. "I will run my ranch as I see fit. And I do not wish to see you insert your advice or yourself into my business. Is that clear?"

She bit at the inside of her lip until she tasted blood.

"Furthermore, I would have you remain here at the homestead, clear of the barn and the cattle, and the *bulls*, from now on. If you can manage that."

Her mouth opened, but only a gasp came forth. Who did he think he was ordering her around? Oh, yes, he was her husband. And, he had every right under the sun to do just that. Whether she thought it just was irrelevant.

She shut her mouth, grabbed at her skirt, and stomped toward the door. Swinging it wide, she proceeded to stomp into the house and slam the door.

If he wanted an answer out of her, he'd just have to keep waiting.

Brandon slammed the stall door closed and pulled at the rope as he wound it. Infuriating woman! What was in her head?

He thrust the rope onto its hook and picked up a pitchfork. Jabbing it into a haystack, he gritted his teeth. Then he hefted a forkful of hay into the stall. His hands gripped the tool tightly, twisting and wringing the wooden handle almost without thinking.

Confounded business this whole marriage. Must he be hitched as such to her for life? He'd rather not lay eyes on her again if he could help it.

A stinging sensation pinched his hand. He jerked it away from the handle. Naught but a splinter. Releasing the tool to its perch next to the stall, he maneuvered his other fingers over to pull the splinter out.

Agh! Such a minor annoyance. Yet an irritant all the same. Just like Amanda. One big splinter. If only she was as easy to remove.

Working with the nail on his opposite thumb, he was able to work the largest portion of the splinter out of his palm. Was that all of it? Surely so. It appeared intact.

He leaned against the stall door and sighed. And begged the Lord's forgiveness for the thoughts he'd had about his wife.

Yes, he was angry. And, yes, she had overstepped her bounds. But she was still his wife and still God's beloved child. As such, she deserved much better consideration from him. Besides, her life had been turned upside down.

Rubbing a hand down his face, he tipped his hat back. How was he to keep his cool against such odds? His heart slowed its racing. And he knew. The same grace bestowed upon him.

That meant that he needed to once again apologize. He pinched the bridge of his nose.

His pride.

That's what had gotten the better of him. Not her.

With renewed purpose, he strode back toward the house. Darkness had started to fall on the ranch. It would be time for dinner soon. He'd have to face her then. Easing the front door open, he slipped inside. A din of voices rose from the dining room. Was she among them?

Maneuvering through the house the long way, he entered the kitchen and pumped water into the sink. His palm stung as he gently rubbed his hands together. Because of the recent trauma? Or because there was still a piece of the splinter there? Holding the injured hand closer to his face, he attempted to see if there was a fleck of brown against his skin. Nothing.

Likely it was only his imagination.

"There you are!" Cook's voice sounded behind him.

He nearly jumped at the unexpected presence. "Why aren't you eating?" Grabbing for a hand towel, he wrung his hands.

"I could ask you the same thing. We were beginning to worry after you. Figured you and Mrs. Miller went off for a moonlit ride."

His brows scrunched. Off on a moonlit ride? That was the last thing he could imagine. He and Amanda, in a tender embrace...

"Couldn't decide what had happened to the two of you."

He spun on Cook. "Amanda isn't here?"

Her eyes widened. "No, sir. We thought she was with you."

He shook his head slowly.

"What...?" Cook started, but Brandon held up a hand.

Moving further into the house, he stepped into the hall between their rooms. As he came to the door, he prayed, *Lord, please let her be shut up in here, safe and sound.* What if she had run off into the night? Would she be so foolish?

He raised his hand, preparing to knock, and then he heard it— muffled sobs. Quiet though she was, he became certain of it. His heart stalled. Was this about him? About what he had said? Or were these tears for Jed?

And what should he do? Leave her be? His heart ached. That

possibility became lost. He had to face her, to at least attempt to right this situation.

Garnering all his courage, he raised his hand once more. And, sucking in a breath, he knocked on the door.

The crying stopped, but he could not discern any movement within.

After several moments, he rapped on the door again. "Amanda?"

Footfalls allowed him to follow her across the room. She soon stood on the other side of the door.

"What do you want?" came her strained voice.

"Please." He leaned on the doorframe, a hand on the latch. "Open the door. I just want to talk."

The latch moved beneath his fingers. Then the door gave way. He stood to his full height.

Her features were revealed in the soft light coming from the kitchen. Even if he hadn't heard her, it was obvious on her face—eyes rimmed in red with puffy circles underneath, cheeks and nose reddened. His heart went out to her. Had his words so affected her?

"Amanda," he breathed.

She turned away, looking toward something in the room. The window? Or something on the wall perhaps?

He reached forth, but thought better of it and let his hand fall.

Amanda sniffled and wiped a hand across her face. More tears?

"You must believe me, I never intended…"

She met his eyes then, hers flashing with intensity. "I must? Must what, pray tell, dear husband?"

He closed his mouth.

A ragged breath was forced through her lips. "I'll tell you what I *must* do. I must learn to live with a man who gives little regard to my thoughts or feelings. Who orders me about like chattel. Jed *never*…" She held a hand over her mouth, and her eyes narrowed as fresh tears pooled in the corners.

Brandon's throat burned. He tried to swallow past it, but was unable.

Her hand fell to her chest. "I am *no one's* property, Mr. Miller." The words were broken with emotion. "Least of all yours." Then she reached for the door and closed it soundly in his face.

And he was once again alone in the hall. Only this time, he stung as if she had slapped him. He wished she had. That would have been better than this.

Amanda sat on the bed that didn't belong to her and stared out the window. How long had she been here, poised on the edge of the bed? The small of her back ached from holding her torso so straight, rigid even.

Her eyes slid closed. What was she to do? Move beyond the door and face the rest of the house? What had Brandon told them?

If only she could hole up in here the rest of the day. But Samuel needed her. Almost as much as she needed him.

Smoothing a hand over the quilted spread across the foot of the bed, she opened her eyes and raised them heavenward. No. She would not pray. Not even for strength. If she didn't have it, she would have to manage without. Or scrape up what she could. There would be no help from above. Never had been.

She stood and took slow steps toward the door, but paused as she set her hand on the latch. Did she have what it took to face him? Her forehead met the door's hard surface.

Why had she exploded? Said things she didn't mean? No, she meant them. She was just sorry for the awkwardness they now created.

A floorboard creaked in the hall.

She jerked her head off the door. Was someone lurking outside her door? Who would…?

Putting an ear to the smooth wood, she held her breath.

The movement stilled, but she swore someone stood just on the other side.

What game was this? Spying on her? Come for more tears? Or an apology? She stifled a laugh. He would have to keep wanting.

Grasping the latch firmly in hand, she readied herself and jerked the door open.

And there stood a wide-eyed Samuel.

"Samuel?" she gasped, hand on her chest.

He worked to right himself. "You scared me, Mama!"

She grabbed for his arm. Once he was steady, she crouched in front of him. "Why were you outside my door?"

"I was worried about you, Mama." His voice was small, timid, and his eyes were still wide and clear; sincerity shone through.

Her heart turned and her whole body sighed. She reached up and straightened his collar, allowing her fingers to linger on his small chest for a moment.

"Listen, I don't want you to worry about Mama."

"But you're sad. I don't want you to be sad." His green eyes, so like Jed's, peered into her soul. What could he see?

"Mama just misses Pa sometimes. Do you ever feel that way?"

He nodded, his brown hair shaking. A haircut would be in order soon.

"That's how Mama feels right now. But I'll be fine. You know why?"

"Cause you got me?" A smile spread over his features.

The same smile tugged at her lips. "That's right. I've got you." Amanda reached across the distance between them and drew her son to her chest.

He wrapped his small arms around her shoulders.

What would she do without him? He was the best part of her. The best of Jed. Proof that what she and Jed had existed. Fresh tears stung the back of her eyes, and she fought them. No need to stir more questions in her son.

He pulled back before she was ready. Such was the price of growing up. As he aged, he needed her less and less. Wasn't that what she was supposed to want?

But as the gentle weight of his arms left her shoulders, she longed for more. How long had it been since she had been held? The day Brandon had rescued her. He had held her tightly then. And she couldn't deny how it had stirred a rather pleasant warmth in her core.

"Let's go see what Cook is making, Mama!" Samuel, his troubles forgotten, bounded down the hall before Amanda could rise.

"Coming," she called after him, straightening her skirt.

She turned to move after Samuel when the door down the hall creaked open.

Brandon stepped out. Did he know she was out here? His eyes met hers, and he paused.

She, too, halted her progress, and then averted her eyes.

"Amanda, I…" His words trailed off. What did he want to say?

She shifted to look at him.

He reached behind himself to grasp the door's latch and pull it closed, but not before she glanced into the room. Had she meant to violate his privacy or had curiosity simply gotten the better of her? She spotted Uncle Owen, still asleep on the only bed in the room.

Where did Brandon sleep? On a pallet on the floor? Surely that wasn't where… Unless he had given up his room for her. So that she and Samuel could have separate sleeping quarters.

Her eyes met his again. Only then did she realize he had continued to talk. But she had missed most of what he had said.

He looked at her expectantly.

She swallowed past the lump in her throat. When she opened her mouth, she feared she wouldn't have a voice as much as she feared what she had to say. "I'm sorry, what was that?"

Brandon's eyes widened, and then his brows furrowed. "I apologized for being hard headed and prideful."

Amanda turned her face away from his. Her cheeks warmed. This was not going well.

She pulled together her courage and forced herself to look at him again. Into eyes that were deep and difficult to read.

His jaw muscles twitched.

Opening her mouth, she prepared to say what needed to be said, hoping it came out the way she wanted.

Crash!

Her head jerked in the direction of the loud sound. A hand was on her arm—Brandon's. He stepped in front of her, placing himself between her and the perceived danger as if by instinct.

Amanda's slender fingers wrapped around the arm that protected her, and she tried to move around him. The sound had come from the direction of the kitchen. Something might have happened to Samuel!

Brandon continued to hold her back as they moved in that direction. As they neared the end of the hall, he turned toward the dining room. She was tempted to veer off toward the kitchen, certain he was wrong.

But as they stepped through the doorway, the source of the commotion became evident.

Cook stood off to one side of the room, Samuel in her arms, A shattered glass vase was splayed out on the floor and wildflowers were scattered among the shards.

"I just wanted to get Mama some flowers," Samuel cried into Cook's shoulder, his voice muffled. Did he even know Amanda had entered the room?

Spotting Brandon and Amanda, Cook nodded in their direction and sidestepped into the kitchen, carrying Samuel away from the mess.

Brandon's shoulders relaxed, and his arm fell.

Amanda stepped around him, coming closer to the disaster created by her little boy's fine intentions. After a handful of seconds, the warmth emanating from Brandon's body alerted her that he had come alongside her.

"I'll clean it up." Where was the strength in her voice? It seemed so weak.

"I'll help." He knelt down next to the glass and began picking up the shards.

"Mr. Miller, you don't have to—" she started.

He looked up at her, his brown eyes soft as he spoke. "It's 'Brandon.' And it's no trouble." As he turned back toward the pieces of glass littering his dining room floor, he pointed toward the front door. "Can you grab that bucket?"

She looked where he indicated and moved to retrieve the metal bucket. After bringing it over to him, she knelt and began gathering what pieces she could.

Some rather large shards lay in front of her. She lifted one, holding it up to catch the light. The vase appeared to have had curved lines with a design on at least one side. A portion of the design remained on the piece she held.

"This must have been a beautiful vase." Her comment surprised even her.

Brandon glanced over at the section she held. "It was a gift for my mother."

Amanda's head jerked toward him, causing her hand to lose its place alongside the shard. It ran down the edge, cutting her delicate skin.

"Your hand!" he called out, reaching for her.

She dropped the glass piece, shattering it yet again.

He took her hand in his as blood pooled in her palm.

She grimaced, not at the pain, but at the amount of blood. And she tried to pull away. No need to get blood on him.

Brandon held her hand firmly. Then, reaching into his pocket, he pulled out a handkerchief. White. Of course. One more thing in his life for her to ruin.

Without a moment's pause, he pressed the cloth to her wound. Now her small hand was clasped between his larger, warmer hands.

Her eyes were on his face, but his attention was on her hand.

He eased the cloth back and inspected the cut. "I don't think it'll need stitches. But I can take you to town to see the doctor if you'd like."

She shook her head, biting her lip. Did she trust herself to speak?

He looked at her, eyebrow quirked.

Letting out a breath, she said what she had been holding in. "I think I've upset enough of your day."

His brows furrowed.

"I intruded on your privacy in the hall, my son broke your vase, I soiled your handkerchief…" She closed her eyes and let the words go. Was there more? Opening her eyes, she peered at him. What was he thinking?

"Nonsense." His eyes danced. "Your wellbeing is more important than any of those things."

She tilted her head and looked at him. Really looked at him. Perhaps for the first time. What she found drew her deeper. And that frightened her. So she pulled back.

"Thank you." Her words were simple, but meaningful.

He nodded.

"I am sorry my son broke your mother's vase."

"And I'm sorry your son wasn't able to give his mother those pretty flowers."

CHAPTER FOUR

Closer

BRANDON AWOKE AND stretched. His back protested the movement. The floor was not his preference, but it wasn't as difficult on him as it would be on Uncle Owen. It just wouldn't be possible for the older man to get down on the floor, much less rise the next morning. His body was worn. Too many years abusing it. And all for someone else's benefit. What had he gained?

Was Brandon doing the same to his ranch hands? Working them hard for his own profit? Or did he deal with them more amicably? What would they say if asked?

He rubbed a hand down his face. The worries of the ranch weighed heavily enough on him without him imagining more.

Uncle Owen groaned in his sleep. The man was sleeping in longer and longer of late. Did his body demand it?

No, that was not the endgame Brandon wanted for himself or his ranch hands. They should all live to enjoy their later years. He needed to be prudent now with the amount of work and stress he took on himself. What was he to do? What could he delegate that he had not already?

Amanda.

Did she not express that Jed had welcomed her help around the ranch?

But the image of the bull came into his mind as well.

No, he could not risk her anywhere near the animals.

What then?

Perhaps some of the clerical work.

The ledgers.

That work had to be done, and more and more Brandon left it as an afterthought. It needed more care than that. Did she know her numbers? How to read? He actually didn't know much about her beyond the few pieces of gossip he collected before marrying her.

But he would find out.

Sitting up, he reached for his shirt. After pulling it on, he pushed the buttons through their slits. Then he rose and jerked on his trousers. Once fully clothed, he stepped into the hall, careful to close the door behind himself.

No one awaited him. The house was silent but for the distant movements in the kitchen.

He took in a deep breath and let it out. As much as he had worked himself up for a confrontation, it would have to wait.

Taking long strides through the house and into the kitchen, he smiled at Cook and poured himself a cup of coffee from the pot on the stove. There was an amiable silence between them. Comfortable, but not deep.

Warming his hands on the mug, he stepped out onto the porch. He welcomed the morning sun streaming toward him over the horizon, its golden rays touching the dark places that remained.

Yes, Lord, chase it away.

The bench to the right creaked.

He turned in that direction.

Amanda sat, blond hair catching the sun, shimmering in the light. Her hazel eyes smiled at him as the corners of her mouth pulled upward.

"I apologize," he said, glancing around. "I did not mean to intrude."

"No need." She shook her head. "You are not intruding."

He glanced at the place next to her on the bench. What would happen if he sat beside her? Felt her near him as he had the day he rescued her from the bull? Would he have the same rush of sensation? Would he become lightheaded?

Jerking his focus away from her, he looked out toward the horizon again. He then brought the coffee mug to his lips and took in the hot liquid. The warmth moved down his throat and into his chest. Yet it could not stop the flow of blood through his body, tingling as it went, bringing his body to a state of awareness.

The bench creaked.

He shifted his gaze to look in her direction.

She had risen. And then ducked her head after meeting his eyes. Was his stare so harsh?

Brandon closed his eyes and let out a breath. Why must things be so awkward between them? They were husband and wife after all. But what should that look like? He did not know. Still, he opened his eyes, hoping that as he did so they were softer.

Her eyes flickered to his but did not catch. "I think I should see if Cook needs help." She moved toward the door, brushing past him.

Brandon turned. "Please…" The word came out rather weak, cracked even. He cleared his throat.

Her head turned, but her body remained as it was—facing the door, weight poised, hand on the latch, ready to proceed at a moment's notice. Was she so eager to flee?

"Please, stay. There is something I would speak with you about."

Her brows arched. And she did not move for a handful of seconds. Did she consider whether or not to take him up on his offer?

At last, she leaned away from the door, and her hand slid free of the latch. She moved back toward the bench, sitting and busying herself adjusting her skirt.

He took another swig of coffee before moving in her direction. Should he sit beside her? Brandon paused by the bench, but only for a second. Then he spotted the chair on the other side of her and opted for the safer, more appropriate choice.

Her eyes were on his movements the entire time.

Once he was seated, he attempted to lean back, but the chair rocked back with him onto two legs. So he pushed his weight forward, landing the chair solidly on all four legs with a thud. Then he tried crossing one leg over the other, resting his ankle on his knee. He didn't like that either. At last, he simply leaned forward, elbows on his knees. It was quite informal, but at least he could be more comfortable.

"What would you speak with me about?"

Her speech sounded so…formal. Was she mocking him? He supposed his vernacular was out-of-place for a local rancher. True, this is not what he was born to. No, he was born to large, fine houses and carriages and a life of leisure. But this was what he was born *for*. Why could no one understand that?

But when he slid his gaze toward her, no malice could be found in her eyes. No hint of farce. So, he shrugged it off.

"I need to ask you something. And I mean no disrespect...it is simply that I need to—"

"Ask me."

He stared at her. She had interrupted him. What had he meant to say? His mind went blank. Yet he continued to stare into those hazel eyes, soft and warm.

Moments passed, and the silence became thick. And awkward. Could she feel it? He needed to say something. Why couldn't he just open his mouth and speak? Perhaps if he started, it would come to him. So, he did. Parting his lips, he forced out a word. Then he was rescued by his memory—the purpose of the conversation came into focus.

"I...do you know your numbers?" Brandon's face warmed.

Amanda's features remained steady, even. Nothing on her face betrayed one bit of a reaction. "I do."

Even her response was measured out.

He let out a breath. "And your letters? Can you read?"

The same mask he encountered before remained intact. "I can."

Though his face became quite heated, a smile spread across his features. Perhaps it would dissipate some of the uneasiness between them.

It did not.

"I would like...that is, I was hoping...if you are agreeable...to have you help with the keeping of the ledgers."

One of Amanda's eyebrows rose slightly. If he hadn't been scrutinizing her face so closely, he would have missed it.

"It's an important job. But I fear I have taken on too much myself and am not giving it the diligence it deserves. Perhaps for a time, we can do it together. The ledgers that is." His features warmed several more degrees.

Amanda's face turned toward the pastures as she sipped her own coffee. Then she nodded. "I think that will suit me just fine."

Shifting her focus back to him, she offered him a half smile. Was this happy? He decided it was. Perhaps the happiest he had seen her since coming to the ranch. Well, the happiest he had made her.

Brandon returned the smile, relaxing a bit more. He leaned back, careful not to upend the chair. "We can get started tomorrow."

"If not today." She tossed him a sideways glance as she tipped her mug all the way back.

"Today?" His brows furrowed. Was she so eager?

"I would be ready and willing to start today. Provided you have some time for me." Now she looked at him full on.

Was this a challenge? A test? His thoughts flew over his day. He truly didn't have time to sit down with the ledgers. Ergo his initial problem and need for help.

Breeding season was coming to a close, they had to inspect the pastures, and he needed to tend to the injured calf among their routine tasks.

But could he tell her he didn't have time for her? That was doubtful. He couldn't form a response in his head that didn't turn him into a louse.

So, instead, he smiled and said, "Of course." He would have to make the time.

This woman was going to be challenging.

Amanda looked over Brandon's most recent figures. They appeared to be in order, as usual. He had yet to let her take on the ledger in full. So she was consigned to watching over his shoulder as he filled it out and then simply checking what he input.

When would he turn it over to her? Would he ever? Or was this something meant to appease her?

It would do no good to think like that. He trusted her. And he was involving her in the running of the ranch. That's what was important.

Jed had never let her near the books. It was just something he kept to himself, an area he wanted to take care of. Sometimes she thought he feared she would find mistakes. And then his pride would be hurt.

Could she help that she had the better education? It wasn't Jed's fault either. He hadn't the aptitude for figures, and the schoolhouse in Wharton City had been limited as far as she could tell. Not that his father had let him attend year round. There had been much need for an extra pair of hands around the farm. Such was the life out here on the range.

Not that her parents needed her hands for anything. No, she had been fairly useless to them. So, she had poured herself into the schooling that was offered to her. And in a big city back east, the education was at least a step above what it had been in small town Arizona for Jed.

No one could fault her for that.

Still, she wanted the chance to impress Brandon with her ability. She was far from inept. When he asked if she knew her numbers, it had been hard to still her hand. How dare he ask her that? Had he made assumptions because she was a poor rancher's wife? That she was nothing more than that?

But she could not escape that he had every reason to ask her, every reason to assume all the same. He didn't know her. Did he care to? Amanda pushed that thought to the side. It did not matter. She would show him just how wrong he was.

Closing the worn book, she then stood, gathering it in her arms and took a step in the direction of the great room. But as she moved to the back of the dining room, she heard loud voices on the porch just beyond the front door.

She turned in time to see Brandon thrust the door open and stomp into the house, followed by Dan and Slim.

"Uncle Owen!" Brandon called. "Uncle Owen!" Then he spotted Amanda at the opposite doorway. "Sorry. Didn't mean to interrupt."

"Not at all." Her eyes met Brandon's. Something wasn't right. His eyes were wide and he fidgeted. Was he anxious?

"Should I get your uncle?" She might as well make herself useful.

With a few long strides, he was in front of her. "No, but thanks. I'll get him."

He passed by her, moving through the doorway, brushing her shoulder. Warmth pervaded her arm where he made contact. What were these touches and sensations? Was she that starved for contact? Ridiculous.

Should she stay and become involved in whatever had upset Brandon? Did she care? She remained rooted to the spot for a moment before deciding that, at best, it was none of her business. But as she turned to leave, Brandon and Uncle Owen came into the dining room, blocking her path.

Amanda stepped back, making an opening for them to come through. She moved over to the table and pulled out a chair for Uncle Owen. Then she backed out of the way.

No sooner had the older man sat then Dan and Slim started in on him.

"We have a problem," Slim said, his eyes widening as he leaned over the table.

"A big problem," Dan agreed, glancing over at Slim, crossing his arms in front of his chest.

"You're exaggerating." Though Brandon spoke the words, it was evident from the paleness of his features that he, too, needed assurances it wasn't the problem they thought it was.

As intrigued as she was, Amanda thought it best she not invade Brandon's privacy. So, she made slow movements toward the door to the hall.

"Hold on a minute," Uncle Owen said, his voice seemed to boom as he spoke over the commotion.

She paused.

"Will someone just tell me what's going on?"

Oh, he spoke to the men. She started inching again.

"It's the cattle. Several of them, especially the calves, have diarrhea. Some of it has blood in it. And they've stopped eating."

Amanda paused again. She was nearly to the door, so she reached for the frame to steady herself. Bloody diarrhea? That sounded serious. Which herd? Closing her eyes, she prayed Brandon would say.

"Is it across the whole herd? Or just in one? Our herd or the new herd?" Uncle Owen voiced Amanda's fears.

There was silence for a moment. Does he not want to say with me in the room?

Amanda jerked her head around, looking over her shoulder at Brandon.

His eyes were already on her. The intensity of his stare made her knees weak.

"Jed's herd."

A sound escaped her lips.

And all eyes were on her.

Brandon was by her side in an instant, an arm around her waist and one clasping her hand. He led her to a seat. A cup of water appeared in front of her, and Brandon helped her lift it to her lips, encouraging her to sip.

She set the glass down firmly on the table and shot a glare at Brandon. He would finish whether he wanted to or not.

Once again, Uncle Own seemed to read her thoughts. "Give her some space, boys."

Brandon pulled away.

And though she thought she wanted him out of her personal space, she felt a bit chilled at the absence of his presence.

Still, she straightened in the seat and looked at the older man. "What could be the matter?"

He scratched the whiskers on his chin. And addressed the men. "Their troughs are not broken, are they? Y'all still keep them up off the ground?"

Brandon nodded.

And the pasture rotation, you're still moving them through the fields like we decided?"

Brandon looked over at Dan and Slim. "We had to adjust that rotation since taking on Jed's herd and coming into breeding season. It turned out that we had to extend the amount of time in the pastures."

"But not the pasture with the pond." Uncle Owen's brows furrowed.

"The cattle needed a water source, sir," Dan spoke up. "That seemed the best field to extend them in.

Uncle Owen looked down at his hands and shook his head.

Amanda bit the inside of her cheek. She had known something like this was coming. Jed had said not to let cows graze near standing water for too long. And while she had not known what might happen, she knew it wouldn't be good.

"It's not good for the cattle to graze near ponds for long periods of time. They can get sicknesses like this. Especially with a herd this big."

Amanda could feel Brandon's gaze on her, but she did not look at him. Could not look at him. The anger in her was too great. Would they lose Jed's herd? All that Jed had worked for? Gone. Just like that?

"Is there anything that can be done?" Dan's voice sounded louder than ever.

Uncle Owen remained silent. Then looked down and shook his head.

Amanda's heart sank, and her head fell into her hands. Why was this affecting her so? It felt as if a piece of her was dying too.

"The good news is, if the sickness is what I think, most of the herd will survive."

"But some will die." Brandon's voice was soft. Did he regret the words as much as it sounded?

Amanda lifted her head just enough to peer over at him. His eyes were still on her. It was almost enough to melt her toward him. Almost.

"Yes." Uncle Owen's voice seemed light. Did he not understand? This was all she had left. She had to see Jed's legacy make it. Or else…or else…

She rose to her feet, almost knocking over her chair. All eyes were on her once more. "Excuse me, gentlemen. I think…" She put a hand on her stomach, suddenly feeling unsettled. "I need to excuse myself."

Avoiding Brandon's gaze, she stepped out of the room and rushed out the front door.

⁕

Brandon watched Amanda run away from him yet again. His gaze caught on where her figure turned as she rounded the front porch, he fought within himself. Did he give her space or go after her?

Everything in him wanted to chase after her, speak words of reason to her. Yet there was that part of him that wanted to shrink away from her, from the fact that he had dismissed her earlier advice and now a portion of Jed's herd was in danger.

His eyes swept the dining room. The men all looked to him. Did they wonder what he was going to do? Did they know the right answer? Should he know? Was it obvious?

"I…" he started.

But when his eyes met Uncle Owen's, the man gave an almost imperceptible nod toward the door.

Brandon breathed a sigh of relief. He was not alone in this. And he had his answer. "Excuse me."

Focusing on the door, he ignored his ranch hands and walked out. Once he stepped onto the porch, he closed the door Amanda had left open. He scanned the area.

She couldn't have gotten too far. His eyes moved over the pastures. Surely, she wouldn't…not after…

But there was no sign of her.

The barn?

He moved in that direction. As he neared, he heard movement. *Please let it be her. Not just the horses.*

Brandon stepped through the large opening in the barn and heard Amanda grunting farther away. He picked up his pace and moved toward the noise.

When he came upon her, he paused. She was near the end of the stalls, pulling on Cutie's horse, Patch's, bridle. The horse would not move.

"Come on," she pushed out through gritted teeth.

Why he didn't announce himself, Brandon did not know. But he stayed where he was and watched her.

She jerked on the horse's bit, pulling, leaning away from the animal with all her weight. It was useless. The horse refused to budge.

Eventually, Amanda wore herself out, and, with an exasperated cry, she threw herself upon the horse's neck. "Why won't you help me?"

Brandon drew closer, the horse looked in his direction.

"What is it, boy?" Amanda pulled back far enough to gaze into the horse's eye closest to her.

"Girl," Brandon corrected as he stepped up to the horse, placing a hand between the horse's eyes, giving the animal a gentle rub there.

Amanda drew back, eyes narrowing.

His eyes were on hers.

"What are you doing here?" she fairly seethed.

"I should think that would be obvious." The words escaped him before he could stop them. He shifted his focus back toward the horse.

"You can't be serious." Her voice was thick with sarcasm.

He chanced a glance in her direction. She had folded her arms across her chest, an eyebrow arched in his direction, lips forming a thin line.

One of his hands dropped to his side. The other held firmly to Patch's harness.

"Amanda, this was not my intention." He lowered his voice. Could he bring the conversation back to calmer, more neutral ground?

"But I told you…"

He raised his hand between them. "I know. I know." Forcing himself to stay calm and not become defensive, he asked gently, "Can you truly blame me for not taking your advice?"

"Yes," came her immediate response. Her eyes were hard.

His hand fell, and he let out a breath, allowing his face to fall. How was he to reason with her? All he could give her was the truth. "My ranch is everything to me. I made the best decision I could. Your advice, though well intentioned, seemed shallow and unfounded. I didn't know if I trusted you."

Her eyes widened, and her nostrils flared.

"If you must be angry with me, I understand. But I speak truthfully."

She opened her mouth, but no words came out. Then she closed it.

"And if you must ride off. May I suggest you take mine? The caramel-colored mount over there—Candy." He indicated the few stalls away where his horse stood. "She is more mild-mannered."

With that, he encouraged Patch back into her stall and shut the door.

Then he turned and walked out of the barn.

As much as he wanted to look back and see if Amanda stood stewing, took his advice, or came after him, he held true to his course.

He would not let this woman get the best of him.

Amanda pushed the horse up the gently sloped hill to the house. Darkness had fallen, but the lights from within the house burned bright. As if some manner of beacon drew her toward it.

She let out a deep breath. Time had passed slowly at first as she wandered aimlessly about the countryside. And then the day whisked away as she made her way back. There had been moments when she feared she would not be able to find her way.

But the horse knew. Of course it did. So, yet again, she proved less useful than a common animal.

Now on the porch, she realized that what had seemed to be a lit up house, was no more than a lone burning lantern in the dining room. Had everyone gone to bed? How late was it?

She laid a hand on the front door. Was she that afraid to go in? Why? Did she fear that she would find Brandon waiting up for her?

Standing on the front porch would not make him less angry. The longer she stood out here, the more his ire would increase.

And what of Samuel? He had never gone to bed without his mother to tuck him in. How had she let her emotions over-run her such that she forgot her son?

The guilt pulled at her core like she carried an anchor in the pit of her stomach. Heavy, unyielding, strong.

Gathering what little strength she could, she pushed the door open and stepped into the house, ready to receive her just dues.

But the dining room was empty save the lantern. And a plate of foodstuffs. She walked to the table and saw that a small note had been scrawled out in Cook's hen-scratch writing.

"Amanda, Some food for you. ~ Cook"

Not much, but Cook didn't know her letters well. She must have had help to come up with that. Amanda lifted the note. Perhaps even Samuel aided Cook with her spelling. He wouldn't start school until next year, but he already knew his letters.

Her hands fell back to the table and the note with them. As much as her stomach grumbled at the sight of food, her worry after Samuel was foremost in her mind. Eating would have to wait.

She moved down the hall and paused outside Uncle Owen and Brandon's room. Uncle Owen's snores could be heard throughout the house each night. This evening was no exception. The corner of her lips tugged upward.

Uncle Owen.

The man was kind, understanding…a good man. He seemed to temper the rowdiness of the ranch hands most nights at dinner and bring out the best in Brandon.

And then there was Brandon. What was she to do? He had hurt her. Truly. But had she not forgiven him already? When he first apologized? And now here she was holding it over him again. That didn't seem right. But how could she just pretend it was all right?

Chilled, she moved her hands up her arms and rubbed warmth back into them. Was it so? Did she harbor resentment unfairly?

But Jed never would have dismissed her. He never would have walked away from her like Brandon did in the barn. No, she had every right to be hurt.

Turning from the closed door, she stepped toward Samuel's door. Working the latch carefully, she opened it with as little noise as possible. Then she was in the dark room. She could hear his deep breathing. Perhaps she should leave him be.

But she wanted to touch him, to know that he was, in fact, all right.

Moving in the direction of where she knew his bed to be, following the sounds of his breathing, she approached him.

Amanda sensed that he was turned away from her. So, she leaned down to press a kiss to the side of his face. And realized too late that she had made a mistake.

Putting her weight forward as she leaned over, balancing her arms on the bed, she lost her footing when the figure in the bed, who was most definitely not her son, jerked onto his back and swiped her arms from underneath her.

Though she fought against the intruder, her back slammed hard onto the wooden floorboards, causing her to cry out in pain.

The figure hovered over her, pinning her.

"Amanda?" came a hazy voice.

She knew that voice.

Brandon.

"What?" she squeaked as she gasped for air.

"What are you doing in here?" His voice was firm.

"I…I would ask you the same thing! Where's Samuel?" When her breath came it was rushed. She panted. Had something happened to her son? Where was he?

The pressure on her arms eased and then hands gripped her under her shoulders and raised her to her feet. She wobbled a moment before finding her balance. Brandon's hands remained under her arms. Would he catch her if she fell?

She gazed into the darkness, wishing her eyes would adjust quicker, but she could only see the faint outline of her would-be attacker.

"My son…where is he?"

His hands grazed her elbows still. Did she dare take comfort from it?

"He couldn't get to sleep on his own, so he's in the room with Uncle Owen."

"Oh." She turned away, wishing she could pull her arms away from his touch.

He remained quiet for a few moments. "He was quite worried about you when you didn't return for dinner."

Amanda looked in his direction again. His features were coming into focus as her eyes took in the little bits of moonlight coming in through the window, but only in forms, no details. "He was?"

Brandon nodded. "We all were."

"Oh?" Why would she bait him? She did not know. But the utterance was beyond her lips before she could stop it. Amanda tightened her lips to keep anything else from coming forth.

"Yes. As was I." His voice was thick.

His confession stirred something high in her chest. Something that spindled and twisted. Something pleasant. It was but a taste, and she wanted more. But how?

"You were?" What was that in her voice? Hope? She barely recognized it.

He stepped closer to her. Heat emanated from his body. "Of course I was."

Her head began to swim as the stirrings in her chest spread throughout her whole body, tangling and weaving into her being. Was he going to kiss her? Did she want him to?

She felt as if they were caught up in this moment. A moment that seemed outside of reality. But they would have to return. Because this was not real.

So, she stepped back. "I'm sorry I worried you. All. I'm sorry I worried everyone."

Brandon dragged in a ragged breath and let it out. "Let's just get some sleep. We can talk about this in the morning."

Looking down at her hands, Amanda nodded. Then she moved toward the door but paused.

When she turned, she halted.

He stood just behind her. And nearly bumped into her when she stopped.

She could see his face better now that they near the hall. His eyes were so dark in the dimness they seemed almost black. "I'm sorry I frightened you."

He let out a throaty laugh. A nice sound. She did enjoy his smile. It was unimaginable how handsome he became when he smiled. "And I'm sorry I attacked you."

That brought a smile to her lips.

Then there was that awkward silence that always seemed to befall them. She watched his eyes as they moved over her features.

He reached up and touched the loose tresses near her face.

She didn't dare breathe.

"Good night, Amanda." Had his voice ever been so deep?

"Good night, Brandon." Had her voice ever been so weak?

⚜

Creak!

Brandon startled in his sleep, stirring to full consciousness. Where was he? The room came into focus. Samuel's room. He had fallen asleep here last night. Turning onto his back, he rose onto his elbows and looked left and right. What made that sound?

The door slammed closed.

Ah, someone had been spying on him. But he was not alarmed. He eased back onto the bed. There was little doubt in his mind that the young boy…Samuel…had come to peek in on him. It would not be the first time he had caught the youngster watching him.

What was it the boy found so intriguing? That Brandon married his mother? Was he so different from Jed?

But he knew he was. Jed, born and raised here in this small Arizona nowhere town, had been largely uneducated and uncultured. Brandon, on the other hand, had his fill of those things. Everything a young man would need to succeed in the world, as his father would put it. Only, his father had had a rather narrow definition of success, as it turned out. And Brandon didn't fit the mold.

Staring at the ceiling, Brandon pillowed his head with one hand and laid the other over his chest. It rose and fell more rapidly than it should. No, this would not define him. Drawing in a deep breath, he held it for a moment before allowing it to flow out through his nose.

It would be best if the boy found someone else to watch. Brandon was no one's hero. If that was the boy's intent. Perhaps he kept watch on Brandon for the sake of his mother.

For Brandon had proved a poor gentleman. He flared and bristled as she bruised his pride. Twice now. And he all but attacked her last night. Fine husband he turned out to be.

And fine wife she, his thoughts taunted. He wanted to reject that notion. True, she had riled him with her challenges and harsh words. Still, nothing justified his reactions.

Reactions he could control. And some he could not. Like the way his body heated whenever she was near. How his heartbeat quickened. And how he couldn't seem to think clearly in her presence. What was this spell she cast over him?

It would not do for him to be incapacitated as such. He would have to push these things to the side. Yes, that must be the thing to do. Then he could manage this wife of his.

Sitting up in the bed, he then turned so his legs fell over the side and his feet landed on the floor. He stretched out his arms, chasing away every semblance of sleep.

Then he made himself presentable to the world before stepping toward the door and pulling it open.

Sounds came from the dining room. How long had he slept? With measured strides, he made his way to the small gathering and to breakfast already in progress.

At first, no one seemed to notice his entrance. Until he reached for his chair. Then all eyes were on him.

Including Amanda's.

His eyes were drawn to hers.

Her face colored and she looked away.

Did he have the same effect on her that she had on him?

"If it isn't the boss," Slim declared, letting out a hoot.

The other men laughed, including Uncle Owen.

"We thought you'd sleep all day," Dan said, taking a big bite of biscuit.

"Or that we'd have to send Cutie in to wake you with a kiss," Slim added. "Just like in that fairy tale. How about it, Cutie?"

Cutie scowled, but didn't give the men any more bait.

"Give it a rest," Uncle Owen warned, his tone serious, and the men quieted. "It's obvious what's going on here," the older man continued.

Brandon's eyes were glued to his uncle. What did he know?

"He needed his beauty sleep." Uncle Owen grinned.

"Back to bed with ya!" Cutie yelped.

The men broke out in raucous laughter and Brandon couldn't help but smile. He chanced a glance at Amanda.

She laughed too, but didn't meet his eyes again, no matter how much he willed her to.

And then he knew…he was in trouble.

CHAPTER FIVE

Secrecy

AMANDA SET DINNER plates at each chair's spot, smiling as each person's face came to mind. Uncle Owen, Samuel, Slim, Dan, Cutie, and Brandon. In spite of herself, she had grown accustomed to this misfit group of riffraff.

Stepping back into the kitchen, she breathed in the scent of dinner. Beef and vegetables. The savory mixture wafted toward her, and she took it in. Cook was good at her job. She fed these men three solid squares a day without fail. They were fortunate to have her.

And to have Uncle Owen, too. He and Samuel were out on the porch working on their latest whittling projects. Samuel had taken to the older man quite well. The attachment took her by surprise. Should she encourage it? Uncle Owen's health was not in the best state.

What was wrong with him? He was much too young to have some of the problems he had—difficulty getting around, dwindling eyesight, hard of hearing, and he seemed to always be in pain. These were the challenges of aging. Yet he did not carry the years needed to experience such ailments.

"Just pull a bit harder. Sometimes it gets stuck."

It was Cook. Calling over her shoulder from the oven as she checked on her main course.

Amanda caught herself. She had been standing by the drawer in the dish cabinet, hands on the knobs, deep in thought.

"Thanks," she muttered, face warming. Tugging on the drawer, it gave way and the contents clattered.

Reaching in, she gathered a sufficient amount of silverware for herself, Samuel, and the men. Then she bumped the drawer with her hip and worked it closed.

"Sometimes it just takes a little effort." Cook grinned at her.

Amanda offered her a small smile before she turned and moved back into the dining room. She distributed the silver, doing her best to stay focused on her task.

As she finished, Cook brought in the steaming containers of food.

Cook caught her eye. "Have Samuel ring the dinner bell, would ya?"

Amanda nodded. Grabbing the triangle from its resting place on the sideboard, she stepped through the front door. The dinner bell had become Samuel's unofficial job. And he thoroughly enjoyed it.

On the far end of the porch, Uncle Owen was speaking with Samuel in hushed tones. As the door shut behind her, he looked up, and their conversation came to a halt. What had they been speaking about?

Frozen to the spot, she eyed Uncle Owen. He wouldn't be sharing inappropriate things with Samuel, would he? The boy was only five!

But Samuel's features had a look of guilt, and he wouldn't meet her eyes. Uncle Owen's face was unreadable.

The older man's eyes scanned her until they stopped on the triangle. "Look what your mama brought, boy!" He elbowed Samuel and pointed with his whittling knife. "You know what that means."

Samuel's face lit up. "Dinner time!"

He hopped from his stool, set his wood block and knife down, and rushed toward Amanda.

"Is it time, Mama? Can I ring the bell?"

Could he what? Amanda's mind still reeled from the possibilities of what Uncle Owen could be telling him. Oh yes, the bell.

Amanda squatted so she was on eye level with her son. Looking into his eyes, she ran a hand through his thick hair and offered him a crooked smile. "Sure." She handed over the metal pieces.

He grinned as he turned toward the barn, raising the triangle as high as he could and banging the metal piece along the inside surfaces.

Amanda watched and marveled at how much he had changed in the short time they had been here. And how well he had adjusted. Could he stop growing and changing for just a little bit?

After some moments, the clanging stopped and he turned back to her, beaming.

"Can I help set the table?" His request was so heartfelt; she wished she hadn't already done it.

"Sorry, pal." She reached out and took the pieces from him. "It's done."

He shrugged. "Maybe I can help Cook with something." With that he took off into the house.

Amanda stood to her full height and watched him go, leaving her alone with Uncle Owen.

When she turned back toward him, he had collected his and Samuel's whittling things into his shoulder bag and secured the knives.

Then the older man attempted to stand. He made a valiant effort, but he soon began to grunt and strain.

Amanda closed the distance and took his arm on the side that Brandon always stood. She worked to pull him up as he tried to stand. Once he was on his feet, he seemed well exerted from the effort.

"It's that old hip of mine." That was the only explanation he offered.

She nodded, not wanting to press further. Wrapping her arm around his, she hoped she made it clear she intended to assist him into the house.

He let out a deep breath and took tentative steps toward the door, more shuffling than anything.

"I guess I sat a bit too long on that stool," he ground out through his teeth. "Not the best seat for my hip."

Again, she did not respond.

They trudged along a few more shuffles in silence.

"Mr. Owen," she started.

"You know better than that," he scolded. "Everyone calls me '*Uncle* Owen.' Including you."

"All right. Uncle Owen," she began again. "I was wondering about something." A unpleasant heaviness fell between her shoulder blades. She didn't want to continue. But she must. It was her job to look after Samuel.

"Yes?" Uncle Owen spoke after her silence stretched for an awkward amount of time.

"What, um, what were you and Samuel talking about?"

Uncle Owen did not respond. Except for his heaves and grunts, there was silence between them.

"Uncle Owen?"

"It is not for me to say."

She jerked her head to look toward him. "What?"

"Samuel likes to ask me questions, man to man. And he trusts that I will be honest and that it will stay between us."

"Man to man?" Uncle Owen couldn't be serious. "He's five years old."

"And he'll never be a man if you won't let him."

Amanda thought on that. Did she baby her little boy?

"You can't shield him from the world any more than you could shield him from the grief of losing his father."

Amanda jerked back as if she'd been slapped. "But…he never said anything to me."

Uncle Owen's eyes met and held hers. They seemed sad. "Did you let him? Did you truly let him be sad?"

Stung. All over. To her very core. Had she not let Samuel grieve? No, she had coddled him and tried to keep him happy. Had he pretended to be happy for her sake?

"I think I can make it from here," Uncle Owen said in a soft voice, releasing her arm.

She nodded, unmoving. Not even watching as he shuffled the rest of the way through the front door.

Amanda fell into the chair nearby and tried to think, but her mind was blank. What had she done?

How long she sat like that before Cutie, Dan, and Slim approached the house, she did not know. Why had they come? And she remembered —dinner. It would be best she return to the dining room, too.

As they approached, she stood, wiping a hand across her forehead, wishing she could wipe away so many errant thoughts.

The men climbed the steps to the porch and greeted her, sliding their hats from their heads.

She smiled and nodded.

Wait. Something wasn't right. Cutie, Dan, Slim…where was Brandon?

"Is Brandon in the barn?"

The men exchanged a look.

"No, ma'am," Dan spoke up. "Didn't you know? He rode into town two hours ago."

Why would he go into town this late in the day? Miss dinner? Surely he wouldn't have business to attend to at such an hour?

Slim held out an arm for her to proceed into the house in front of him. She offered him a half smile and turned toward the front door. Whatever had caused Brandon to ride into town, she hoped he would be safe.

❧ ⚜ ❧

Night had fallen. It was better that way. Brandon hugged the sides of his horse with his knees and dug heels into her flank. She gave him more speed. The sooner this errand was concluded, the better.

The town came into view in a matter of minutes, and he pulled on the reins. No need arousing suspicion from the passers-by. As he came onto the main stretch, his caramel-colored steed was in a slow trot. Steering her toward the saloon, an all-too-familiar feeling slaked across his shoulders. Something about this wasn't right.

But it wouldn't be, would it? No, what he was about to engage in was of ill repute.

He tied his horse by the saloon. One horse among others. Perhaps she wouldn't be noticed. Perhaps he wouldn't be noticed. Glancing from side to side, he watched for any sign that others eyed him. The few men around him were intent on their own business. And that business, for the most part, included drinking.

There was no judgment in Brandon. There could not be.

Pushing those thoughts to the side, he removed the saddlebag and stepped toward the far side of the building, ducking into the alley between the saloon and the barbershop.

The lights from the saloon did not extend far into the alley, and the moon offered precious little illumination into the space. Fitting.

He didn't travel far before sensing he wasn't alone. There were others here. At least three.

Brandon stopped several feet short of the silhouetted figures. Doing his best to gain more height than his five-foot-nine frame, he attempted to appear looming.

"All right, I'm here." Brandon fought the urge to look around him. Were others watching? Had he been followed?

"Do you have the money?" a gruff voice said.

"Of course." Brandon reached into his saddlebag.

The click of the hammer of a gun gave him pause.

He jerked his head up.

The men on either side of the leader had raised their arms. Brandon saw the glint of metal in the moonlight.

He raised his hands. "I'm just pulling out the money."

The leader nodded, but his lackeys kept their guns trained on Brandon as he pulled out the stack of bills.

"Is that all of it?" the harsh voice roughed out.

The men let off the hammers of their pistols and re-holstered them.

Brandon let out a breath. "I can count. It's all there."

"It better be."

Brandon swallowed. If this man intended to intimidate, he was doing a good job. But Brandon dare not show it. He squared his shoulders. "It is."

The man jerked his head, and one of the other men approached Brandon, hand outstretched.

A sick feeling settled in the pit of Brandon's stomach. He needed that money. Badly. But he had no choice. Turning the bills over, he watched as the man counted them in the dim light.

The man looked back toward his leader. "It's all here, Will."

"Good," the dark voice said.

Brandon tipped his chin upward. "I don't expect I'll be hearing from you again, then."

The man let out a stifled laugh. It was not a pleasant sound. "We can part amicably."

Why did that not sound like the nice thing the man in the dark made it out to be? Either way, Brandon took that as his cue to leave. But as he spun, leaving his back open, he immediately felt vulnerable. These men were armed. And this was not a man to be trifled with...or trusted. Yet he could do nothing but quicken his steps as he moved further from danger.

Once free of the alley, he stepped toward the saloon, slipping inside. The cold sweat he had broken out in ceased, and his nerves calmed.

But he found himself surrounded by a raucous uproar of men drinking, playing poker, and flirting with the wrong kind of women. As much as he was relieved in this anonymity and wanted to remain until the other men were surely gone, he should probably leave.

Yet in the moments that passed, he found himself not in the saddle, but on a barstool.

Squeak! Clang!

Amanda bolted awake. What was that sound?

Yet again, she cursed her inability to sleep through anything as she slipped from underneath the covers.

She tiptoed to her bedroom door and opened it just a crack. More sounds came from the great room. Fear gripped her. Was there an intruder? Were they in danger? Should she wake Brandon? Was he even home? There was the slim possibility that it was him making those noises. Regardless, she had to do what she could to keep Samuel safe.

That meant she had to act on what information she had. She was not assured that Brandon was home, and she suspected someone was in the great room. While she was no damsel in distress, she wasn't sure she was Calamity Jane either. But she would have to be. For her son.

Slipping out of her room, she looked for anything she could use as a weapon. Could she make it to the kitchen? There would be more possibilities there. Sneaking through the hall, she continued to hear movement in the great room, but made it to the kitchen.

Amanda surveyed the situation. There were the knives—an obvious choice. But could she truly cut someone? Perhaps. Her eyes continued to scan. An iron skillet caught her attention. She picked it up. Heavy in her hands, it would fall heavy on someone's head. Yes, this was a better choice for her purposes.

Moving from the kitchen into the dining room, her heart thundered in her ears; she rallied her courage. She had to protect Samuel.

The silhouette of the figure became visible in the moonlight. A man. Hunkering around the great room, bending over and looking at something on the floor. But it was too dark to make out anything more.

Creeping up behind him, she raised the skillet over her head and steeled herself. Just one swing. That's all it would take. She pulled her arms downward, bringing her only weapon toward the man's head.

Then he stood and turned on her before she made contact. Amanda's hand was then pinched between his. The skillet fell. Her arm became twisted behind her back and she found herself pulled up against his warm body. And the cold metal of a pistol was unmistakable through the thin cotton of her nightdress.

The face drew near hers and let out a breath. Alcohol.

"Amanda?" The voice was rough.

The pistol was withdrawn.

"Do you realize I could have shot you?"

Though the voice was disguised by its harshness, and the night still shaded his face, the man whose hands held her captive was undeniably Brandon.

"What are you thinking, sneaking up on someone in the dark? You are going to get yourself killed!"

Amanda opened her mouth, but nothing came out. She trembled. What made her so fearful? Was it the alcohol on his breath? Or the grating quality of his voice? Perhaps the roughness of his hands?

Wriggling, she tried to free herself from his grasp.

He pulled her tighter against himself.

"Let me go," she plead.

Brandon leaned over to the right and the world became light again as he brought the lantern to life. Was that why he had bent over?

Then she stared into deep brown eyes. Fathomless.

"I need you to understand what danger you put yourself in," his voice softened.

"You're drunk," she spat at him, pressing her free hand against his chest. She needed to create some distance. If only just a little. Did he know how this affected her?

"And you're trouble." His eyes fell on her lips.

She raised a hand to slap him, but he caught her wrist.

He leaned toward her, his lips moving for hers. But he paused just short of touching. Had something gotten through to that whiskey-soaked brain of his?

Still, she couldn't stop herself. Pulled in by the warmth of his body and by the pleasant sensations shooting through her whenever he was near. Her eyes slid shut, and she closed the remaining distance between them, pressing her lips to his, melting into him.

The hands on her wrists loosened, and strong arms came around her. Sheltering, protecting…and then he was gone.

Amanda looked up at him. Why had he withdrawn his affection? Had she done something? Was something wrong?

His head was in his hands. "You're right. I am drunk."

"But I…"

"Go back to bed." He did not meet her eyes, but looked off into the dark recesses of the room, hands on his hips.

"Brandon, I…"

"I said…" His eyes flashed as he looked at her. "Go back to bed!"

She could not stop the tear that escaped. This feeling was all too familiar. Unwanted. Not needed.

Slapping the tear away, she turned before he could see any more and ran for the safety of her room.

Somewhere in the thick haze of his inebriation, Brandon knew. As soon as the words were out of his mouth, he knew. If only there were some way to take them back.

He watched her move away from him, run, in truth. Was she afraid? Hurt? Both?

That alone caused his fogged brain to clear. A weight lashed itself to his neck. Would he be able to move? It seemed so tight. Would the load on his chest suffocate him?

But he found himself trudging forward somehow. And, step after step, pursuing Amanda. Until he stood outside her door.

The cries coming from within were unmistakable.

"Why?" The question, muffled by the door, could have been a prayer. "Why?"

He couldn't bring himself to knock. So, he laid his forehead against the door and tortured himself with the evidence of her pain.

What had he done?

Slamming his hand against the wooden surface, he beseeched the Lord. *What a pitiable creature I am. How deserving of every grievance against me. Every accusation ever levied upon me. I will never refute them as unjust. My sinful nature is laid bare before me.*

Only then did he realize all was silent. Her cries had stopped.

He had slammed on the door.

What must she be thinking? Had he terrified her anew?

Nearly overcome with the urge to hit the surface again in anger toward himself, he held back. That would only make matters worse. But he seethed through clenched teeth. How could he be so ignorant?

"Amanda?" he called, forcing his voice to remain calm, gentle.

Nothing.

"Amanda, I didn't mean to frighten you."

Not a sound.

God, help me.

"I was angry. At myself. About this whole thing. I wasn't trying to scare you."

Still, she did not respond.

"I'll leave you be, but just know that I meant you no harm." His heart sank. While this statement was true, he had now attacked her twice. And then banged on her door. He wouldn't blame her if she packed up Samuel and disappeared into the night.

His heart constricted at that thought.

And then clarity came. She wouldn't. Couldn't. Because she had nowhere to go. No way to live, to provide for her son. Did she feel as trapped as she seemed to be? He had not made her situation any easier on this night.

Turning, he moved down the hall and toward his shared room. He couldn't do this. Hadn't he vowed to take care of her? And that's exactly what he must do. No more of this. She deserved better.

***

The sun tipped the horizon and the sky exploded in color. Pink-tinged clouds spread over the earth and gave way to the climbing orb of light, dissipating as its reaching rays touched them.

Those same streams of warmth woke Amanda's body as well. She closed her eyes and let them fall on her face, too long in the dark. How long had she been here? Her horse shifted underneath her, but she didn't care. If only everything in life could be as simple as this: the sun rising and shattering the night.

No corner of the sky was safe from its piercing light, unveiling all that could be known of the world around her. Even the stars sought refuge, as if their glow paled in comparison.

Rolling her shoulders back and closing her eyes, she pressed her chest forward. Could the light not expose every dark thing in her as well? Warm her very core? Touch the things in her that were wounded and hurting with its brilliance?

Though she felt heated, the tightness within remained.

Her head dropped to her chest.

What was she going to do?

She stared at the small structure in front of her, so familiar. And yet a chill came over her body. Should this house seem so strange to her? The place she once called home?

Amanda urged the horse forward then pulled her to a halt just short of the porch. Once the horse stopped moving, she strained her ears, as if she could still hear Jed's voice echoing through the thin walls.

But she could not. Did she truly want to?

Why had she come here? It had not been her intended destination when she saddled Brandon's caramel-colored steed in the wee hours of the morning. In truth, she had not known where she would go. But here?

The grasses were overgrown. No cattle or horses to keep them under control. Other than that, it appeared to be just as she had left it. What would become of it? Would Brandon sell it? It had been a fine home.

Her eyes caught on the door. Dare she go inside?

She slid off the horse before she had decided.

The animal began munching on overgrown clover by the porch.

Amanda tied the reins to a post, but her eyes were locked on the door. Her slipknot completed, she moved toward the porch steps. With slow movements, she climbed onto the raised area but stopped.

Her hands grazed the nearby post. And she remembered. The day Jed died she had rushed through that door, down these stairs, her hands covered in blood. His blood. She had tried to tend to him so faithfully. But that day. That horrible day. Why had she left his side?

Because he told her to.

Just like Brandon had last night.

Jed was never the most compassionate soul, but he was good to her. He needed her. They were a good team. But when he became sick… He just wasn't right. Especially that day. She had been tending to him, pressing cooling cloths to him. And then he spoke.

Her eyes slid closed. Amanda could still hear his words. The words that accused her, spat blood at her, and demanded she leave. She hadn't wanted to. But they both needed a moment.

It was only a moment.

Amanda blinked. She stood in the bedroom, staring at the place Jed had lain in his last days. How did she get here?

Falling to her knees by the bed, she laid her head and arms across Jed's pillow as tears poured down. How could she ever forgive herself? She had abandoned her husband. Her husband. And when he'd needed her most.

In her heart, she felt the urge to cry out. And though cry she did, she would not beseech the Lord. She had seen enough in life to know that

He didn't concern Himself with her.

And then she was angry. Angry at herself. Angry at God for His uncaring nature. Angry with life.

All she had done for the last few months was cry. And she hated it. She was not weak. Why should she be forced to play the part?

She did look heavenward then.

"No more."

She stood, bumping into the night table. Something clanged to the floor. What was that? Dropping to her hands and knees, she searched under the stand. A glint of light shone off the thin metal band.

Her wedding ring! The one Jed had given her.

And she remembered. After she had wed Brandon, when they returned to gather their things, she had decided to leave the ring here, in Jed's home.

She stood, holding the precious ring in her palm. With her other hand, she rubbed the cool metal.

Jed had been a good man. More than she deserved.

Her hand closed over the circlet of silver.

She would not leave it here again.

Perhaps she was joined to Brandon and would have to find a way to live with him, but she would remain faithful to Jed. He would never have treated her the way Brandon did. No, not Jed. That man only ever wanted to care for her and love her. He never meant to hurt her.

With these thoughts firmly planted in her mind, she marched out of the house. But she would not leave these memories behind. The space between her shoulders tightened and her throat filled. No, not even if her body betrayed her.

Amanda strode onto the porch. The horse no longer stood where she had been. No sign of even the reins remained. A cold chill ran down Amanda's spine. Was she not alone? Tingles rushed through her body as she backed into the safety of the doorframe while looking from side to side.

No sign of anyone else, but she spotted the horse several feet away, still munching. Had she not tied the knot properly? The wave of dread subsided, but she continued to glance around, leery of an attack.

Once satisfied that there was no one on the property except her, she stepped back onto the porch and moved toward the horse. Her steps were slow. Best not to startle the animal. What would she do if Brandon's horse were to get spooked and run away? How would she explain that?

Perhaps if she talked to the horse, it would remain at ease.

"Come here…" Then she realized she didn't remember the animal's given name. "Horsey. That's a good girl. Just stay calm."

With slow movements, she raised her arms wide. Not for any reason other than this was how she always saw people approaching animals.

The horse raised her head and looked at Amanda.

Amanda halted her progress.

A snort was the only response she got from the animal.

"Yes, that's a good girl." Amanda took another step forward. And stepped onto a stone in her path. Her ankle turned, pitching her to the side and throwing her to the ground.

The horse took off.

"No!" Amanda reached after the horse, ignoring the pain shooting through her injured foot.

Dust was all she saw.

Amanda slammed her fist onto the ground and then rolled onto her back, staring into the clouds.

"How could you?"

CHAPTER SIX

Found

BRANDON'S HEAD HURT. A lot. He pressed a hand to his forehead, clamping fingers over his temples. Perhaps that would calm the throbbing.

It did not.

His mouth was dry. Parched. He attempted to sit up. That was a mistake. Queasiness overcame him immediately. Lowering his body back onto his pallet, he moved the back of his hand over his mouth.

Why? Why did he do it? He never drank. Not even a glass here and there, certainly not enough to get drunk. Then why last night?

But he knew. All that money. Gone. But he probably had enough cushion with Jed's herd. He'd make what he needed to pay off the bank and save the ranch. He had to.

His stomach eased, and he maneuvered to stand again, only this time, he moved more slowly.

The happenings of the previous evening came back to him—the exchange in the alley, the bar, the whiskey, and his confrontation with Amanda.

Amanda…

That was the other reason he never drank. The morning shone light on the mistakes of the evening. Had he forced his affections on her? Or had she kissed him? He couldn't be sure. But he did remember her tears and his words spoken in anger.

He was a cad.

Could he face her? Did he have a choice?

Drawing in a deep breath, he ran a hand down his disheveled shirt he had not bothered to remove the night before and stepped toward the hall. Pulling the door open and setting foot into the open area, he breathed in the aroma of breakfast.

The queasiness returned. But his stomach twisted in hunger as well. An odd combination.

He moved toward the kitchen. Voices filtered in from the direction of the dining room, causing his head to pound even harder. The light coming in through the windows of the bigger rooms seemed to pierce his skull as well. Brandon wished he could return to the dimmer, quieter recesses of his room, but his thirst drove him onward.

Now in the kitchen, he thanked God that Cook was not there to disturb him. He rushed for the coffee on the stovetop. After pouring himself a generous cupful, he downed the hot liquid. His stomach churned and lurched, but he kept it down.

The door squeaked, and Cook swept into the room. Her eyes landed on him.

"Mr. Brandon, I do declare, you look a sight!" Her eyes widened and her nose wrinkled. "And that smell…" She paused. "Mr. Brandon!"

He cringed as her shrill voice sliced through his brain. Did she have to yell?

She closed the distance between them and grabbed his arm. "You best sit yourself down, mister." Leading him toward the great room, she paused only when they arrived at his armchair.

Brandon landed in the chair and found himself looking up at Cook's hard eyes, nearly hidden under furrowed brows.

"You best finish that coffee, and I'll bring you another."

With that, Cook turned, skirt flaring, and whisked away.

Brandon's face heated. How he wished Cook didn't have to see him like this! If only Amanda hadn't come out of her room last night. If only…

Thump, thump, thump.

The sound grew louder and closer.

Thump, thump, thump.

Brandon could pretend that he didn't know what it was, but that would be foolish. Those were the uneven steps of Uncle Owen. Couldn't Brandon just disappear?

No, he could do nothing but sit and wait as the only elder relative he respected drew near. Once he sensed Uncle Owen had entered the room, Brandon raised his eyes to face his fate.

Uncle Owen's stare was intense.

Brandon looked away.

Thump, thump, thump.

Then there was a plop as the armchair next to Brandon gave under Uncle Owen's frame.

"I know what you're going to say," Brandon started. Perhaps he could avoid the scolding he was due.

"Do you?"

Brandon glanced at his uncle. His face was as stern as he'd ever seen it. And there was no sign of any give.

"Have some mercy, Uncle Owen. You don't know what I've been through." Why was he trying to defend himself?

"What you've been through?"

"Yes, what I've been through."

"What about them?" Uncle Owen's tone was even, calm.

"Them?" Brandon furrowed his brows.

"The wife and child who depend on you."

Brandon hung his head. "They deserve better."

"You deserve better than what you're doing to yourself."

"What do you know—?"

"More than you think." Uncle Owen's voice became soft.

It gave Brandon pause. He turned curious eyes on his uncle. "What do you mean?"

"You don't know much about Jedidiah Haynes, do you? Or what his widow has been through?" One of Uncle Owen's eyebrows raised.

Brandon opened his mouth, but then shut it and shook his head. In truth, he knew little of Jed. And most of it was rumor.

"He was a cantankerous sort of fellow. Never pleased with anything or anybody. And he would let you know exactly what he thought. I wonder if that wife of his ever thought she was worth anything."

It hurt to think. But Uncle Owen's words made Brandon do just that. And he didn't like it. Was it true? Amanda, treated as if she was useless? Made to feel less than she was? It stirred such an anger in him, he could hardly see straight.

But then Brandon had done nothing but reinforce those messages, not through words, but in the way he treated her. Out of his pride. Again, that pride.

He looked at his uncle again. "What am I supposed to do?"

"Only you can know that." Uncle Owen leaned back in his chair.

Brandon nodded.

"But I will tell you this: it's not what you're doing." Uncle Owen's finger pressed onto Brandon's leg then retracted.

Looking down at the floor, Brandon nodded again.

Hurried steps rushed into the room.

Brandon lifted his head. It was Dan, his chest heaving. Had he been running?

"Pardon, sir." He spoke to Brandon. Then he turned his attention toward Uncle Owen. "Cutie just got back from a ride over the property. She ain't nowhere on the grounds."

"What?" Brandon rose. His head swam a little, and he thought he might lose what he had kept down, but it soon calmed.

"Mrs. Miller. She come up missing this morning. Along with Candy."

"My horse?" Amanda could be anywhere by now if she was on horseback. Could she be in danger?

Dan nodded. "Cutie wanted to ride down to the stream at least before we alarmed anyone. But she's not there. Or anywhere else on the ranch."

A hand fell on Brandon's shoulder. He turned his head, but he already knew it was Uncle Owen.

"You're not in any condition to ride out just yet. Let the boys go to town and scour the countryside. You best stay here in case she comes back."

He should argue. It was his job to look after her. But Uncle Owen spoke wisely. Riding out in his condition would only bring on more problems.

Nodding, he turned back to Dan. "Saddle three horses. You head to town and search there. Ask if anyone has seen her. Have Cutie follow the stream further north. And tell Slim to check out Jed's homestead."

Uncle Owen squeezed his shoulder.

Dan nodded and moved off on his errand.

Brandon fell back into his chair. What would this day bring?

Amanda had to get up. At some point. There was nothing for it. Lying here in the dirt. A mess.

The clouds moved overhead. White against brilliant blue clarity. Could she see to the heavens? No. Her eyes slid closed. What a mess she had made. Of herself. Of her life. Of Samuel's life. Of everything.

Her arms stretched out on the ground, she clenched her fists tighter. The cool metal of the band in her right hand reminded her of its presence. She drew the closed hand to her heart.

Would Samuel have been better off if it had been her and not Jed? The question stung. Her inability to answer hurt more.

Tears pricked at the backs of her eyes.

No. Enough. No more.

Wiping a hand across her eyes, she sought to restore herself to a more controlled state. Where was such solace for her mind?

Samuel. She had to get back to Samuel. Regardless of what would have been better, she was all he had left in the world.

Pulling herself into a sitting position, she kept her hand clamped tightly around the ring. She would not lose it again. Staring at her fingers, she wondered what she was to do. The band belonged on her ring finger. But Brandon's held that place now. Should it? Did he deserve to hold her in such a way? Dare she remove it? How would Brandon react? Did she care?

Gripping Brandon's ring tightly, she pulled at it. At first, the metal clung to the bend at the bottom of her finger. But that only increased her determination to have it gone. Twisting and maneuvering, she worked the circlet off her fourth finger then placed Jed's band where it belonged. The offending ring sat in her palm. Unassuming. One would never guess it had fought so hard to retain its hold.

A simple gold band, whereas Jed's bore faded silver, marked and marred with scrapes from years of working alongside the man who welcomed her assistance. He thought she was worth something. Had.

Not Brandon. He made sure she was quite aware that she was only in the way. Insufferable man.

Her fist closed around the innocent piece of metal and raised over her head. Best to be done with it. Into the brush with it. Never to be found again.

As she pulled her arm back to give her throw distance, she halted. Why should she pause? Brandon's ring wasn't worth the metal it was forged from. Much less any promise he made to her.

Still, she found herself lowering her arm.

And her father's face appeared in her mind's eye.

She attempted to blink away the image. He was the last thing she wanted to think on. Truly the last thing. After everything she had endured, Amanda wanted nothing to do with that man.

Was this one of the rash gestures he would have made?

No. His wedding vows meant everything to him. He had stayed by her mother's side for better and for worse. And they experienced mostly worse. The man worked himself to the bone to provide for a sickly wife and a child who was unfortunate enough to be born a girl.

Still he stuck it out. He never went back on his vows. No matter how tough it got.

Amanda had made vows, too. Could she just throw them away?

Looking at her hand again, the light brightened Jed's ring, but it didn't shine off the metal as it had Brandon's newer ring. She touched the dull silver, but couldn't bring herself to take it off again. No, she belonged to Jed.

Then she glanced to Brandon's ring sitting in her other hand. The ring she couldn't toss into oblivion. What was she going to do? Was there more of her father in her than she dared admit?

Her hands closed into fists and her eyes shut.

"Why do you taunt me so?"

The chain—the one Jed bought her their first Christmas together. It was the most prosperous year they'd had at the ranch. And he'd been so proud of her.

Opening her eyes, she reached for her neck. There it rested. She grasped for the clasp and unhooked it. From there, it was a simple matter to thread Brandon's ring through the chain and tuck it into the top of her dress. It would be invisible there.

Now for the matter of getting up and heading for town, several miles away. Amanda drew her throbbing ankle closer. Testing it, she decided there were no broken bones, simply a sprain. Would it hold her weight? She'd rather not try to stand only to fall over again.

Scanning the area, she caught sight of a large stick nearby. She would risk ruining her skirt if she dragged herself over to it. Looking down at her dress, she let out a little laugh. Too late to worry about that.

Using her forearms and her uninjured leg, Amanda maneuvered her way to the stick. Leaning on the sturdy piece of branch, she worked herself into a standing position. Soon enough, she was testing the ability of the ankle to hold weight. Not bad. Certainly not as bad as she had first thought. Perhaps she could make it to the main road. Perhaps.

Setting one foot forward, she grimaced as pain shot through her leg. Could she do this? Yes. She was determined. More than that, she had no choice.

Step by step, cry by cry, she made slow progress. After some moments of difficult work, she touched her forehead. Wet. Was she sweating? Her dress clung to her in places.

As she heaved her body forward, her breathing became heavy, labored. She paused often, taking deep breaths and expelling them with force.

A soft thundering sounded in the distance. Was a storm coming? Stopping, she looked to the sky. It appeared blue as far as she could see. Holding her breath, she listened. It could be…perhaps it was…hoof beats? Yes! It was! In the direction of the town. She had to get to the main road! If not, they would pass her by, and there may not be another chance for hours.

Biting her lip against the pain, she hobbled as fast as she could toward the road. With each step, she teetered on disaster. How was she ever to make it? But she had to.

Her ankle screamed, the sharp pain stabbing with each step. Her lungs seared from the effort. As she leaned on the stick, her hands became scraped and filled with splinters But she couldn't think of these things. She had to get to the road. Only her body wouldn't obey.

Amanda stepped once more on the injured ankle and it gave way under her weight. She tasted dirt as the earth rose to meet her.

Still, the hoof beats drew nearer.

Though tears stung her eyes and her shoulders ached, she rose up on her arms. The lone rider took shape.

He was coming this way!

Was it Brandon? Come to rescue her?

Amanda's tears became those of joy and she regretted every terrible thing she ever thought of him.

As the rider neared, he pulled back on the reins and slowed the animal to a stop.

"Mrs. Miller?" The face took shape.

Her heart dropped. It wasn't Brandon.

"Mrs. Miller, are you all right?" The rider dropped off his horse.

She turned onto her back. "No, Slim, I've injured my ankle."

He knelt beside her and took her wrist to help her sit up. "That ain't all, ma'am."

She nodded, turning away so he wouldn't see her tears.

"Can you walk?"

Amanda shook her head.

Slim nodded. He slid an arm under her knees and another behind her back. Expelling a breath, he lifted her and placed her on the saddle. Then he jumped up behind her.

"Thank you," Amanda said, as Slim steadied her in front of himself. "For coming for me."

He nodded. "Mr. Brandon has us all out looking for ya. He's real worried. And terrible frustrated he couldn't come himself."

Amanda furrowed her brows. Couldn't come? Why? Ah, because he would be suffering from too much drink the night before. What kind of man had she hitched herself to?

Slim spurred the horse into motion, making any further conversation more difficult.

Tucking her raw hands close to her chest, Amanda longed for the comfort of a fresh bath and the sight of her son.

❧

Where could she be? Was she in danger? Was it because of him? Brandon hung his head, running his fingers through his hair.

"They'll find her."

He had forgotten Uncle Owen still sat in the great room. Instead of turning eyes on his uncle, he gazed out the window and across the horizon. Barren. Emptier than he had ever seen it. His heart dropped. The sun was high in the sky. How much longer would he sit here and let his ranch hands do the task he should have undertaken?

Footsteps neared the great room. He neither moved away from the window nor let his gaze wander from their target.

The footfalls came to a halt just inside the room. But he needn't look to know it was Cook. Her gait was unmistakable. Unhurried, yet brisk, as if everything must be done the most efficient way possible.

"Pardon, Mr. Brandon, Mr. Owen, I've prepared lunch."

"Thank you, Cook." The smile in Uncle Owen's response was evident.

"Brandon?" Uncle Owen's entreaty did not seem like a request.

Brandon tore his gaze from the edge of the dirt road and turned to face Cook. "I thank you. But I am not—"

Uncle Owen cleared his throat.

Brandon caught his uncle's eyes.

They were hard.

"That is…lunch would be great."

Uncle Owen nodded.

Brandon stepped toward the older man as he started to rise from his armchair.

Uncle Owen struggled, grimacing as he fought to regain his feet. But a mask fell over his features. Brandon could only guess that it was for Cook's sake. Why would Uncle Owen be so concerned about what the older woman thought? Yet there was no mistaking the way Uncle Owen both sneaked glances in her direction and avoided her eyes. Yes, Brandon had his suspicions.

Cook stepped toward the pair, hands extended. Would she attempt to help?

Brandon held up a hand. "Could you see to Samuel?"

"Of course." Her voice wavered, brow quirked. "He has refused to leave his room for anything."

"Please, entice him if you can. Offer him a sweet roll."

Cook gave Brandon a long look, but turned toward the hall and swept from the room all the same.

With Cook gone, Uncle Owen became much more cooperative and was soon on his feet. After the grunting silenced, Brandon heard what he believed to be hoof beats in the distance. Were they? Or was his mind playing tricks on him?

He and Uncle Owen exchanged a look.

Uncle Owen shifted his grip to the back of the chair, and Brandon rushed for the window.

There, where the land met the sky, a cloud of dust and a rider. Brandon narrowed his eyes but still couldn't make out the figure in the saddle. Was it Amanda? One of his ranch hands? Were there more upon the horse? Two perhaps?

Glancing over his shoulder at his uncle, he shrugged before stretching out his legs and moving toward the porch. There he remained, though it became more and more difficult for him to do so.

As the horse neared, he discerned that it was Dan. And that he alone occupied the saddle. Brandon's heart weighed heavier. Amanda had not been found.

Dan slowed as he approached the porch, pulling on his horse's reins.

"Mr. Brandon," he yelled as he drew the horse to a halt.

"Dan," Brandon dipped his head briefly, hoping to disguise how his heart pounded. "No sign of her in town?"

Dan shook his head. "Sorry, sir. I searched, asked questions, even checked the church."

He meant the graveyard. A chill went down Brandon's spine. His eyes fell on the ground as if the answers would appear there. But nothing did. Except what had been driving at him all along.

Brandon had to go, to search for her himself. Standing by was useless. He felt useless, helpless even.

Raising his eyes to meet Dan's once again, he nodded. "Please, take your horse to the barn for a rest and yourself inside for a well-deserved meal."

Dan turned the animal in the direction of the barn, but paused. "What about you, sir?"

So his ranch hand knew him well.

Brandon stepped off the porch and moved alongside Dan's mount. "I must seek her out myself."

Dan's features became stoic. But his mouth turned down. A grimace. Though he dared not speak.

Brandon ignored the displeasure in his hired hand's gaze and set his sights once again on the barn. Moving in that direction, he considered which horse he would saddle. Were there any horses left to his disposal? He halted. There weren't.

Turning on Dan, whose horse snorted and shifted, Brandon tipped the brim of his hat.

"I might need your horse."

Dan's gaze hardened. But they both knew he could do nothing to stop his boss from taking the animal and roaming the countryside no matter his condition.

The ranch hand opened his mouth to speak.

And gentle thunder rumbled as the ground vibrated. It was no ordinary thunder. This was the sound of a horse galloping.

Eyes on the horizon once again, Brandon spotted the rider barreling toward them. Who was it? That was not the direction of the stream. It must be Slim.

Brandon sent up a million prayers in that moment. Most of them involved Amanda being on the quickly advancing steed.

There—a flash of blond hair. His prayers had been answered. Relief washed through him, and his eyes slid closed. But only for a moment. Was she well? What had happened to her? He held his breath as he awaited the answers.

The moments that passed were lengthened by his trepidations. But mere moments it was until Slim pulled the horse alongside Brandon.

Slim's breath came in gasps. The ride had taken it out of him.

But Brandon's eyes were on Amanda. Her form huddled against Slim's chest, arms pulled into herself. She seemed smaller somehow. Was she injured? The words were on his lips, but Slim's voice broke into the silence before he could.

"It's her ankle. Twisted it." That was all he managed as he shifted in the saddle. Maneuvering Amanda's limp form, he slid her down into Brandon's waiting arms.

She was lighter than he would have imagined. Was that only perception? Holding her to himself, he let out a breath as she murmured into his shoulder. Still, she made no move to steady herself in his arms.

When he was able to tear his eyes from her, he raised them to Slim once again. "Ride for the doctor."

Amanda's hand slid up, grasping the collar of his shirt.

His focus shifted to her. Warm hazel eyes met his.

"No." Her voice was weak. Too weak.

"I must insist." His gaze drifted over her face, scanning features that he hoped would betray more information about her condition.

Her lids fell. "Please, do not. I am not so injured that Cook cannot attend to me."

What could he say? It wasn't in him to argue. Neither would he back down. "Can you walk?" The question slid from his lips in an almost muted tone.

Eyes once again on his, she shook her head.

"Then I will have the doctor see you." That would be the end of that. Brandon caught Slim's gaze and nodded in the direction of the small town.

Slim tipped his hat and spurred his horse onward.

Brandon hated it. For his ranch hand had already ridden hard this day and was in need of rest. Yet he moved after his task without a word. Nor did Brandon relish defying Amanda's wishes. But he must.

Turning toward the house, he cradled her impossibly closer as he stepped toward the front door. Could she sense what he tried so hard to hide? The depth of his concern after her? Concern that went far beyond anything he claimed to feel?

But he couldn't deny that his heart beat stronger now that she was in his arms. Every nerve ending seemed more alive. Yet it was as if someone melted the very core of him at the same time.

Stepping into the house, he was first faced with Cook.

"I'll declare, it's Mrs. Amanda! Where…"

Brandon moved past her, setting his sights on Amanda's bedroom. Even the appearance of Uncle Owen out of the corner of his eye could not slow him.

He strode directly into her room, pausing by the bed only for a moment. Why? Was he reluctant to release her? Afraid he would never hold her like this again?

Turning his face to hers, he enjoyed the gentleness of her breath on his cheek. Was it his imaginings, or did she lean ever closer?

Regardless, he could think of no logical reason to linger in the moment, so he settled her on the bed, allowing her weight to become supported by the mattress. Only then did he pull his arms out and step away.

Amanda's eyes opened. There was a question in them.

His heart pulled him in the direction of those hazel eyes.

"Are you angry with me?" came her simple words.

"Angry with you?" He moved toward the bed again, kneeling to better engage her.

"For running off." She bit her lower lip. "And losing your horse."

He gazed into her eyes; the urge to reach forth and touch her golden tresses almost overwhelmed his better senses. "Do not worry yourself with the horse. She will come home in time."

Silence fell between them.

"But, no, I am not angry." He took in a deep breath and let it out slowly. "I am thankful you have returned, safe."

Her eyes glistened. He had not intended to make her cry. Should he turn his focus to something else? His gaze moved about the area before fixing on her hands, still close to her chest.

Brandon reached for the hand closest to him and gently pulled it toward himself. He watched her features for any sign of pain.

Her lips quivered, but no protest was forthcoming.

Turning the smaller hand in his, he examined her palms. They were raw and covered in splinters. His eyes flicked to hers, brow quirked.

"A walking stick. I tried to get to the main road to seek help."

As he continued to watch her, he brought the offended hand to his lips and pressed a gentle kiss to the injured flesh.

Her breath caught, and her fingers curled, tips touching the scrapings of his unshaven face.

The moment was perhaps more intimate than anything Brandon had ever experienced. What had caused him to do such a thing? That was unclear, but he soon realized he had not pulled away. But he must.

So, he drew back. Only then did the ring on her finger shimmer from the light coming in through the window. Her wedding ring. The ring that bound her to him.

With equal tenderness, he turned her hand over and leaned over to press a kiss to the ring that symbolized their vows.

Only it had become tarnished.

That gave him pause.

Was it possible for a gold ring to tarnish silver?

No, it was not.

Amanda tugged at her hand, but he would not yield it.

Brandon examined the ring. Silver. Scratched and etched with years. As if it had been worked with. Like Jed's ring would have been.

This was Jed's ring.

She had put Jed's ring back on.

He released her hand.

She pulled it to her chest and slid it under the other. Was she trying to hide it?

"It's not…" she started.

He held up a hand.

That silenced her. But not her tears.

Brandon stood, swaying but a moment in his decision. Should he hear her out? The hurt won over. And he walked out of the room, closing the door behind himself.

He heard her muffled sobs through the sturdy oak. And he leaned against its frame, laying his head back as his heart bled out into his chest.

The night gave way to dawn. It did not fight the break of light as it came. No, the darkness yielded to the coming sun, bowing out ever so graciously and taking its turn to rest. As if the only thing for it to do was to lay down any power it had over the sky.

Stars disappeared, drawing farther away into the breaking dawn; the moon made its own get-away across the horizon. Yet, it was a peaceful display. A daily lesson on this grand partnership between the day and the night, this delicate balance that had existed since time began.

But on this day, Amanda did not gaze out her window to greet the coming day. Though her absence from this age-old mystery was not because she slumbered, but because her mind had become deeply occupied.

She sat on the edge of the bed, facing the window, poised as if to take in that very scene. A quilt was wrapped around her shoulders, fighting against the chill in the air. Still, her feet and hands, protruding from what warmth the thin blanket offered, were as ice. Her eyes were fixed on her outstretched hands. For in the palm of each hand lay a ring —one taken from her finger, the other from around her neck.

How long had she sat in this position, considering these metal objects? Most of the night. Had she slept at all? It was uncertain. Her mind had been much engaged in this battle: the gold ring or the silver.

The previous day, she had been so certain. Everything had been much clearer. She knew who she belonged to. But then, as she returned to this place, to that man… His arms, his care for her, the feel of his lips on her skin… It became unclear.

Why had she not just thrown the ring away and been done with it? Because she had spoken vows to Brandon. Vows that meant something to her. And apparently, to him as well. He was concerned after her well-being. Was there more?

His hands, his eyes, the feelings he evoked in her…such tenderness. And this was new.

Jed had been many things, but tender was not one of them. He had been a good man, a hard-working man, her savior in so many ways. The man had rescued her and given her purpose. But was that all?

Her eyes slid closed. And she shook her head.

No, of course not. Jed had loved her. Perhaps in his own way.

Memories of his sharper admonishments rang in her ears.

But he hadn't meant those things. He was always sorry. And he had never made her feel useless the way Brandon had. Or completely dismissed her.

Her eyes popped open and her hands squeezed around the metal bands. Clarity returned. She slid Jed's wedding band onto her finger and left Brandon's on her necklace. Fastening the chain around her neck, she ensured that the ring was well hidden beneath the folds of her dress's neckline.

Her decision was made. And this is where she stood.

CHAPTER SEVEN

Tension

BRANDON STOOD AS the calf continued struggling to breathe. He ran a hand over his brow, fingers slicking across perspiration there.

"There's nothing for it, Boss," Dan said from his position on the ground next to the animal. He tipped his hat, giving Brandon a better view of his stricken features. "She's lost."

Looking off into the nearby herd briefly before turning his attention back to Dan, Brandon nodded. Then he bent down, picked up his hat, and sat it on his head.

"Do what you must," he instructed his ranch hand.

Dan jerked his head, a hollow look in his eyes.

Brandon turned and walked away. There was no relief in it, though. Dan would not let the calf suffer. And it would have to be buried with the others.

He didn't have to think too hard to figure up that this made the second one this week. And nearly a third of the calves from Jed's herd since the incident with overgrazing.

How could he have been so blind? So stubborn? Amanda had tried to tell him. But he wouldn't listen. This was his due. And he so desperately needed that cattle. How many more would they lose? The bank wouldn't take excuses as payment. They had extended him too much for far too long already.

Stepping into the barn, he found his way to Candy's stall. His faithful horse had made her way home the next morning after Amanda's return. Taking up a brush, he slipped into the stall with the animal and began brushing her body and mane.

His breathing evened and deepened. Spending time with the horses always helped. He spoke words of encouragement as he moved along Candy's flank. If only everything in life could be as easy as communicating with a horse.

But nothing was as complicated as women. That was for certain. Hadn't he done everything possible to make a home for Amanda? Provide for her? Care for her?

And then for her to return his kindness with such a gesture! Replace his ring with Jed's, indeed! What had she even done with his ring? Did he care? But he did.

As he continued to brush Candy, a breeze blew over him. Odd. The way the stalls were situated in the barn, there wasn't much direct wind flow to this area. This was not just any wind.

He closed his eyes, halted his movements, and let it pass over him. The breeze, which started out as a refreshing, cool bit of wind, became warm and penetrating. It seemed to blow through him. But it soothed and comforted him.

Father, I have done wrong. I have been wrong. So horribly wrong.

The breeze let up to a gentle whisper of a movement.

Brandon opened his eyes but turned them upward, toward the roof of the barn. Then he spoke out loud.

"Help me," he pled. "I don't know what to do. Where to go from here. I just know that I need Your help."

The movement of the wind stopped altogether. But Brandon felt at peace.

What would happen between him and his wife? He did not know. But he was determined that his actions and words would honor the vows he had taken in the sight of God. If only he could rein in that pride.

<hr />

Amanda tried to keep her eyes open as she stirred a pot of beans for Cook. But it wasn't easy. Her body ached for the comfort of her mattress and the license to close down for sleep.

Why had she stayed up so late? It had made sense last night, but in the light of day, she had to suffer the consequences. Maybe it wouldn't be so bad if she closed them for just a second…

Clang, clang, clang!

What was that? Amanda jerked and scanned the area in the direction of the attack. After some moments, she relaxed. Just the dinner bell.

Sure enough, Samuel bounded into the kitchen in short order.

"Did ya hear me, Mama? Did I do a good job?"

She placed a hand on the top of his head and did what she could to stifle a yawn. "Yes, you were wonderful."

He moved off into the dining room, and she turned her attention back to the beans. One stir and a quick sniff made her aware that something wasn't right. A thin layer of burnt beans had settled at the bottom of the pan.

Her nose wrinkled. She would not hear the end of this. Cook's prized beans. Ruined. All because she couldn't stay awake to stir them properly.

Couldn't she do anything right?

Cook rushed into the kitchen. "Them men folk are already coming in. Let's get this stuff on the table."

"Cook, I…" Amanda started. Surely Cook could smell the burnt beans.

"No time for that," the woman insisted as she reached for the cornbread and brisket. "Get those beans to the table."

With that, Cook disappeared through the door.

Amanda stared at the pot. Perhaps they didn't taste as bad as they smelled. Maybe they were just a little burned. Scooping a small amount onto a spoon, she lifted them toward her mouth. And, closing her eyes, took a bite. Then gagged and spit them out into her hand.

They were awful.

Truly awful.

She couldn't serve these.

"Mrs. Amanda!" Cook called from the dining room. "We got some hungry men in here waiting on them beans!"

Pot in hand, Amanda pushed open the door. "Cook, I need to speak with you."

"There you are!" Cook grabbed for her free arm. "I was just telling the fellas here how much you helped with making the beans today."

"That's what I need to talk to you about, I…"

"Pretty much made the beans herself." Cook beamed at the men.

That's when Amanda caught Brandon's eyes. He sat at the head of the table, fairly unassuming. But when his eyes reached hers, they flickered away.

Her face warmed and she looked the opposite direction.

Cook's hand pushed on the small of her back. "Go on, Mrs. Amanda, you know how this goes. Mr. Brandon gets served first."

Amanda stepped forward as she was prodded, but closed her eyes in a mock prayer. *If there is a God, please don't let Brandon hate me for this.*

Then she was next to Brandon's chair. He glanced over at her before holding up his plate.

Her face heated a few more degrees, and she spooned some beans onto his plate. They looked every bit as awful as she imagined. Bits of black had flecked off the bottom and now swam in the bean mixture. Everyone could see it.

Brandon picked up his fork and gingerly touched the beans. Couldn't he see the burnt bits? Was that why he delayed taking a bite? After only a handful of seconds, however, he dug his fork into the pile and scooped some into his mouth.

She wanted to die.

Miracle of miracles, instead of gagging or spitting them out, he kept them in. And swallowed.

"Mighty fine," he declared, his gaze moving over each of his ranch hands.

Their features betrayed their curiosity...and their chagrin. So, she wasn't the only one who could see the black, burned pieces in there. But no one would dare speak up against their boss.

"Pass them around!" Samuel said.

"Yes," a reluctant Slim spoke up.

Cook nudged her. "Don't keep them all for yourself now. Dish them out."

And so she served each of the men a small amount of beans, making sure Samuel's was the smallest and gathered from the topmost portion of the pot.

When she was able to sit, she deflated into her chair, wishing she could disappear. Instead, she found herself meeting her husband's gaze. How could it be that once again, she found herself indebted to him? That he once again proved himself not to be the kind of man she imagined him to be but instead a gracious soul?

And that confused her all the more.

Brandon pressed his heels into Candy's flank. The horse gave him a little more speed. Not so much that they galloped, but enough to hurry along their trot. Nothing seemed amiss today. The cattle were well enough. Finally.

And everywhere he looked, the fence line appeared to be in good condition. He had taken this task upon himself today for the sake of a few moments of solace. Something he'd gotten precious little of this past week.

Cook had hovered over him as if he were a sick puppy. Uncle Owen was ever near. And Amanda…he could hardly breathe when she was close at hand. Was it so unpleasant a feeling though?

But here…here he could fill his lungs. He urged Candy over the final hill and came upon the stream that fed his pastures. Pulling on the reins, he halted the horse before dropping his connection to the harness. Then he leaned back, arms wide, opening his chest to the sky.

Lord, fill me anew.

This was frequently his prayer in this place. When naught but nature surrounded him. Was there anything standing between him and his Creator? Yet in his heart, he knew something else resided there. Something had changed in him. A new thing grew within.

Straightening in the saddle, he gazed across the stream, watching its slow movement over the rocks in its way. If only the water would baptize him in such a way—release him from the distractions, from the pain, from these feelings.

After sliding down off his horse, he made short work of securing her to a nearby tree. Moments later, his feet and chest were bare, and he worked on rolling his trouser legs. The water called to him.

Stepping from the security of the bank and into the pleasant coolness, he closed his eyes and let stream work its magic. First one foot, then the next, he began to immerse himself in the gentle rush of water. Dare he go deeper?

He longed to feel the chilled liquid on his bare shoulders. Bending over, he thrust hands into the swirling stream and sprayed as much upward onto his arms and chest as possible.

It brought him back to life.

More. He needed more.

Once more, he dug hands into the water and scooped some of the liquid onto his upper body. Letting out a deep breath, he gazed into the sky. He was revitalized. Alive.

Then the hairs on the back of his neck rose. Was someone watching him? Turning to the side, he spotted movement in his periphery. Who? And for how long? Did he have a weapon?

He frowned. His pistol still rested in his gun belt lying with his shirt on the bank. What could he do if this person's intentions were malicious? If they were armed?

Best to face his fate.

Running his hand across the droplets of water gathering on his arm hair, he called out, "Are you brave enough to shoot an unarmed man in the back?"

There was some scuffling in the direction he had spotted the figure.

"What do you do when you're truly feeling bold? Rob children in their sleep?"

Silence.

"Nothing to say?" He turned his head to the side, but did not look back.

Still silence.

He started to turn.

"Please!" A woman's voice said. "Don't!"

Startled, Brandon completed his turn. Eyes widened as he took in the scene. There stood Amanda, huddled in the shade of a tree. She was dripping from head to toe and trying desperately to cover herself with her discarded dress.

He should be embarrassed at his state of undress. He should be embarrassed for *her* state of undress. But all he could do was chuckle. The situation was so uncomfortably embarrassing for them both, he couldn't help it.

Amanda's eyes, wide when he met them, narrowed, as he was no longer able to suppress his laughter.

Raising her chin and flinging wet hair behind her shoulder, Amanda all but stomped her foot. "Excuse me, Mr. Miller, but I fail to see the humor in the situation."

"You fail to see the humor, do you?" He tilted his head back and laughed even harder. "I bet you do."

Surprising even himself, he strode through the water toward her.

"Come now, my wife, 'tis not so unseemly. We are married after all, are we not?" He quirked an eyebrow at her.

As he moved closer, he saw that she was clad in her chemise, though it was soaked. Thereby it likely left nothing to the imagination. If naught for the blue dress she clung to.

She worked with the fabric to cover more of her vulnerable figure. "That may be, but we are not exactly…amiable."

"No?" he drawled in his most charming voice. What was he hoping to gain here? He did not know. But he stopped an arm's length away.

"That is," she stepped one foot closer to him, chin raised. The strap of her chemise fell off her shoulder. She quickly righted it. "We are not living as husband and wife."

He, too, stepped closer. They were well within reach of one another. Close enough to feel the heat of each other's body. And he was all too aware of that fact. Fighting to keep his head clear and his eyes on hers, he glanced but briefly at her lips. What would it be like to taste them again?

As if sensing his thoughts, her mouth parted slightly.

"That, Amanda dear, can be arranged." Without thinking, he reached out and pressed a hand to the side of her face. What was this boldness? Was it stirred by her presence? Would she slap him?

Her eyes darkened. Or was it that her pupils dilated? She drew closer, now up against him. He became all too aware of the places where their bodies touched. Was this a game? If so, would he take the bait?

Watching her eyes with intensity, he began to lose hold on his inhibitions. What strange drunkenness was this? His face moved ever nearer hers.

Her eyes slid closed, breaking his connection with her. It was more than he could resist. So, he captured her lips.

She did not pull away, but instead her mouth moved beneath his. Inviting him. Enticing him. For several long wonderful moments.

His arms wrapped around her, pulling her against himself. After all, she was the only thing keeping him standing upright.

Her arms surrounded him. One hand tangling itself up into his hair.

Then they were gone. Her hands were no longer caressing him. She was pushing against his chest. Pulling away from him.

"Please," she pled as she created a small space between them.

He released her. "What…?" Had he hurt her somehow?

She backed away from him, hitting the tree's trunk. "I…"

"What is it?" What had happened? Had he done something wrong? His heart pounded and his arms already ached to hold her again.

"I...I can't do this." She reached down and grasped for her dress.

"Amanda, I don't understand. If I—"

"No." She shook her head and drew a shaky hand through tangled, wet hair as she struggled with her dress.

"Let me help you." He stepped toward her again.

She jerked away as if he would burn her. "No!"

He halted, hand in midair, then drawing back as if stung. It seemed as if he had been.

Her features softened, and she moved to reach out to him, but stopped. "It's not what you think."

The metal on her finger glinted in the sunlight.

And he understood.

His heart sank. And something in him burned at the same time. "It's Jed, isn't it?"

She pulled the hand to her chest and frowned.

"You won't give me a chance because you won't let go of him," Brandon ground out.

Amanda looked at the ring on her hand and sniffled.

"There is life after loss. He's gone, and you can't change that." Why did he have to push her? Yet he did. Because she needed to face the truth.

Her eyes flicked to his. There was nothing comforting there.

He pushed a breath out through his teeth. "I'm here now. Let me in."

Amanda looked toward the ground. She seemed so lost.

A part of him wanted to pull her back into his arms and chase the pain away. But a burning within gave him pause. The way she continued to treat him was unjustifiable. How was it his fault Jed had been lost? Why must he be punished?

"Where is my ring?"

Amanda remained silent. Her hand moved to her chest and her eyes widened. He must have hit the target. Looking down at her chest, she then glanced around herself frantically. What was the matter? Had she dropped something?

He tried to catch her eyes. "What did you do with *my* ring, Amanda?"

She still didn't answer, nor would she look at him.

"You threw it away, didn't you?" His nostrils flared. He could hardly control the emotions welling inside. How dare she? Who did she think she was? Did their vows mean so little? "We may not have been in love, but we spoke those words before God, and they meant something."

She sank to her rear at the base of the tree and laid her head in her hands. And then the tears came.

But they were tears he refused to hear.

No more.

Not from her.

Amanda set the bowl of eggs down on the table and moved back toward the kitchen.

Cook met her at the door. Arm outstretched toward the table, she ushered Amanda back into the dining room.

"Now you sit yourself down right now. You've been working yourself to the bone this morning."

Amanda wanted to resist, but that would not get her anywhere. So, she allowed Cook to lead her to the chair between Samuel and Brandon.

She paused. Dare she take the seat beside Brandon? They had not spent time in each other's company since that day by the stream.

The day he took her in his arms and pressed his lips to hers.

Just the memory caused her body to flush. She kept her eyes glued to the table. Though she was keenly aware of Brandon's presence to her right, she dared not look in that direction.

"Are you warm, honey?" Cook said as she passed by the opposite side of the table.

Amanda pressed a hand to her cheek. Her face heated all the more with everyone's eyes were on her. "Maybe a little."

"Mama?" It was Samuel's voice.

She inclined her head in his direction. Why did he have to see her humiliation?

His green eyes stared up at her, a question already forming.

An unnecessary question. There was nothing for it but for her to take her seat. So, she placed a hand on his shoulder and pulled out her chair. Then settled into the seat.

Samuel offered her a grin. A pang in her chest told her how much that smile reminded her of his father. Why must it? Why must his memory still haunt her?

Her body was all too aware of Brandon's presence. Every nerve ending came to life. Yet she refused to look at him. And she doubted he would even glance in her direction the entirety of the meal. Would the others notice?

The meal commenced, and they ate in relative silence. There was the banter of the ranch hands and the simple conversation between Brandon and Uncle Owen, but Amanda kept to herself.

She could not help but notice every time Brandon's arm brushed hers as they reached next to their plates—his for coffee and hers for her knife.

Was he as affected as she? It did not matter. She had done irreparable damage to whatever flicker there had been.

"You all right, Mrs. Amanda?" Uncle Owen's voice called across the table.

She glanced in his direction.

He stared at her.

As did Brandon.

Whereas Uncle Owen's eyes held a question and concern, Brandon's were hard. What was that Uncle Owen had said?

"Yes, I am well." Why would he ask such a thing?

Uncle Owen's eyes settled on her hand, which lay between her collarbones.

She forced it into her lap.

And he moved on with his conversation with Brandon. Their focus returning to their nearly empty plates.

She let out a breath. Had she been holding it? Fighting the urge to raise her hand back to her chest, she shoved another bite of bacon into her mouth.

The ring, Brandon's ring, was gone.

It had been securely around her neck when she got into the water to bathe yesterday, and then it was missing when Brandon asked after it. Was it gone forever? Lost in the stream?

She had stayed and searched as long as she felt prudent, but to no avail. The ring and chain had vanished. So now the only thing that could possibly assuage Brandon's ire was lost to her.

How stupid! How thoughtless! What had she been thinking replacing Brandon's ring with Jed's? How could she not have considered the trouble she would stir?

She had only been thinking of herself and her feelings in that moment. As usual. Impulsive, selfish, fool.

"You done?"

The words startled her. She turned toward their source.

Brandon's brown eyes stared at her.

Jerking back, she nearly toppled the chair.

His expression did not change. But he repeated his words. "You done?"

"Done?" What did he mean? Had she spoken out loud?

He reached forth and slid his fingers underneath the dish in front of her. "Your plate. Are you done?"

Her face warmed. "Yes." She turned away as he took her plate and walked off.

The others around her did likewise—gathered dishes, moved around, headed out of the house.

"Mama, can I go play with Daisy in the barn?" Samuel looked up at her.

Amanda smiled into her son's face. He had adjusted so well to life here. Nodding, she released him from the table.

He all but jumped out of his chair and bounded out of the room.

Then she watched as the rest of the men moved out the front door as well. Everyone had their tasks to perform, their ways to be useful. What did she have to do? Sit around and sulk?

No, Brandon had wanted her to help with the bookkeeping. Now seemed an opportune moment to bring it out.

Moving toward the small bookcase, she grabbed the ledger and brought it to the dining table. She sat and opened it, going down each column, checking off the balances and amounts.

All the while, she became more and more concerned as she did so. Brandon's most recent entries didn't add up. Should she speak with him about this? Or should she talk to Uncle Owen and have him share her findings with Brandon?

What cowardice! She dug a hand into the hair at the crown of her head. Brandon had entrusted this job to her, and she would fulfill it, even if it meant she had to face him when she'd rather do anything else.

But where was he? Out tending to the cattle? How long would it be before he returned to the house? She would just have to wait to speak with him.

Closing the book, she gathered it to her chest and moved toward the great room.

As she passed by the front door, however, it opened and she dropped the ledger as she slammed into something solid.

Umph!

Hands were on her arms, steadying her. When she raised her eyes, she found herself staring into deep brown eyes: Brandon's.

He released her and stepped back.

She bent down to pick up the book. "Sorry I—"

"No, the fault is mine," he interrupted.

Straightening, she met his gaze, but briefly. "Were you…that is…are you…I mean, do you have a minute?"

He searched her features, his eyes not betraying his emotions. At last, he nodded.

She turned toward the dining table, taking strides over to the chair she had just vacated. Once seated, she opened the logbook to the page where she found the first discrepancy.

Placing a finger on the number, she said, "This amount here doesn't seem correct. Not only that, nothing in this column," she ran her finger down the page, "seems to add correctly. Certainly not to this sum here."

He leaned over her, placing a hand on either side of the book, his face so close to hers as he examined the page.

She turned her face ever so slightly, intoxicated by his nearness and by his masculine scent.

"You must be adding this incorrectly." His voice was gruff.

Amanda swallowed past the lump that had formed in her throat. Part of her wanted to back down, but still, she knew she was right. "I summed it several times. This is not the only number that cannot be right. Look here," she turned the page and pointed to another figure. "And here." She pointed further down the page.

The muscles in his jaw twitched.

She eyed his features as they became more set. Was he angry? Or just concerned?

He pushed back from the table. "I think this was a bad idea."

Jerking around in the chair to look at him, she followed his movements. "Bad idea?"

"Having you look over the books." His eyes were hard on her, his arms crossed in front of his chest.

"What do you mean?" What had she done wrong?

He reached around her and plucked the logbook from the table. Clapping it shut, he held it to his chest and backed away a few paces. "I just don't think it's working out."

She stood up, knocking over her chair. "Because I found a few mistakes that you don't understand, then I must be wrong? Because I'm a woman and you're a man?"

His eyes held hers, but he did not respond.

"Well, I never!" She walked up to him, raised a hand and slapped him soundly across the face.

He didn't flinch.

She turned on the balls of her feet and stormed off to her room.

Brandon had nerve. Imagine! To suggest that he was smarter just because he was a man. That her figures were inferior. Because of her female mind. Once in her room, she made sure to slam the door. Only, did he even care?

CHAPTER EIGHT

Danger

AMANDA AWOKE TO another day that held nothing for her. Void of any hope. Every bit of it had drained away. All that lay before her was to care for Samuel. To watch him grow into the man he would become and pray he did more with his life than she had.

Life had stolen everything from her. Every last bit of it. Not that it had given her much to start with. She began her life with little, had come to know deep loss, and now…now had tasted something sweet only to have it taken from her.

She dragged herself out of bed and forced her way through her morning regimen. She would be useful this day. Regardless. No one would care. Brandon certainly wouldn't. But it mattered to her. To Samuel. He would need to see her making something of herself.

Moving through the hall of the house that was silent but for the stirrings in the kitchen, she wondered at the hour. Perhaps she had overstayed the morning in bed. Had she missed breakfast?

As she stepped into the kitchen, Cook nearly knocked her over moving past to put a pot away.

The older woman jerked back, hand over her heart. "Land sakes alive, Mrs. Amanda! You gave me a fright."

"My apologies." Amanda laid a hand on the woman's shoulder. "Am I late to breakfast?"

"Lawd, child. All the menfolk done ate and gone." Cook moved off to the cabinet.

Amanda strode toward the stove, scrounging for something to fill her empty stomach. All the pots appeared to be clean. "Gone?"

"Yes, ma'am. Said they had business in town. Left Cutie here to mind the cattle, but the rest of 'em took off for town 'bout two hours ago." Cook tossed her a look, but moved on to the washtub, stacking more dried dishes and putting them away.

Amanda glanced around the countertops. Was there even a basket with a biscuit left? "What about Samuel?"

"That old Uncle Owen took him to the barn to help Cutie. They're mucking the stalls."

"Mucking the stalls?" That was hard work. Too much for her small boy.

Cook waved Amanda's concern away. "It's good for the boy. You should've seen how excited he was."

Giving up on her search for food, Amanda leaned her backside against the closest counter, folding her arms across her chest. She watched as Cook continued to clean. Should she offer to help? But Cook seemed to be in her own routine, and he last thing Amanda wanted was to get in her way.

So, she wouldn't have to face Brandon this morning. Was she pleased? She should be. Yet a weight settled in her stomach. Could she truly miss the sight of him that much? No. Amanda shook her head and let her gaze fall to the floor. Not after yesterday when he…when it was clear he didn't trust her.

"Look at me, rattling about when you hadn't a bite to eat," Cook said. Amanda looked up.

Cook reached for a covered plate sitting behind some pots. She then presented the saved food to Amanda. "Goodness, dear, whatever could be the matter?"

Where did that come from? Then Amanda felt moisture on her face. A tear had escaped. Had she been so moved? She wiped it away. Why did this still bother her so?

"Do not worry yourself, Cook. I am well."

Cook set the plate down and took Amanda's hand. "I've been watching you for some time. You are not well."

Her lips upturned in a kind smile. The sort of smile others described as motherly.

"Now if you don't want to talk, I understand. But if you need an ear…or a shoulder. I've got two…of each."

Amanda wanted so badly to share. She was bursting at the seams. But could she trust Cook? The woman had been a long time in the employ of Brandon. How well did she know him? Would that be to Amanda's benefit? Or would it be to her detriment if she said something she shouldn't?

The woman's eyes seemed so sincere, and Amanda's heart was so burdened… Her eyes pricked with emotion. And soon she lost the ability to choose as tears poured forth.

"I have made a horrible choice," she cried as she threw herself into Cook's open arms.

"Come now, my dear. It can't be all that bad. Certainly nothing we can't put right again." The older woman rubbed her back. It did soothe her aching heart. And almost made her believe the words she spoke. Almost.

Amanda pulled back and shook her head, sniffling. "It can't. It's done. And now I've ruined my life, and Samuel's…"

Cook shook her head and tipped Amanda's chin with a gentle hand. "Let's get some coffee and we'll sort it out."

Amanda nodded but doubted that coffee and talking would make anything better. Still, it couldn't make anything worse.

"You just go settle yourself in the dining room, and I'll be along in a minute." Cook stepped to the sink and put a pot under the pump.

Amanda nodded again and moved into the adjoining dining room, carrying her plate. She stepped over to her favorite seat and allowed her mind to wander.

It hadn't been long ago that she and Brandon were in this room. When he had pulled the ledger from her and deemed her unfit to mind them. What had drawn him to such a conclusion? Her figures were right. She knew they were. What then?

Had he been embarrassed they escaped his notice? But then he shouldn't have been. He had missed numbers before and not reacted thusly.

Or was it…it couldn't be. She wanted to dismiss the thought. But there it was…staring her in the face. He knew about the miscalculated numbers. Because he hid something?

Missing money. A drunken night. Was he gambling their money away?

Is that why he needed Jed's herd so badly? Because he had gambled away his earnings and needed the extra money to pay off the bank?

Her stomach sank. She felt sick. But the pieces fit. And fit well.

The door creaked, and Cook came in with two steaming cups. "There now, let's see if we can solve this problem of yours."

Just then the ground began to rumble. They both turned toward the window. There on the horizon were at least five horsemen. Coming fast.

Was it Brandon? Was something amiss? No, Brandon, Slim, and Dan made three. This was five.

Who rode on the homestead? Should they be afraid?

⁂

Stepping out into the sun, Brandon shook his head. He couldn't deny that he was as thankful as he was frustrated that Mr. George C. Perkins had been unavailable to meet with him. What kept the banker so busy these days? Foreclosing on some unsuspecting farmer?

He shouldn't think such thoughts. The man had extended Brandon more than once. But it was not without a pound of flesh. Brandon always had to give up something. Something bankers called 'collateral' or some such nonsense.

Moving down the main stretch of Wharton City, Brandon sought out the café. Not only did he need some coffee, it was almost time to meet up with Dan and Slim. Being the only eatery in the small town made it popular. So, when Brandon walked in, he had to hunt for a place to sit.

Moments later, Brandon settled into the café's last available table. Part of him hated taking the whole table for himself, but Dan and Slim should be joining him soon enough. He hoped. They needed to make their way back to the homestead before too long.

Not that he looked forward to it. This trip to town had been a nice excuse to avoid Amanda this morning. But the longer they stayed away, the more his heart ached.

Nonsense. It was all nonsense. He hated to be away, yet he dreaded facing her just the same.

The café owner, Mrs. Kate, looked in his direction. He signaled for coffee. She nodded and held up a finger before turning.

That left him to his thoughts once more. Removing his hat, he ran a hand through his hair. How could he be so thoughtless? Amanda was bound to discover that the numbers didn't add up at some point. She wasn't some empty-headed schoolgirl. If he had come to learn anything about her, it was that not much escaped her notice. Still, he had been thoughtless in trying to hide in the ledgers—the very place he invited her.

It was only a matter of time before his secrets were laid bare. How long until she pieced it together? He prayed she wouldn't. Perhaps there were not enough clues. This, too, he knew was a hope in vain. For she was sharp. She would figure it out. His secret. The one he had guarded so well. Until now.

A hand landed on his back and startled him out of his reverie. So deep in thought and focused on the grain of the table, he had not noticed that Slim and Dan had entered.

Trying to cover his surprise, he nodded to his ranch hands as they took seats opposite his. They continued their spirited discussion. From the snatches Brandon caught, it was something to do with town gossip.

"Can you even imagine? One minute you're playing cards, thinking the man is cheating and then *bang*, you're dead." Slim crossed his arms over his chest and eased back in his chair.

"It's got this town shook up, that's for sure." Dan's face fell as he leaned over his arms on the table.

Just then, Mrs. Kate walked over with the cup of coffee. She set it in front of Brandon and nodded to Dan and Slim. "What'll ya have, boys?"

"Same," Slim said, indicating Brandon's steaming cup.

Dan grunted and jerked his head in that direction.

"Two coffees coming up." She turned and moved off.

"Did you hear about last night's happenings?" Dan's gaze was on Brandon now. Why couldn't they leave him out of it?

He picked up his cup and took a sip. "Nope. Haven't been asking questions myself."

"Haven't been asking questions?" Slim's eyes widened. "No need to ask questions! Everyone's talking about it."

Brandon then noticed the somber mood about the townsfolk and that everyone was speaking in hushed tones. But he wrote it off as idle gossip. Was there more to it?

Mrs. Kate brought the two additional cups. The men nodded and she left them to their conversation.

Dan leaned toward Brandon. "There was a murder here last night."

Brandon's brows raised. "A murder?"

Slim nodded. "Seems the blacksmith and a good-for-nothing got into some sort of disagreement over a poker game, and the man shot the blacksmith."

Brandon couldn't help the iciness that ran through his veins at the cold-bloodedness of the crime. But shouldn't they stay out of it? He had enough on his mind without concerning himself with the town's troubles. "It's none of our business. Best let the law enforcement take care of it."

Dan and Slim exchanged a look.

"It doesn't bother you that a *murder* happened in our quaint little town, just miles away from where we lay our heads?" Slim's voice rose as he spoke.

Brandon eyed his features. So his ranch hand was a bit skittish. He had every right to be. "Who is this man? Is he at large? Did they not capture him? Have we reason to be concerned?"

Another look passed between Dan and Slim.

"No, the man is in custody at Camp Grant waiting for the law." Slim rubbed the stubble on his face.

"See now, there is nothing to worry ourselves over. The man will get his just due." Brandon started to raise his cup again.

Slim turned to Dan. "What was his name again?"

"Henry…" Dan looked toward the ceiling. "Henry something."

"No, his criminal name. That real catchy name." Slim elbowed him.

"Oh, yeah. That one. I remember. Calls himself 'Kid Antrim'."

Brandon froze, cup touching his lower lip. A cold chill went down his spine. There but for the grace of God…

He tried to swallow past the lump in his throat as he released the cup. Could the others see? He hoped not. Forcing his face to remain neutral, he pushed his cup to the side.

Dan and Slim seemed too engaged in banter about the possible origins of the man's alias.

After some moments, Brandon cleared his throat.

The two men turned toward him.

"If we're done with our coffee, I suggest we head on back toward the ranch." *And put some distance between us and these happenings,* he decided.

Brandon set his hat on his head and put some coins on the table to cover their coffees.

Dan and Slim nodded, gathering their hats and following Brandon out of the cafe without question. He hoped they didn't suspect that anything was amiss.

Lord, please help them not think any more on it. Let this day pass without notoriety in their minds that they may think on it no longer.

The horsemen rushed toward the homestead, stirring a cloud of dust as they came.

"Who…?" was all that escaped Amanda's lips. A sense of foreboding settled in her being, all the more as they drew nearer.

Cook let out a grumble, a deeper sound than Amanda had ever heard from her. "This won't end well."

Amanda's gaze on Cook was intent. "What are we to do?"

Cook's eyes remained trained on the coming posse. She stood still as a statue. "Ain't nothin' we can do."

Amanda forced a breath out through her teeth. She wasn't going to just stand here and wait for whoever these men were to come and take the homestead. Could she make it to Samuel in the barn? It might be up to her and Cook to defend everyone. Perhaps it would be best if she found a way to do so. Standing, she searched for a weapon, anything that could be used to defend life and limb.

"Cook, where does Brandon keep his shotgun?"

The older woman merely stood and stared out the window.

Amanda stepped directly in front of the older woman. "Cook!"

She glanced in Amanda's direction.

"Where is Brandon's shotgun?"

The woman shook her head. "In his room I s'pose."

Amanda rushed for the back bedroom, searching her memory for the only lesson she'd had on one of the confounded things. Jed had wanted to make sure she knew how to defend their home. She'd noted everything he'd said, prepared to be useful, but it had been so long ago. And she'd not laid hands on the weapon since.

Stepping into Brandon and Uncle Owen's room, she scanned the interior. There was nothing in sight that she could easily spot as concealing a gun. Rummaging quickly gave her no hope either.

Heaving from the effort and running out of time, she shifted her focus. If the shotgun was not to be had, then another weapon must be found. How she wished she carried a knife of some sort. Not that she thought she could hurt anyone any more than she could the other night. But it might make someone think twice. The only knives in the house she could lay hand to were the cutlery in the kitchen. Then that was where she must go.

But as she passed out of the room, she spotted a long metal tube hanging above the door. She took a step back. It was the shotgun. Just there, above the door. In plain view. How could she have missed it?

Pushing a chair over to the doorway, she grabbed for the weapon that would surely be their only hope. Then, rushing back into the dining room, she found Cook just as she had left her.

The men, however, had reached the pasture and began to slow their horses. Amanda took as long of strides as she could and closed the curtains, preventing anyone from seeing into the dining space.

Then she turned her attention to the weapon. Was it loaded? She checked the chamber. Two shells rested in the barrel. Silently thanking a deity she wasn't sure she believed in and promising to thank Brandon should she see him again, she moved the curtain aside just far enough to see out.

Should she ask Cook to search for more shells? Would that be a wasted effort? It would be best to make wise use of the ammunition she had. Perhaps a warning shot would be all she needed. After all, killing a man wasn't something she was sure she could do.

The men came to a halt in the front yard. One of the men, young by the looks of him, motioned for two of the others to head for the barn.

Oh no! Samuel!

How was she going to help him?

This young leader and the other two headed toward the house.

When should she utilize her warning shot? How best could it be used? As they approached the porch? Amanda wanted to scare them away before they mounted the stairs. But they needed to be close enough to get the full effect. Could she aim for their feet? Would her aim be that good? She dared not hit anyone.

They stepped closer to the stairs.

She held her breath and shoved the shotgun's muzzle through a windowpane. "Stop where you are!"

What had she said? She hadn't intended to speak.

The men did seem startled. They turned their heads in her direction, eyes landing on the piece of shotgun protruding from the house.

There, that would intimidate them.

The leader laughed.

He *laughed*.

At her.

"Ah, a woman sent to do a man's job. And just where is your man, little lady? He bent his knees slightly as he searched for her."

The other men with him snickered and elbowed him.

Amanda swallowed and pushed down her fear. "Don't be foolish, ruffian. I will shoot you."

"Shoot me?" The young man stood to his full height and held a hand to his heart. "Well, that's not very nice now, is it?" Then he turned to his men. "Hear that boys? The big, bad lady is going to shoot me for my bad behavior."

They continued to laugh as he turned back toward the window. His expression dropped. Eyes darkened and his mouth became a thin line. "Go ahead. I dare ya'." Nodding his head toward the front door, he took a step in that direction. "C'mon boys."

The shotgun shook. Or was it her hands? Beads of sweat formed on her forehead. How did he know her so well? Could he see through her ruse somehow? Still, she could not let him get into this house. Could not let him get to her son.

She fired. The bullet hit just at his feet.

Perhaps she wasn't the best aim.

The young man rewarded her with a look of surprise as he jumped back and drew his own gun. His men rushed for cover.

"Well now, the lady has spunk." He gave a hard look in the direction of the window, but he still seemed unable to pinpoint exactly where to stare. Did he want to intimidate her? If so, he was doing a good job. But she dared not let him know that.

"I've got more."

He offered her a crooked smile. "I bet you do."

Just then the two men emerged from the barn dragging Cutie behind them. But it was not due to a struggle. He seemed unable to walk.

Amanda gasped as they moved closer. Had they broken his legs? Cutie's face was red and swollen. What did these men want from them? What had they done with Samuel? With Uncle Owen?

The shotgun's muzzle rattled against the windowsill.

And the young man's gaze moved from his men back to her. And his eyebrow quirked. "Bothersome, is it?" He motioned for the men to drag Cutie over to him.

Amanda gripped the shotgun more firmly, but her hands were slick. She brushed hair out of her face and felt moisture gathering underneath her eyes.

"Dearest Lord Almighty!" Cook's breathing became ragged.

That didn't help.

The two men dropped Cutie at the younger man's feet.

Was he dead? Amanda held her breath. There, a slight movement as he tried to roll over. It wasn't much, but it was something.

The young leader cocked his pistol and lowered it, aiming at Cutie's head. Turning to face the window, he addressed Amanda, "If you don't want a mess out here, you'll give it up."

Did she dare? Dare she not? She and this shotgun, with but one shot left, may be their only hope. But could she let Cutie's death be on her conscience? And for what? This man wasn't going to give up. He would force his way into the house regardless, and Cutie's death would be for nothing.

"You have one minute." The man sneered.

The two who had beaten Cutie smiled at each other. The others came from their hiding places. All together now, they were quite the intimidating group. What chance did she stand against them? Cook would be no help. And she had no idea what may or may not have happened to Samuel and Uncle Owen. Her heart burned at the thought. No, she would not think on that. Not now. Not while there was still hope.

"Minute is up." The man shifted his gaze to Cutie and straightened his arm.

"Wait!" Amanda called. She retracted the shotgun, pulling the muzzle through the window.

The young man looked at the house, pausing.

Amanda moved to the door and laid hand to the latch, lingering for only a brief moment. "Cook, go, now! Hide yourself!"

Cook looked to Amanda. "Where, my dear? We are all lost."

Fighting back bitter tears, Amanda pushed forth her anger. How could Cook just give up? Amanda pulled the door open and stepped forth, shotgun held above her head.

Five pistols were immediately pointed at her.

The world spun, but she held her ground.

With a jerk of his gun, the man with the young face signaled to one of his men. The one with the partially grown-in beard.

He stepped forward and relieved her of the shotgun, moving a little too close to her than necessary and jerking the weapon from her grasp.

She stumbled.

"All too easy, eh, Henry?" he said as he stepped back in line.

The younger man shot him a look. "I said we ain't gonna use names," he flashed. His gaze was on the man for a moment before he turned to Amanda.

Could she use this to her advantage?

When the leader again set his eyes upon Amanda, he seemed to soak her in. "So, this is what a brazen woman looks like." He began to circle her. Closely. "Pity."

She closed her eyes as his breath fell on her ear. "Pity for you or for me?"

He stood to his full height and seemed to consider her words. "That, I fear, only time will tell. But the odds are in my favor." The half grin he gave her showed teeth that were clean and straight. She had not expected that in an outlaw.

"What do you want?" She faced him, refusing to show fear.

"Now that's more like it." He took her arm about the elbow and pulled her up the stairs. "I want the money."

"The money?" What was he talking about?

"I know there's more, and I want it."

"More?" More than what?

They were in the house now, and he pushed her ahead of him, thrusting her against the dining table. Cook was no longer in the room. Had she taken Amanda's advice and disappeared?

"Don't play coy with me, woman. I know your man has more money than he gave me. And I want to know where it is."

So, this is who Brandon had owed his gambling debt. All of this was because of Brandon.

She turned, putting her rear against the table. "I don't know anything about that."

He rolled his eyes and grabbed her by the arm again, pulling her further into the house as he rummaged around.

Amanda interjected after Henry crashed a lantern in the great room. "If he owes you more, I'm sure Brandon will find a way to pay you."

The man halted his search and looked at her. "Brandon? You think Brandon owes me a debt?"

"Isn't that why you're here?"

He dropped his head back and laughed. "It's almost too precious."

What was he talking about?

"I...I don't understand."

"Don't." A voice behind them warned.

Henry turned, pulling Amanda along with him.

Brandon and one of Henry's men stood in the room, a gun to Brandon's side.

"We had company," Henry's goon said.

"Ah. Glad you could join us." Henry motioned Brandon further into the room. "We were just getting acquainted."

Brandon's eyes took in Amanda as if he thirsted for the sight of her. He searched her top to bottom. Did he seek out injuries?

"Is Cutie...?" she started, but was stopped when Henry jerked her sharply.

Brandon pulled forward, but Henry's man held him back.

"I'm the one asking the questions here," Henry yelled. "And I've got a good one."

Amanda's gaze drifted to Brandon. She wished she could assure him that she was well. Yet the reminder that they were in this mess because of his gambling debt drew her anger to the surface once again.

"How is it that Mrs. *Miller* doesn't know the truth about the gambling debt?"

The muscles in Brandon's jaw twitched. "Don't."

"And just why would you care to conceal it? That is an even better question." Henry's gaze flickered between Brandon and Amanda.

"I care not." Amanda shifted her gaze away from the men.

"No?" Henry asked, pulling her face back toward him with his fingers on her chin. "Not even if you found out it was Jed's debt?"

It wasn't possible. She tried to jerk her face away, but Henry held it fast. Was he getting some sick pleasure from taking in the fullness of her reaction? He had to be lying. It couldn't be Jed's debt. Jed died. Why would this Henry tell lies about Jed?

"Liar!"

"Oh? I'm the liar?" Henry's gaze shifted to Brandon while still holding Amanda's face where he wanted her to look. And right then, he wanted her eyes on Brandon. "Tell her, praying man, if you love the truth so much. Tell her whose debt you paid."

Brandon's eyes softened as he looked into Amanda's.

It couldn't be. All this time. All the terrible thoughts...were meant for Jed, not Brandon.

"Tell!" Henry's anger flashed again.

His man jabbed his pistol into Brandon's side.

"I will not play your game." Brandon's tone was level, even.

He couldn't say it. Even now, he couldn't betray Jed's memory. For her sake.

Amanda's head jerked back when Henry pulled at her hair. The cold muzzle of his pistol dug into her neck. The impulse to cry out was great, but she fought it.

A scuffle followed. She could only imagine that Brandon fought against the man holding him.

"What do you say now?"

"What do you want from me?" came Brandon's breathless plea.

"Cooperation."

"Fine." Brandon blew out a long breath. "Yes, it was Jed's debt. Now, will you leave her be?"

All was quiet. As if the victory was as empty as it seemed. Crushed as she was, Amanda would not give Henry the satisfaction of having bested her again. She fought for a neutral expression.

"No." Henry's voice was hollow. "I want the rest of the money. Now." He pulled Amanda tighter against him.

Brandon's eyes widened. "What money?"

"You know what I'm talking about. Your nest egg. I want it."

Brandon's eyes shifted to Amanda's. Was Brandon hiding money? What else was he hiding?

"When you release her."

Henry seemed to consider it. Then shrugged and shoved her toward Brandon.

He caught her. The relief was plain on his face.

The urge to wrap her arms around his neck was irresistible. She put her face in his shoulder but did not allow herself to linger there. They were still in danger.

But as she pulled back, a loud *bang* echoed in the room. Then there was searing pain cutting through her shoulder. What?

Brandon's eyes went wide. "Amanda!"

He fell to the ground with her. "Antrim, what have you done?"

Antrim? Wasn't his name Henry? These thoughts confused her as everything around her became hazy.

Brandon's face loomed over hers. His eyes were the last thing she saw before everything went dark.

"Amanda!" Brandon tried to rouse her as he gently laid her on the floor. There was nothing for it. Blood pooled under her shoulder, marring her dress and staining the floor. What was he going to do? He couldn't lose her! Emptiness filled his chest, and an ache like he had never known filled him.

He glared up at Kid Antrim. "Why?" Brandon thrust his jacket off and tore at his sleeve, pressing the cloth to the back of her shoulder.

"Amanda, can you hear me?" He touched her face, her hair, her neck. Was she even breathing?

"Enough." Kid Antrim's voice broke through Brandon's desperate thoughts.

Hands grabbed for him, pulling him off Amanda. He fought against them, landing a solid punch on the man's jaw. And he was free once more. Leaping for Amanda's still form, a pistol intercepted him.

Staring down the barrel of a gun, Brandon shifted his gaze to its owner, Kid Antrim.

"You know she needs a doctor. And the sooner you get me my money, the sooner you can send for him."

Brandon's hope sank. He was caught. Nowhere to turn, to hide. If there was any hope for Amanda, it was in the care of the town's physician, but every minute that ticked by lessened her chances of survival.

Antrim cocked the hammer of his gun as rough hands shook Brandon from behind, securing a hold on him.

"What'll it be?"

"I'll take you to the money. Just leave her alone."

Antrim nodded, but slowly. Could Brandon trust his word? He had no reason to, but he had no choice either. They were at the mercy of this lawbreaker, a man who had lied, thieved, and just last night murdered a man. Would he have any qualms about doing so again?

Brandon swallowed hard, past the lump in his throat, and took one more look at Amanda. She was still. Too still. And pale. He wanted to go to her and reassure himself that she indeed lived. But even that was denied him.

The hands on his arms gave him a good shake.

"I grow tired of these games." Antrim moved over to Amanda,

crouched down and moved her hair to the side with the muzzle of his pistol. "Perhaps I should just finish her off now."

Brandon ground his teeth. "The money is out back."

Antrim stood, brows quirked, shoved his gun into its holster, and motioned that they would follow him.

Thankful for his foresight in not hiding the money in the house, Brandon moved toward the front door. His ranch hands were in no better position. Dan and Slim were on their knees, hands on their heads as they had been when he left them.

As they had ridden to the homestead, they realized something was afoot. But it also became apparent that fighting against the contingent, which had already taken possession of his home and his people, would not end well. So, they gave themselves up, having already been spotted.

Cutie still lay on the ground, breathing, but not making so much as a peep. Where were Uncle Owen and Samuel? And Cook? Had they somehow escaped? Hidden in the field? He prayed they would remain concealed.

Brandon walked Antrim and his man out to the back of the homestead. Then he brought them to an odd-looking tree, the only one on Brandon's land like it. It had been damaged at some point and forced to grow at an angle. It made for a great climbing tree, and a rather unique looking tree all the same.

Pacing himself between the tree and the outhouse, Brandon found the spot.

"Here."

"Here?" Antrim looked around. They were somewhat exposed.

"Yes, here."

Antrim stared at the ground, and Brandon could almost hear his questioning thoughts—the ground was undisturbed. How, then, had Brandon accessed the money to pay Jed's gambling debt?

"It's all there. Trust me." Brandon's shoulders slumped. What was he going to do? Now it would be near impossible to pay the bank back. He was relying on this money. The ranch was as good as lost to him.

But he couldn't have let Antrim hurt Amanda. The weight he bore over what she already endured was heavy upon him.

"Dig," Antrim ordered.

Brandon eyed him. "With what?"

"Your hands if need be."

Sighing, Brandon knelt and began pawing at the earth with his fingers.

"You too." Antrim glared at his henchman.

"But, Boss…"

"You heard me!" The click of a cocked pistol tempted Brandon to look up, but he continued his work.

Soon enough a second pair of hands joined him.

After some moments, Antrim let out a long breath. "This is going to take forever! Go get a shovel." He nudged his man with his knee.

The man took off toward the barn and returned with a shovel. He then started to dig. Moments that stretched out longer than necessary revealed the first tin.

Antrim shoved his man out of the way and pulled his gun out of its holster. Pointing it at Brandon, he jerked it toward the hole. "Retrieve it."

Brandon crouched and grasped the tin firmly around the edges. Pulling it out, he thought just for a moment about attempting to make off with the sum. He could use the shovel as a weapon. Perhaps he could…but it would be pointless against two armed men.

So, he relinquished the canister.

Antrim tore off the lid and pulled out the money. His eyes were then hard on Brandon. "This can't be all of it."

"It isn't. There's another alongside it. To the right or left."

Antrim dropped the arm holding the tin. His eyes scanned the horizon. Was he concerned about something? Perhaps those who might come looking for him?

"You," he indicated Brandon, picking up the shovel and tossing it in his direction. "Keep digging. And you," he glared at his hench man. "Keep an eye on him."

The man nodded, pulling his gun free of its holster.

"I'll be back."

Brandon watched Antrim head toward the house.

The man watching Brandon held the weapon up and stepped toward him. "You heard him. Dig."

Brandon chose to dig to the north side of the canister's location. There would be nothing there. As soon as it was determined as such, the man looked in the direction where Antrim had gone and turned quickly back to Brandon.

"Keep digging."

But Brandon saw the sheen of sweat that had started to form on his features. And there was a slight shake to his voice. There might be an opportunity. If he could just bide his time.

As he continued to dig, he chanced glances at his overseer. Sure enough, the man cut his eyes frequently to where Antrim had gone. What was he so concerned about?

Brandon landed the same depth as the other hole, once again empty. "Nothing."

The man glared at him. "Nothing? Didn't you bury these canisters? How can you not know where they are?" With a shaking hand, he pointed his pistol at Brandon's face.

Brandon raised a hand, feigning fear. "I...I did. I'm just so nervous."

The man gave him a hard look. "Keep digging."

Brandon leaned over the shovel once more, but did not put it into the dirt just yet.

As the man turned toward the homestead, Brandon raised the shovel with one fluid motion and slammed the man's chest with the blade.

A shot rang out, but cut wild as the man's arm flailed about.

He went down. As he landed, the pistol fell from his hand.

Brandon jumped for the gun, grabbing it easily as his overseer was then gasping for breath.

Then it was Brandon who stood over the man, leering down at him, pistol aimed at the other man's heart.

Regretting the action almost immediately, he knocked the butt of the gun against the top of the man's head, and he was out. Why did he have to take such action? But he needed the man to be incapacitated.

Rushing toward the homestead, he prayed he wouldn't be too late. Sneaking around the side of the home, he crept along the easternmost wall.

Hoof beats sounded.

No!

Now running, he made it to the front of the home to see Antrim and his posse, now less one man, take off.

With his money.

But they did not take any of his people.

His gaze flickered around the yard. No one.

Taking quicker strides than he ever had before, he stepped into the house. There, in the dining room, his ranch hands were tied to the chairs. Including Cook. Where had she been?

And Amanda? She still lay in the great room, unconscious. He fell on his knees beside her. Hands moved over her, wishing he knew what to do. Did her heart beat still? He pressed his ear to her chest. There it was. Faint, but sure.

He ran a hand over her hair. "I'll get you help. I promise. Just don't die. Don't leave me."

Her eyelashes fluttered, and her eyes opened slightly.

"Amanda?"

"Brandon…"

Something pleasant flooded his spirit, but he was still weighed with the danger of her situation. "Shh…don't try to talk."

"…with me." The first part of her sentence was spoken with words too weak to discern.

"No," he stroked her hair again. Would that comfort her? "Save your strength."

She cleared her throat. Whatever she wanted to say, she seemed quite determined. Her hazel eyes met his and held them. Whatever she requested, no matter how outrageous, he would give it to her were it at all within his power.

"Please…stay…with me."

CHAPTER NINE

Concessions

ACHE. THAT'S ALL Amanda knew as she came to awareness. Hurt and horrible ache. It seemed to come from all over, but she couldn't move her arm.

Her eyes opened, and the world was bright. Blinking several times, she allowed her eyes to adjust to the room. Then she realized that what had been bright to her eyes was truly dimness.

But where was she? This was not her home. Either of them. Not Jed's homestead. Or Brandon's. This was a different place altogether.

The room had a bed, a nightstand with a lantern, and a chair. But someone occupied it.

As her eyes became more accustomed to the light, she made out the dark brown hair and the form that belonged to her husband.

Brandon.

Why had he stayed with her? After everything they had said to one another, why would he stay here?

A strange memory came to the forefront of her mind, a dream really…that she had asked him to.

Had he honored that?

The hour must be late, for he dozed in the chair. How long had he kept vigil?

She shifted in the bed, and pain slammed into her awareness.

A cry escaped her lips.

Tender hands were on her arm in a moment. Brandon's fingertips. And his face was over hers, deep brown eyes searched hers.

"You're in pain?"

She turned away so he wouldn't see more in her eyes than she wanted him to. "It is not so bad."

He sat on the edge of her bed. Such familiarity. Was it warranted? Then he slid a warm hand over her unwrapped one. "I was so worried, Amanda."

Her name sounded heavenly sliding off his lips. She moved to sit up.

Brandon placed gentle hands on her shoulders. "No, please don't. Allow me." He shifted the pillows behind her and slid an arm underneath her back and legs, moving her until she was sitting.

"Thank you," she said, smiling as she rearranged the blankets so that she was more covered.

He resumed his seat on the bed's edge.

She met his gaze until it became uncomfortable. Then she looked out the window.

"You are sure you are well?" Brandon's voice was low. "I can fetch the doctor if you need him."

Perhaps she was in the clinic then. She turned toward him again. "No, I thank you. I'm just rather sore."

Brandon's gaze fell. "I'm so sorry. For that. For everything."

Sorry? What had he done? Then it all came rushing back. The outlaw, the pistol, Brandon's attempt to help her...

She reached out and touched Brandon's cheek. "It is I who should be apologizing to you. I said...and did some rather mean things. I judged you, I blamed you...and the whole time you..." Her voice broke.

He caught her hand in his. "It is all forgotten."

Her eyes widened. "What about Samuel? What happened to Samuel?"

"He and Uncle Owen hid in the hay loft when they heard the men coming. How Uncle Owen managed to get up there, I'll never know. But it took three of us to get him down." Brandon let out a little laugh. He brought Amanda's hand to rest between his in his lap.

Amanda breathed a deep sigh of relief. "And now?"

"Cook is making sure they get what's due them. In her eyes, Uncle

Owen is the ranch hero, taking care of your boy like he did."

"I'll have to be sure and thank him."

Brandon nodded then looked down at her small hand captured between his. His fingers massaged her more delicate ones.

The simple motions were intoxicating. Amanda found herself quite entranced by the gesture. Unable to think about anything else, yet unable to pull away.

Did he know the effect he had on her?

"What…" She cleared her throat. "What happened to Henry?"

"Henry?"

"The leader of the posse? That's what his men called him—Henry."

"Kid Antrim? That's the name he goes by. He took off while I was detained. We captured one of the members of his gang though. Turned him over to the sheriff."

Amanda nodded. Chances were they'd never see or hear from him again.

"Did he…get your money?"

"Some of it." Brandon focused on her hand, but let out a deep sigh. Was he so burdened? He had Jed's cattle. Wasn't that enough?

She told herself to stop thinking like that. He wasn't the man she made him out to be. Brandon was simply trying to make his way in the world, and he needed that money. It *was* his money after all. And he had used it to get her out of trouble, and because of that, he had lost more, nearly all of it.

"I'm sorry." The words were weak on her lips.

His eyes sought hers again, brows furrowed. "Why? You didn't take it."

"But it's my fault you lost it. My fault you had to pay. My fault Henry…er…Kid Antrim even knew about it."

Brandon's eyes became serious. "Let's get one thing straight. That was Jed's debt. I paid it off to protect you. But it was not your fault. And I don't know how Antrim knew about my stash, but I intend to find out."

Amanda choked back further words of apology. Why would he not hear them? Let her shoulder her portion of the blame?

Instead she settled back into the pillows and allowed herself to rest in just being with him—for the first time.

Brandon winced as Cutie let out another yelp. He hated watching his ranch hand go through this. But he trusted the doctor's capable hands, just as he had with Amanda. There was nothing else to be done.

The medical man continued to work the braces on Cutie's limbs, ensuring they were secured properly. And he cleaned the ranch hand's wounds. None of it was pleasant. But once he finished, he looked over to Brandon. "We'd best let him rest now."

Brandon nodded then held up an arm for the doctor to step out of the small room. Following the doctor, Brandon then secured the door behind himself.

Once they were several paces away from the barn, out of earshot, both of the ranch hands and the house, the doctor turned to Brandon.

"I will be honest with you, Mr. Miller. It doesn't look good."

Brandon furrowed his brows. "Will he recover?"

"The scrapes and cuts won't be the problem. It's the deeper wounds — the torn muscles and bones that will take more time to mend. Much more than I think you will want to harbor an invalid worker."

Catching himself lest he bristle visibly at the callousness of the doctor, Brandon forced his eyes toward the house. Were all doctors cut from the same cloth? Uncle Owen had a doctor once. A doctor who told his ranch master that he was no longer worthwhile. Brandon's heart ached. He would not put Cutie out. No matter what it cost him. They would find a way. Together.

"Perhaps the man has family who can take him—"

Brandon held up a hand.

The doctor paused.

"We will manage."

A doubtful expression passed over the doctor's features. He quirked a brow at Brandon, but said nothing further on the matter.

"Shall I check in on my other patient while I am here?"

"Please," Brandon moved in the direction of the house.

The doctor picked up step beside him once again.

They walked the remainder of the yard in silence. And once they entered the house, Brandon wasted little time leading the doctor to the back hallway.

Amanda's door was open a crack, and he heard snippets of the conversation from within.

"I don't know." It was Amanda's voice. "This is our home now."

"But I don't like it."

A young voice. Samuel?

"You're sad here, Mama."

Definitely Samuel.

The pitifulness in the smaller voice tugged at Brandon's heart. Was he right? Was Amanda sad here? Brandon wanted her to be happy. He wanted Samuel to be happy. If only he hadn't been so distracted with the expanded herd and the problems they had encountered. And the challenges he'd faced with Amanda. Had he even considered Samuel at all?

Doctor Norwood coughed behind him, and Brandon remembered why he was there. Raising a hand, he knocked on the door. Through the thin opening, he saw movement.

"Who is it?" Amanda called.

"Brandon. I have the doctor. He wants to check on your progress."

Amanda whispered something to Samuel that Brandon couldn't make out.

Moments later, the door swung open and Samuel stared at him. The young boy's deep eyes were wide as they gazed up. Did Brandon intimidate him? Scared? That was not Brandon's intention at all.

Should he speak first? Or let the boy say something? What would be less overbearing on the child?

"Please, come in." Amanda's voice held a smile as she waved them farther into the room. "Samuel, mind your manners. Let Mr. Miller and the doctor in."

It seemed rather uncertain for a moment that Samuel would, in fact, move out of the way. Perhaps it was not that the boy was so much unnerved, but that he intended to throw Brandon off balance.

After his mother admonished him, however, Samuel slowly stepped to the side. Once Brandon and Doctor Norwood moved past him, he bolted out of the room and down the hall.

Brandon looked after him. Where was he off to in such a hurry? Or did he simply intend to escape the two grown men? His gaze shifted to Amanda's.

Her eyes softened and she mouthed an apology.

This, too, struck him as odd. Was there something he wasn't privy to? Did everyone else know?

"Well now, Mrs. Miller," Doctor Norwood started as he moved farther into the room, coming alongside the bed. "How is the shoulder?"

Amanda shuffled herself in her seated position to allow the doctor better access to her bandaged arm. "I am better today, I think. The medicine helps a bit. But I haven't tried to move it much."

Doctor Norwood took her arm in his hands and maneuvered it this way and that.

Amanda grimaced, but did not make a sound.

Brandon watched, not liking this any more than he did the doctor's work on Cutie. Rather, he liked this even less. Amanda's discomfort affected him in a way that Cutie's did not. It was almost as if he felt every pang she did. And if he could take the pain for her, he would. Gladly.

At last, the doctor finished that portion of the examination and started to undress her shoulder. In that moment, he seemed to forget that Brandon was in the room. For he removed her sling without pause and moved to unbutton her dress.

Amanda startled.

Brandon stepped forward.

Doctor Norwood pulled his hands back. "My apologies. I just need to look at the wound."

Amanda's eyes were on Brandon's. Should he leave? The doctor didn't seem to think there was anything inappropriate about him remaining. But then there wouldn't be, would there? He was, after all, her husband.

Yet as Doctor Norwood assisted her with the buttons at her collar once again, she turned away from Brandon, features coloring.

"I, ah, need to check something in the…um…field."

"No worries, Mr. Miller, I've got everything under control here." Doctor Norwood didn't so much as glance in Brandon's direction as he slipped from the room, careful to leave the door wide open.

After finding Cook and instructing her to assist the physician, Brandon set his sights on the barn.

So much had happened in the last few days. He hadn't the time to process it all. Amanda…Cutie…Jed's ring…Kid Antrim…the loss of his money…it was almost too much to even begin to think about. But he would have to sort it all out. Too much depended on it. On him.

He found himself in the barn. The lifeblood of the ranch. But he was not here to work. No, he needed some space to think. And this was not the place. Then why was he here?

A horse snorted off to the right, and he knew. His mind would be clearer once he was back with his beloved companion. Nothing but the two of them and the wind to resist them. Together, they could solve anything. Moving over toward Candy's stall, he grabbed for a harness and bit.

Something gave him pause. Was this truly the right thing to do? Abandon his ranch when he was already down one worker? Leave Amanda in the hands of the doctor before learning of her updated prognosis?

Glancing down at the leather straps in his hands, his heart fell. He wasn't the kind of man who could ride off and leave it all behind. Not even for an afternoon. No, he cared. Too much.

Besides, there was work to be done. Especially with Cutie out. What would he do? He couldn't afford another worker. And he couldn't exactly ask Uncle Owen to step in. Or lean on the others more than he was already. Brandon would not risk Cutie's future by pushing him out of recovery for selfish gain.

Brandon sank to the ground, back against the stall door. What was left for him but to forfeit his ranch? Was it reasonable that he, Dan, and Slim could manage everything minus Cutie? Was that even fair? And would it even work? With a portion of his nest egg gone, forever in the hands of Kid Antrim, could they even survive with what they would add from auction? Even with Jed's herd?

There were so many unknowns. Too many.

One thing was certain: he was not ready to give up.

***

Cook helped Amanda secure her blouse into place and re-button her collar.

"Everything looks good, Mrs. Miller. You can resume normal activities as long as you wear the sling. Even that can come off in the next week or two."

Amanda smiled. Wouldn't Brandon be glad to hear that? She had made a great recovery! And he had been so worried. It had been evident in his eyes.

"Thank you, Doctor." She nodded as he stood.

Cook led him from the room. Amanda heard their voices as they traveled down the hall and toward the front door, but she wasn't able to make out exactly what was said. Not that she concerned herself with what Cook might say to the doctor or vis versa. No, there was only one thing on her mind: Brandon.

Where had he gone? Back to his duties at the ranch? Perhaps he didn't concern himself with her well-being as much as she would like to believe.

But he had appeared so bothered…

He cared. Of that, she was certain.

Standing, she shifted the weight of her arm in the sling, trying to find the most comfortable position to bear the load on her neck muscles.

The front door snapped shut in the distance.

Was that the doctor going? Or someone coming?

She glanced out the window. Did dinnertime draw near?

Stepping out of her room and into the hall, she looked this way and that. No sign of anyone.

"Cook?"

No answer.

That was odd.

Perhaps the door shutting was Cook stepping outside.

Amanda took steps toward the kitchen. She would gain access to the front door by way of the dining room through the kitchen. And moments later, she stood at the front door, hand on the latch, preparing to open it.

"What did the doctor say?" A voice called out from behind her.

She jumped.

Fighting to compose herself, she turned. Brandon sat in the great room adjacent to the dining room, brows furrowed. He seemed rather troubled.

"I didn't mean to startle you." He rose, placing something in the seat he had just vacated. A book of some kind.

"It's all right." She took in a deep breath, only then realizing her good hand was over her heart. Was she as drained of color as she felt?

"I, um," he looked to the window off to the side of the room and ran a hand through his thick hair. "Couldn't seem to think straight."

Amanda eyed the book he had been reading. Was it a Bible? *Spare me.*

"He said I'm well recovered."

Brandon met her eyes again, a brow quirked.

"The doctor. He said I can go back to my regular duties as long as I wear the sling and that I'll be out of the sling in a week or two."

"That *is* good news." Brandon offered her a half smile.

For as much as he spoke the words, he didn't seem to believe them.

The distance between them seemed rather…awkward. Should she close it? Could she be so forward?

Closing her eyes for a moment, she wondered if it was prudent. After everything they'd been through. All the fighting, the odds between them.

But when she opened her eyes, she found that he had moved toward her. "Amanda?"

She waved him off. "I am well. Just thinking."

"What about?" He was close enough now that all he had to do was breathe the words. But they were still spoken deeply. Their bodies were mere inches apart. If he would but reach out, he could touch her. Would he?

"You." She couldn't help but be honest.

"Oh?" He took another step toward her.

Now there was precious little space between them. She felt the heat radiating off him. And it was delicious. Would her knees hold her up? They became soft and liquid.

"You know what I think?" he muttered, leaning toward her, cupping her face in his strong hand.

"Hmm?" was all she could manage; her eyelids became heavy.

"That I've been thinking a lot about you. And you've been thinking a lot about me."

Was it true? What was this spell he held her in?

He pressed his forehead to hers. The contact was both satisfying and but a taste of what could be.

"But I can't," he whispered.

Her eyes flew open.

He pulled back far enough to look at her. Reaching down, he grasped her hand and rubbed her ring finger. "You're wearing his ring. You belong to him."

She whimpered as her heart dropped to the floor.

He drew back further.

Amanda couldn't stop her outcry as he turned away. "And so you will punish me?"

His eyes were glazed and sad as he turned back toward her. "No. I have to do what is right by my heart. Until you are ready to let him go, I cannot risk it."

She bit her lip and watched as he gathered his Bible and walked out of the room. Only then did she let loose the cry that had built in her heart. Closing her eyes, she tossed her head back. What was she going to do?

Brandon maneuvered Candy out of the way of a passing heifer. Blinking several times, he rolled his shoulders back, trying to sit straighter in the saddle. The days ran longer and longer as the workload stretched farther into the night. What else could they do?

He couldn't ask for more from Dan and Slim, they were giving him all they had. They had stepped in as if Cutie were their flesh and blood brother. Perhaps, he wondered, they thought of themselves, too—that their situations could have been switched.

True to what the doctor said, Cutie's progress was slow. Painful and slow. Painfully slow. But Brandon was determined he would not rush the man's recovery in any way. Not that he needed to. Cutie clearly struggled with his invalidity. Yet his body kept him from denying it.

So, Brandon, Dan, and Slim pulled long, hard days. And still the quality of the ranch floundered. Even Uncle Owen saw it and wanted to step in. But Brandon forbade it. For purely selfish reasons. The last thing he needed was greater medical expense. Or to worry after the older man's health more than he already did. No, it was better this way.

Dan rode past Brandon off to the right and nodded in his direction. At last, Brandon was relieved. For a moment.

He could be out of the saddle and doing something with his hands. The horses needed their afternoon meal. And the stalls would have to be mucked at some point. That would at least help him fight off sleep.

"C'mon, girl," he urged Candy as he pulled her reins in the direction of the barn. "Let's get you fed."

The horse picked up her step, moving a bit faster than Brandon would have liked. He leaned a little too far to the left, a bit off balance. It took some work to right himself. Apparently, he wasn't the only one who was tired and hungry.

Trotting into the barn, he worked to slow the horse. As she came to a halt, he slid out of the saddle. He rubbed the animal's muzzle before walking her toward her stall.

As they neared, swishing sounds cut through his over stimulated, overtired brain. Was someone amidst the stalls already? Slim? He was supposed to be resting. The man had been up half the night with a sickly cow and all morning doing his ranch chores.

As he moved closer to the stall, the scraping sounds became sharper.

Shovel against ground. Someone was mucking the stalls. He drew in a breath. Slim would get a word from him. They needed to take care of themselves when they could. No one needed a hero here.

But as he came around the side of the stall and to the opening, the blond braid being flung over her shoulder caught his eye. Amanda.

With her back to him as she hunched over her work, she could not see him. Did she not hear him come up behind her?

She half turned to put her shovel-full into a bucket in the middle of the stall. Startling, she jumped.

"Why must you always sneak up on me?"

He looked down at the ground before meeting her eyes. "It's not my intention."

A silence fell between them. But it lasted only long enough for Brandon to collect his thoughts.

"What do you think you are doing?" He furrowed his brows.

She waved an arm about the stall. "I should think that would be quite obvious."

He glanced around. She had done a good job, he had to admit. But she shouldn't be doing it. "You know that's not what I meant."

Her eyes caught his. They were soft and sad. "You and Dan and Slim are wearing yourselves too thin. How can I not do what I can to help?"

Help? What was she thinking? Brandon opened his mouth, but Amanda held up her hand.

"I know you are hesitant to let me get involved in the ranch. But surely you can't—"

"I can."

She quieted, licking her lips, holding his gaze for a few moments more, and then looking off to the side.

Candy butted her nose against Brandon's shoulder. Brandon hooked her reins to the stall door's latch and stepped in, closer to Amanda.

He crossed his arms in front of his chest and then lifted a hand to rub his brows. Why was it so difficult to argue with her? This was nonsense. Watching her work herself alongside his ranch hands would be too difficult.

"Your shoulder—"

"Is just fine." She moved and flexed the arm as if to prove it was indeed well. The doctor had let her go without the sling well over a week ago.

He held her eyes then. Why did he find himself wanting to give her what she wanted? As if it started to make sense?

Amanda took several steps toward him. "I know it's not what you want. But I am capable."

How could she not understand? It wasn't that at all. He swallowed hard as she drew closer.

"I won't let you down." Now she stood directly in front of him. So close he could smell the sweetness of her. It intoxicated him. He couldn't think straight.

The urge to draw her into his arms was almost irresistible. Almost. His eyes traced along her features, down to her lips, and to the hand that held the shovel. Jed's ring still shone on that finger.

He took a step back and dragged in a breath, his lungs aching as if deprived. Had he not been breathing?

"All right," he conceded.

She smiled, eyes gleaming.

"But," he said, holding up a hand, "There will be limits."

Amanda nodded and her eyes glistened. Was she going to cry? He prayed not. How would he handle that?

"And this will only work as long as you are honest with me about what you can handle. I do not want you overtiring yourself."

"But you and Dan and Slim—"

"I don't care. We are ranchers."

She opened her mouth. Was she going to protest? Seeming to think better of it, she closed her lips and nodded.

"All right, then. Back to work." He gave her a wide grin.

She threw her arms around him.

Had she tripped? He caught her, clutching her waist to steady her.

Amanda tightened her grip around his shoulders.

No, she hadn't fallen. She just embraced him.

Holding her to himself, he breathed in the scent of her hair and relished the feel of her body against his. How he wanted it to last! But it was not possible.

Before he was ready, she drew back. It was for the best. He would be lost to himself before long, his boundaries forgotten.

Amanda turned and moved the shovel along the ground again, collecting the things that needed to be removed from the stall.

The warmth drawn from his body was tangible. Her absence from his arms created an ache, a longing that would not be satisfied by anything he could do.

So, he forced himself to pull back from the stall and move on to the next thing. And while he knew he would worry after her the entirety of her working, he thanked God for the provision of the extra help. Perhaps, just perhaps, there was hope.

Amanda shoved her hands under the running water and closed her eyes. The cool liquid felt good. But it stung. Her skin was raw. It had been months since she had tended to the ranch with Jed. Was her skin getting soft? She should inquire after a pair of gloves. Would that make Brandon worry?

Looking down at her hands, she noted the scrapes. Blood, though only small lines, marred her skin. Not the stains that had marked her hands when Jed...

Movement behind caused her to draw her hands to herself. Jerking her head around, she breathed relief. It was only Cook.

"Did I frighten you, dear?"

"Maybe a little." Amanda smiled slightly at the older woman.

Cook closed the distance between them before Amanda could cover her hands.

"Land sakes alive, child! What have you done?" Cook grabbed for her wrists.

Amanda attempted to pull away. "It's nothing."

"I can see with my own eyes it ain't 'nothin'." Cook pulled Amanda's hands closer to her face.

"Please don't tell Brandon," Amanda said before she could stop herself.

Cook gave her a hard look with quirked brow.

"Please, Cook. He wouldn't understand."

"Understand what?"

Amanda took in a breath. "That I just want to help."

Cook continued to stare at her, but didn't speak further.

"You see it, too. He and Dan and Slim are killing themselves to keep this ranch going. I have to do something. I have to help."

The older woman's fingers rubbed at the outer sides of Amanda's hands. What was she thinking?

"Please say something."

Cook bit at her lip.

Amanda's eyes pricked with unshed tears. But they were coming.

A great sigh came from Cook. "Let me get some salve and bandages."

Nodding, but not trusting herself to speak without crying, Amanda tried to smile her gratitude.

"And if I see this again…"

Amanda nodded. "I understand." A tear escaped.

The front door opened.

"That'll be the menfolk coming in for dinner." Cook urged Amanda toward the door to the back hall. "Go to your room. I'll tell them you're not well."

"Won't that worry Brandon more?"

Cook paused. "More than seeing bandages on your hands?"

Amanda hadn't thought of that. "I suppose not."

"I'll tell him it's your head aching."

Nodding, Amanda moved toward the safety of her bedroom. Breathing a sigh of relief once she was out of the kitchen, she cradled her hands close to her body. She would have to be more careful.

She heard Samuel's small voice speaking loudly to Cook. That urged her to move on to her room. Passing on a lie to her son was not something that she relished, but she didn't want him worrying after her either.

Why had she spent so many hours hard at it today? She should have eased into the work. Should have recognized that it wasn't as easy as jumping back in as if no time had passed. Her hands had become unaccustomed to work.

Just then a figure stepped out from the door to her left and blocked her path. She nearly knocked into it, pulling back at the last second. Looking up, the image came into focus: Uncle Owen.

"Forgive me, I did not know anyone would be back here."

"No need." Uncle Owen smiled. "Are you unwell?"

Must be her face. She must look a wreck.

"I, um, I have a headache." Best go with the same lie.

He appeared doubtful; eyebrows gathered on his forehead.

She turned away. He had her. But what could she say? Wouldn't he tell Brandon anything she admitted to him?

When she shifted her gaze to meet his again, he was no longer looking at her face. His eyes were on her hands, huddled close to her stomach. She turned her palms into her dress. Had he seen?

His eyes were on hers then. But he didn't speak.

"It's nothing." A stray hair fell into her face. She almost moved to put it back behind her ear. Only then she remembered. And stayed her hand.

Uncle Owen's mouth became a thin line.

She went to move past him, but he stepped into her path.

"I…" Tears threatened to come. Why wouldn't he just let her be?

He held out his older, weathered hands, open and waiting.

What was he doing? What was his plan? Should she trust him?

Licking her lips, she stared at his calloused skin. What lay there for her? A confidant? Mercy? She needed some understanding right now. So very badly.

Cook was her ally, but even she did not understand. Would Uncle Owen? Should Amanda chance it? Dare she?

Without meeting his eyes, she hesitantly put forth first one hand, and then the other. And, closing her eyes, she set them in Uncle Owen's roughened hands. Though her eyes were shut, tears forced their way out.

Uncle Owen remained as he was, holding her hands gently in his. What did he intend to do? March her straight to Brandon? Examine her wounds himself?

At length, she opened her eyes and gazed into his soft, almost gray eyes. There was a deep sorrow there. As if he knew. How could he?

Something in her resonated with that sadness. All of a sudden, she wasn't alone.

Leaning toward him, she only hoped he would catch her.

His hands released hers and took hold of her arms as her face met his shoulder. And the floodgates opened. Was this what it was like to be cared for by a father? To be embraced?

And her wound opened. Hot liquid poured from within her. Aching pain seemed to burst from her core and fill her. Would she ever stop crying?

Her sobs did, after some moments, subside. Then reality settled. This was Uncle Owen. Not her father. How could she have let him see?

Amanda pushed these thoughts to the side. Being known and cared for soothed those sore places in her too well for her to turn her back on it.

She did pull away from Uncle Owen enough to offer him a smile. "I'm sorry. I didn't know—"

He waved a hand. "Your apology is not necessary." Those kind gray-blue eyes once again settled on hers.

She nodded, wiping at the remnants of her tears. It burned. Jerking her hands away, she wondered at the sensation. Perhaps the salty liquid stung her injuries anew.

Uncle Owen reached once more for her hands, closing around her wrist. "Come. I have something for that."

She obeyed, allowing him to lead her into his and Brandon's bedroom.

He left her just inside the doorway while he moved toward a small cabinet by the bed.

Amanda's eyes wandered about the room. Not much had changed since the day she had come in search of the shotgun. The room even appeared as if it had been rummaged through. Brandon's pallet was disheveled and clothes were strewn about. Uncle Owen's bed was the only thing in order.

"I use this on Brandon's cuts and nicks. Seems to help." Uncle Owen held a small tin canister in his hands as he limped back toward her.

Brandon's cuts and nicks?

Did he have them often? How hard was this life he led? Jed had his share of scrapes and cuts…but that was different. Somehow. Why was it different though? The thought disturbed her. And then realization hit her —because she also bore the brunt of the labor. When Jed had injuries, she was also tending to her own? Something that Brandon wanted so badly to protect her from. But it hadn't bothered Jed. Had he even cared?

Struck. Amanda froze to the spot. Everything around her seemed hazy. And then it started to spin.

She reached out to steady herself, and Uncle Owen's arm caught her. "Are you all right?"

Amanda put a hand to her forehead. "Yes. I…I think so." She caught Uncle Owen's eyes.

"Let's get you to your bed."

She didn't argue, but let him lead her.

How could she have been so blind?

CHAPTER TEN

Choices

BRANDON RUBBED THE bridge of his nose. His prayer time had been a struggle. Had been for quite some time. Was it the exhaustion? Or his own fight against the line he'd drawn with Amanda? The line God told him to draw?

He sucked in a deep breath and closed his eyes. It was no use. Would there ever be reconciliation between them? Or would there always be this longing, this emptiness within him?

Only God knew. So he would just have to trust.

Gazing toward the night sky from his seat on the porch, he prayed once again. If the God Who crafted each of those twinkling stars cared for him like the Bible promised, everything would work out. He'd just have to have faith.

Lifting his Bible, he stood and turned toward the front door. The house had long since fallen quiet.

Stepping into the dining room, he startled. A clatter sounded from the kitchen. Cook had already left for her home. Who was up and about? Samuel need a snack?

Perhaps now was as good a time as any to become acquainted with the boy. Brandon set his Bible on the dining table and made his way toward the kitchen. Pushing the door open, he entered the smaller room.

But a flash of long hair and a white nightdress caught his eye.

"Amanda?"

She spun on him, eyes wide, mouth open slightly.

He couldn't help but take her in. Her eyes were puffy and swollen. Had she been crying? Why? What had happened? His heart turned.

As his eyes moved over her figure, her hands caught his attention. They were bandaged. Had she been injured? Cook said she had a headache. Everything in front of him spoke otherwise.

"Are you unwell?" He moved toward her.

She stepped back, bumping into the counter. "No. I am well enough." Amanda pulled her hands around her back.

Was she frightened of him? He halted his progress, and she seemed to breathe easier.

He opened his mouth, but the right words wouldn't come. Floundering for a moment, he closed his lips and swallowed past a lump in his throat.

Couldn't he just reach out and take her in his arms? Wouldn't that make everything better? But that was not the answer.

She bit at her lip, but held his eyes. "I…was just looking for something to eat."

Brandon nodded. She had missed dinner. "Are you better?"

Nodding, her face turned in the direction of the floor. Her hair fell in waves to both sides of her face. Did she not usually gather it in a braid for bed? His face warmed at the realization that he knew something so intimate about her. At length, he spoke into the silence, "I was worried."

She met his gaze again. Was that moisture in her eyes? Had he made her upset?

Brandon took a step forward. "Please." He held out his hands. "I know we haven't always had the best of understanding between us. But I wish…" Pausing, he looked off to the side. Then secured her eyes again. "Tell me what's wrong?"

Amanda appeared as if she were ready to climb on top of the counter to escape him somehow, but after some moments, her shoulders relaxed. And then a tear fell.

He held his breath, praying she would speak.

"I just didn't want you to be angry." She held out her hands, palms up, displaying the bandages. Her eyes were set.

This happened as she worked the ranch. A familiar sensation welled within him. But it was not anger. At least, not for her, but for himself. It wasn't right to work her like this. To the point that she was injured. If she would push herself to this point... He drew in a breath through his nose and held it for a moment before letting it go.

Brandon closed the distance between them and took her hands in his. Then he unwrapped the bandages one at a time. He would see with his own eyes what damage had been done.

Once the skin was laid bare before him, he let out a sigh. It was not as he feared. Though the ugly crisscross marks marred her skin, there would be no scars.

With gentle fingers, he traced over the lines of her palm. Uncle Owen must have attended to the injuries. There were traces of his salve on the cuts.

An audible breath escaped Amanda's lips.

He stopped his movements. Had he hurt her? His eyes flew to hers. But he did not find hazel orbs. Her eyes were closed.

Looking back down at her hands, he glanced over to her left hand. Jed's ring was gone. Was that because her hands were healing? Or because she was ready to move on?

Though it was unclear, and he should stop here, help her find food, and send her back to bed, he could not help himself. She so captivated him; surely, he was under a spell.

He lifted her hands toward his lips and pressed them first to one palm and then to the other.

A gasp escaped her.

It thrilled him.

How could he stop? How could any warm-blooded man?

He angled his head and then kissed her wrists.

"Brandon," she breathed. She moved her body closer to his. Her arms slid around his shoulders and her face drew near his.

Her lips were inches from his. And he longed to taste them again. Only tonight, he would take his time.

His eyes flickered over her features. Something gave him pause. Something in his core.

Her red, swollen eyes. There was more to this story. More she wasn't telling him. Was she not ready to trust him?

She stood on her tiptoes, leaning into him.

Brandon moved his head, pulling her to his shoulder, embracing her.

At first, she resisted, but soon melted to him.

He had to resist the urge to hold her more tightly, to feel the curves of her body. That would only lead where he could not follow…yet. It was not time. She wasn't ready.

Amanda sighed into his shoulder and leaned into him even more. Was she tiring?

He pressed a kiss to the side of her head. "Let me take you back to bed."

"No," she protested. "I want…I…"

He lifted her easily. "What you need is the sanity that comes with a good night's rest."

She murmured something else, but it was muffled in his shoulder.

Cradling her in his arms, he walked her back toward her room. But nothing could keep him from enjoying the feel of having her in his arms, the intoxication of her scent, and the thrill of what may come.

But there was also fear. Fear that when the day broke, this would dissipate into a memory.

Had she really tried to…?

Amanda stared at the ceiling in her room. As dawn woke her and the events of the evening came racing back, she recoiled at her behavior.

Turning to her side and pressing her face into her hands, she let out a groan. What must he think of her? It couldn't be good.

Moving her hands down over her mouth, she blinked several times as if that would make the memory go away. But it was firmly planted in her mind. How was she going to face him?

Maybe she could grab a biscuit from the kitchen, excuse herself from breakfast, and head out to do her chores, missing Brandon entirely.

Would he try to check on her this morning? He had been concerned after her hands last night. She glanced at the skin on her palms.

It couldn't be.

Amanda jerked them back farther. Her vision must be going. But even gaining some distance between them and her eyes did not change what she saw.

The scrapes and abrasions were all but gone.

What was in that salve?

Or perhaps it was Brandon's kisses?

Her face warmed at her silly schoolgirl thought. She pulled the covers over her head. Ridiculous. Just ridiculous. She was hopeless.

After some moments of hiding from herself, she peeked out. Yep, she was still there. As were her thoughts about Brandon. Why couldn't she push him to the side? *This* is hopeless!

She thrust the covers to the side and sat. Gazing out the window, she welcomed the warmth of the sun streaming in. What would today bring? The uncomfortable confrontation with Brandon that she feared? Or simply a satisfying work day?

It would be easier to avoid him by doing her chores rather than at the breakfast table, she decided.

She pushed herself out of bed and hurried through her morning rituals. Once dressed with hair braided and out of her face, she stepped quietly out of her room.

Moving through the house, she was comforted by the sounds of Cook in the kitchen. Pushing open the door, she put a smile on her face for the older woman. She owed her a great deal of thanks for her assistance yesterday evening.

Her heart stopped at the sight that greeted her. Cook indeed moved about the kitchen. But Brandon stood to one side, leaning against a counter, coffee in hand, comfortable as could be.

Couldn't she just die right there? Her face heated several degrees as her eyes met his.

"I…ah…didn't mean to disturb you two." She spun to step back out the way she came.

"You ain't disturbing anything, honey," Cook said. "Stay."

Amanda paused, breathing deeply.

"I was about to set the table anyway."

Amanda turned to see Cook walk to the cabinet and pull down plates.

"I can do that…" Amanda said, taking a step in that direction.

"No, ma'am." Cook shook her head. "You are doing quite enough around here. Get yourself some coffee and enjoy your morning while it lasts."

Amanda sighed, wringing her hands. Wasn't there something she could do? Anything but stand in this room with Brandon?

Cook finished gathering the plates and moved into the dining room, leaving Amanda and Brandon alone.

Amanda glanced at him.

He offered her a smile as he lifted his mug to his lips. "Did you sleep well?"

What was that supposed to mean? She paused. Perhaps she shouldn't read into everything. "I did."

"Good." His smile radiated from his eyes as well as his lips. As if he had a secret. And he continued to lean against the counter as if he were as comfortable as could be. Did he not feel the awkwardness?

"Care for some coffee?" He indicated the pot on the stove with his mug.

"Sure." She stepped in that direction.

"Allow me." He was closer, so he got there first.

She watched the muscles in his arms work as he set his mug down and transferred hot liquid into a fresh mug for her. Then he walked it to her, stepping a bit closer than he needed to.

Did she mind? His presence had become rather comforting. Even in the awkwardness of the earlier moments, having him so close soothed her.

He handed her the cup and, placing his other hand on her arm, leaned in to press a kiss to her forehead.

Her eyes slid closed.

His lips lingered for a moment. His breath tingled and warmed her skin.

Why did he do that? It seemed so…intimate. Is this where things were?

"I best get back to my morning chores," he whispered as he pulled away.

She swayed toward him as he did so, almost tipping her balance before catching herself.

His movements were somewhat stuttered as he moved across the room. He didn't turn until the very last second, when he was at the door to the dining room.

At that point, Cook came back into the kitchen and they collided.

Amanda couldn't help but giggle. So much for him being calm and confident.

It was time for his face to color as he ensured Cook was all right.

"Gracious, Mr. Brandon, where is your head?" she muttered.

He glanced toward Amanda.

Cook's eyes followed his, and a knowing smile broke out across her face.

"Sorry," he stammered. "I…just…my mind was somewhere else."

Amanda put the back of her fingers against her mouth to keep from laughing out loud.

Brandon gave a quick nod and then he was gone.

Cook's eyes were wide as she turned toward Amanda. "What was all that about?"

What should she say? These were the things she wanted to keep in her heart. Just for her. So she drew the cup to her lips and took in a long sip. That would give her a moment.

"It's like that, is it?" Cook smiled. "Well, I declare!"

Amanda smiled. Today was turning out to be quite all right.

***

Brandon closed the fence and secured the latch. He heaved from the effort of the morning's chores. Another long day. His shirt clung to him in places, but only because he had accomplished much.

Turning back toward the barn, he moved in that direction. There were other tasks that awaited him. Taking long strides, he kept his eyes trained on the structure. It wasn't long before he saw a figure emerge.

The skirt and long braid gave her away—Amanda. He squinted to get a better glimpse. She walked to the water pump with a large bucket. Once there, she placed the bucket down and began working the pump. Were her hands better?

It had been his intention to check on their progress today. He had been too…distracted this morning to ask after them. And he hadn't another chance yet today. But as he watched her, he noted that she worked without much concern after them. That was a good sign, right?

How he hated that she had to assist with the ranch work. But her offer might very well save the ranch. Only time would tell. At auction.

He shifted his steps and aimed to intercept her. What did he intend to say? That was unclear. But his heart raced at the thought of being near her again, of speaking with her. What was this thing between them? Did she feel it, too?

Brandon neared her position as she filled the bucket. She stopped pumping and reached down for the handle. But she took notice of him in that moment. Standing to her full height, she put a hand over her eyes. Was that a smile that graced her features? Her other hand raised in a slight wave.

His heart did a flip-flop and he waved too, grinning. Why did he feel as if he were a schoolboy again? That he was about to ask her to the town's Sweetheart Dance?

Her face fell then. Was something amiss? She seemed to look past him. It gave him pause.

He turned. A small carriage appeared over the horizon. His heart fell. Whoever it was had just taken away his moment with Amanda.

Looking back at her, he offered her a half-smile and a shrug.

She smiled as well before bending over to gather the bucket. Then she moved back into the barn.

Brandon shifted his focus to the coming visitor. A fine carriage like this could only be one of a few people. None of whom he wanted to see.

He continued walking toward the front of the house to intercept his guest there. As the carriage came closer, he could make out the markings on the vehicle and some of the details of the driver—Mr. George C. Perkins. So, the banker had come at last. Would he want his next pound of flesh now?

Brandon worked to keep his features as neutral as possible. The man's presence made that all the more difficult. As if the situation wasn't trying enough…

The banker fairly slithered. His eyes were filled with dollar signs. If they cracked open his chest, would they find a loan document?

Lord, please forgive me for such thoughts. He is just a man doing his job.

But this man seemed to enjoy what should be the more unpleasant parts of his job too much for Brandon's liking.

The carriage came to a halt alongside the front porch. Mr. Perkins set the reins down.

"Good day, Mr. Perkins." Brandon tipped his hat and offered the man the only smile he could force onto his face.

The man touched the brim of his hat. "And a find day to you, too, Mr. Miller." Perkins maneuvered his somewhat clumsy body out of the carriage. It wasn't because of his size. He just always seemed awkward in his own skin when doing such things.

Brandon had seen him falter getting on or off a horse more than once. It made him wonder if he should assist the man. But then he thought better of it.

After some moments, the man was on solid ground. Relief was evident on his face as he turned toward the porch.

"And how are things here at your little ranch these days?" Perkins held up his arms, waving them about as if to encompass the whole of the property.

Brandon bit his tongue. He was proud of his ranch. And had every right to be. This land was not inherited. No, he had built his ranch. How dare this man make light of it.

And Perkins had certainly heard of the robbery and Cutie's injuries. He was not ignorant to their hardships. Was he here to taunt? Brandon was not in the mood to play games.

"We do as well as we can. As you know, we've had some hard luck."

Perkins' face fell. But he recovered quickly. He shook his head and made a tsk-ing sound with his tongue. "That's too bad."

Brandon did not respond. That left the two men staring at each other in an awkward silence.

Perkins took out his handkerchief, pulled off his hat, and wiped at the sweat on his brow.

Brandon shook his head. The man was not cut out for any kind of life of hardship. Not even house calls to his debtors.

"Might I trouble you for a glass of water?"

"Certainly." Brandon's reply was curt. As much as he wished Perkins would speak his peace and leave, he would not deny any man the simple comforts he could provide. That's not the way Christ would have him treat others.

Brandon stepped onto the porch and into the house. He made his way to the kitchen where Cook was already working on lunch.

She seemed startled to see him.

He went straight for the cabinet to get a glass.

"I don't often have the pleasure of your company at this hour." Cook continued to stand and stare at him.

Brandon didn't so much as look at her. "Mr. Perkins is here from the bank. He requested some water."

Though he knew Cook would want further details, he offered nothing else. But he felt her eyes boring into his back while he finished filling the glass. So, he was careful not to glance in her direction as he finished and headed back outside.

When Brandon stepped onto the porch, he found that Mr. Perkins had helped himself to a seat there. Brandon handed over the glass, but didn't bother sitting.

Mr. Perkins drained half the water with one sip. How thirsty could he be after so little effort? But as Brandon looked at him, he saw that the man continued to sweat rather profusely. More so than he would have imagined possible.

Brandon folded his arms over his chest. And when Mr. Perkins didn't speak, though he had paused in his refreshment, Brandon's patience wore thin. "Mr. Perkins, I don't mean to seem unneighborly. But I can't imagine you stopped by just to ask after the ranch."

Perkins eyes burned into Brandon. Did he hate being put on the spot as much as Brandon hated the games?

The banker used his handkerchief to blot the corners of his mouth and set the glass on a side table. "I am loath to be the bearer of bad news, Mr. Miller. And I had hoped to speak genially to you about this. But you seem to wish that I tell you straight." Perkins' sarcastic tone betrayed that he was anything but loath to share whatever tidings he brought.

"Please," Brandon ground out.

"The bank is not able to make any further extension to you." Perkins eyes narrowed, and there was a slight upturn to the corner of his mouth. He enjoyed this.

So that was that. There would be no mercy, no grace extended for their circumstances. Regardless of the robbery, regardless of losing a ranch hand, their loan would still be due on time.

Brandon forced himself to breathe. In and out. In and out. His hands curled into fists, but he kept them secured in the pockets of his arms, still folded over his chest.

Everything in him wanted to lash out toward this man, whose grin was becoming more apparent by the second. But he stilled himself. Nothing good would come from that.

"I do have a proposition for you." Perkins now made no attempt to hide his glee. "Turn over the ranch now, and I'll just take the property and the cattle. You keep the money."

Give up? When there was still a chance? What was he to do? Could they make it at auction time? Was there any hope? Could he risk losing everything for the chance he might save it all?

"This offer won't be good forever." Perkins' gaze moved over the pasture, the cattle. "After all, it is such a sad little piece of property. I'll have to sell off what I can a piece at a time."

"I'd like you to go," Brandon seethed.

Perkins shifted his focus back to Brandon. "I can see you're upset. But you must think like a businessman. Be reasonable. Save what you can while you can."

"I'd like you to go. Now."

Perkins' half smile fell. It was replaced by an uneasy expression. Was he afraid of Brandon? He got to his feet. "Just remember what I said. This offer won't be good for long."

"Good. I won't be taking you up on it." Brandon stepped closer to Perkins.

The man stepped back. "You'll regret it. Mark my words!" Perkins stumbled down the stairs and to his carriage.

Brandon continued advancing toward the man. Was it his intention to intimidate or simply to make the man leave him alone?

The banker seemed to have a rather difficult time getting into his carriage, fumbling with his own limbs. Once he was seated, he straightened his jacket and looked back at Brandon. "It's only a matter of time before this ranch folds."

"Good day to you, Mr. Perkins."

Perkins frowned.

Just then Amanda came from the barn, leading Candy. It drew not only Brandon's attention, but Mr. Perkins' as well.

It was a moment before Perkins turned back toward Brandon. "My, what a lovely wife you have there, Mr. Miller. Does she come with the ranch?"

Perkins slapped the reins and his horse jerked into action, moving into a trot before Brandon could react.

He burned in his heart toward Mr. Perkins. Deeply. It was as if he could go out of his skin after the man. His head spun. Still, the carriage moved off into the distance.

What could he do? What would become of them all? Of the ranch?

***

"See, Mama. See how she loves it?" Samuel called from the yard. He waved a stick in the air.

Daisy knocked him over.

Amanda stood, preparing to rush to his aid.

But he simply laughed as he got to his feet. Then he threw the stick and the dog bounded after it.

Samuel turned to look at her. "Come on, Mama. You try."

Amanda's body ached from her work, but the guilt of neglecting her son won out. Between grieving Jed, her transitioning challenges, and taking on a more active role at the ranch, Samuel had been under the care of Uncle Owen and Cook much of the time.

This weighed on Amanda. Never had she imagined that she would leave the care of her son to someone else. Not that she wasn't grateful. She was. It was just one more thing for her to regret.

"Mama?" Samuel's small voice broke through her thoughts.

"Coming." She stood, making her way off the porch and into the yard. Muscles sore from overuse protested. *Just a few moments*, she promised.

Daisy had returned with the stick in her mouth, tail wagging to boot. She brought the stick to Samuel, pushing on him with her nose.

"You take it, Mama." He stepped to the side.

Amanda closed the gap between herself and the dog, reaching toward the animal's slobbering mouth with some hesitation.

Daisy pulled away, lowering her head to the ground, a low growl emitting from her throat.

Amanda's eyes widened. Was this dog about to challenge her right here, right now?

"What is it, girl?" Samuel attempted to soothe the animal.

Not willing to back down, Amanda leaned further, stretching toward Daisy again.

The dog's growl became louder.

Samuel stepped forward, hand outstretched.

Amanda put an arm in front of Samuel, pressing him behind her.

"What's the matter?" Samuel's voice rose.

"I don't know, but let's not upset her."

"She wouldn't hurt me," Samuel argued, attempting to push Amanda's arm away.

Amanda grabbed his shoulders.

Another rumble came from the dog. This time, she dropped the stick and bared her teeth.

"We're going inside." Amanda gripped Samuel's arm, but kept her eyes on the dog.

"No! You don't understand. She's just trying to protect me, Mama."

Amanda moved toward the porch with Samuel in tow. "Protect you? From what?"

Daisy barked as she stood and followed them.

Samuel tried to shrug Amanda's hands off. "Stop it! She's my friend."

"Don't fight me." Amanda continued to pull at him. Much to her relief, the dog didn't climb the stairs onto the porch. But Amanda didn't stop until they were in the house. Only then did she release her hold on her son.

He raced toward the door.

"Samuel Isaac Haynes, don't you dare move one step closer to that door."

The boy paused. But he stared at the door. Was he trying to decide?

Amanda watched him from across the room. What had happened to her sweet little boy? The one that hung on her every word? Where did this defiance come from?

He took another step toward the door.

"Go to your room." Her command was sharp.

Samuel whipped around, eyes narrowed as they glared at her.

She widened her eyes. "Now."

He opened his mouth. Was he about to sass her? Then he closed it, folded his arms across his chest and stomped off to his room, huffing as he went. A handful of seconds later, a door in the back hallway slammed.

Amanda let out a breath and deflated into one of the dining room chairs. The encounter with the dog and Samuel began to sink in. What might have happened to Samuel? To her? Was the dog truly safe?

Just then shuffled footsteps moved toward her. Was Samuel out of his room?

She rose, prepared to send him back. But as she turned, she saw that it was Uncle Owen limping into the great room.

Moving toward the larger room where she could see him better, she looked at the ground as she apologized. "Were you resting? I'm sorry if Samuel—"

He waved her off. "I just came out to make sure everything was all right."

Amanda sighed. "It is."

Uncle Owen maneuvered his frame into a sitting chair in the great room. "Please, come join me."

It wasn't what she wanted to do. She'd rather take some time to think through what happened and what she would say to Samuel in the next ten to fifteen minutes.

But she had a lot of respect for Uncle Owen. Both for his place at the ranch and for the way he had treated her. So, she pushed that to the side and took the seat beside him.

A silence fell between them, but it was pleasant, companionable.

"I never had kids," he said after some moments.

Amanda didn't know how to respond. She was unsure about his relationship with Brandon. Had he raised Brandon as a surrogate father? From what age?

"I always wanted more." Her response surprised her. It was true. She had wanted more. And though Jed had never said it out loud, she sensed that he blamed her for the fact they hadn't had more.

Uncle Owen smiled. "There's time."

Amanda's face warmed. What would it be like to have that kind of marriage with Brandon? To have children with him? Or were Jed's suspicions correct? Could she not have any more?

"Samuel is a special young man." Uncle Owen turned his head to meet her gaze.

"Yes, yes he is. But he's growing up too fast."

"Is he?"

That was an odd question. "What do you mean?"

"Is he growing up too fast? Or are you having trouble letting him grow at all?"

Taken aback, Amanda couldn't think of anything to say. She could hardly think at all. Not let him grow at all? Of course she wanted him to grow. What mother wouldn't?

"It's okay," he continued. "You're still learning to let go of your late husband. Acknowledging such big changes in your son must be even harder in the midst of that."

Would he just stop talking for two minutes? Her chest constricted. Was the room getting smaller? She wanted to get up and leave the room, but she was weighed down, anchored to the seat somehow. Closing her eyes against the shrinking space, she took a deep breath. It hurt her lungs to do so. But she did. And then took another. "I...I don't understand what this has to do with—"

"Just a thought. That's all." His eyes met hers again. "Just a thought."

Part of her wanted to reject it. After all, what did he know about raising children? He said it himself—he never had any. But the louder part of her knew better. Though he may have never had children of his own, he was wise beyond her years. And he had spent more time with Samuel these last weeks than she had. It would be foolish to dismiss him.

So, she faced him and nodded. "I understand."

He turned toward the front door.

It opened. In walked Brandon, Dan, and Slim. How did Uncle Owen know they were coming?

Amanda reached over and patted Uncle Owen's hand. "I think I need to have a talk with my son now."

He winked at her, but his face remained neutral.

Rising, she caught Brandon's gaze. She was tempted to give him a little wave. But that seemed like such a schoolgirl impulse. Instead, she satisfied herself with a smile.

He returned it.

Her heart expanded. Was that what she needed? A little tenderness and encouragement? Either way, she was more prepared for her talk with Samuel.

CHAPTER ELEVEN

Changes

BRANDON HAD A plan. A silly plan. Was it too forward? Would Amanda think him hopeless?

Cook smiled from across the kitchen. He turned back to the task at hand as his face warmed. What was she thinking? Did it matter?

When he looked in Cook's direction again, she was hard at work. Would his plan leave a void, a hardship for Dan and Slim? He had risen especially early to ensure his portion of the work had been completed.

It was no matter. This was important.

He finished with his immediate task and stepped back, admiring the basket, filled to the brim. Had he packed too much? His hands moved over the items within. And then fell.

Cook leaned against his side, placing a hand on his arm. "It's perfect."

Brandon nodded, gaze still on the contents of the rather large basket.

"Now quit putting it off. Go ask her." Cook elbowed him before she stepped to the sink.

He smiled in her direction. An uneasy smile. Where was his confidence?

But he couldn't think of any reason to delay longer. Lifting the basket, he was surprised at its weight. Should he lug it all the way to the wagon now? That seemed a bit premature. So, he set it on the floor instead, his hands thanking him for relieving them of their burden.

His palms had become slick. He rubbed them on his pants legs.

"You still here?" Cook turned her head as she pumped water into the sink. "Go!"

"I am," he muttered. Then Brandon set his sights on the door and let his feet follow.

Before long, he was outside and headed to the barn. Much of Amanda's work was kept to the barn: mucking the stalls, feeding the horses, tending to the general cleanliness and maintenance of the interior of that structure. It was a big job, but one she had handled well, and without complaint. More than that, he knew where she was at all times and had some sense that she was safe.

Now, as he approached the building, his heart began to thunder in his ears. There was the real possibility she wouldn't respond well to his invitation. Would she outright refuse him? That seemed unlikely. But would she accompany him out of pity? Now, that would be worse.

Stepping into the barn, he searched for movement. The horses shifted in their stalls, but there was no sign of Amanda.

Curious.

He glanced toward the hayloft.

No one.

Then he heard her voice, faintly. It seemed to come from the other side of the barn. Taking long strides, he walked out the other door.

There she stood, facing the opposite direction. One hand on her hip, the other shielded her eyes.

"Daisy!" she called.

Why would she seek that dog? Hadn't the animal attacked Samuel? That was what Brandon had been given to understand.

Closing the distance between them, he touched her shoulder.

She startled, turning with hand over her heart. "You frightened me!"

"My apologies."

Waving her hand, she shook her head. "I haven't seen Daisy for a couple of days. Any idea where she is?"

Brows furrowed, he watched her face. "I was told that she attacked you and Samuel. So, I had to take care of her."

Amanda's eyes widened. She reached for his shirt. "You didn't..."

"Didn't what?" He put his hands on her arms.

She swallowed audibly. "Have her…shot?"

"No. We tied her up outside the ranch hands' bunk house."

Amanda's shoulders relaxed, and she put her forehead against his chest.

"We needed to make sure she—"

Straightening, Amanda waved a hand between them. "There is no need. It was a misunderstanding. And I fear the fault was all mine."

Brandon watched her features. Her fault?

"I over-reacted. She was just trying to protect Samuel."

He still wasn't ready to forgive the animal everything. Daisy shouldn't be exhibiting aggression toward the mistress of the ranch. She needed to learn her place. But Amanda's concern touched him. Her heart was in the right place.

Rubbing her arm, he lowered his eyes to meet hers. "It will be all right. No harm will come to the animal. She'll be running wild soon enough."

"Not now?"

Brandon sighed as his eyes scanned Amanda's features. "No. I thank you for telling me, but Daisy behaved poorly toward you. I won't have that."

Amanda looked away. It seemed as if her concerns were not assuaged.

"Perhaps we can arrange some time for the two of you to get to know each other?"

She met his eyes again. "That would be good. Samuel adores her so. She's his best friend."

Brandon smiled. "Thought she was supposed to be my best friend."

Amanda returned his grin. "Are you disappointed?"

He brushed a stray hair out of her face. "No. Not at all." His fingers grazed her cheek.

Her eyes slid closed at the contact.

She was a vision. The sunlight set her hair aglow and warmed her skin tone. Her lips upturned, and his heart swelled.

It was her lips that held his attention.

He moved toward them.

But stopped himself and pulled back, taking her hand in his.

Her eyes fluttered open and the hazel orbs stared at him.

"I came to ask you a question." He kept his voice low.

"Oh?" She quirked an eyebrow. With a smile on her face, she made quite the endearing picture. It put him at ease.

"Yes." He took hold of her other hand, drawing them both to his chest, rubbing his calloused fingers of her more delicate skin. "Amanda Miller, will you go on a picnic with me?"

Her eyes danced. Did that mean she agreed? She squeezed his hands.

"Is that a 'yes'?"

She nodded.

Why wasn't she speaking? As he watched, she actually bit at her lip. What wasn't she saying?

"May I...do I have...Can I take a few minutes to get ready?"

He let out a breath. "Of course." And then he released her hands.

She moved in the direction of the house. But then paused. Turning, she took the few strides that separated them and, raising on her toes, pressed a kiss to the side of his face.

And then she was off.

Brandon watched her go. This was the beginning of something wonderful. He could just feel it.

***

Amanda dipped her hands into the water bowl. Grabbing for the soap, she tried to clear her skin of the dirt streaks. Did her face show the effects of the day as clearly as her hands? She hoped not. Now that her skin was clean, she turned her attention to her attire. The mud-caked skirt and stained blouse just would not do.

Kneeling in front of her trunk, she rummaged through the few dresses she had. The blue one would be perfect. Pulling it out, she ran a hand over the folds of the dress. Would she have time to press it? It took little effort to exchange her dirty clothes for the fresh dress. The last matter to attend to was her hair. She picked up her hand mirror and gasped. It was a mess. What must Brandon have thought? She had pulled it back that morning but several strands had come loose as she worked.

Grabbing for her brush, she smoothed out the errant strands. She wished she had more time. A braid was the quickest way to tame her hair. As she braided, her fingers fumbled. Why was she shaking? Excitement? Was she nervous? What was she expecting from this time with Brandon?

Forcing her fingers to obey, she finished. Then, taking a deep breath, she picked up the mirror once more. There. Everything was in place. She set the mirror down and stepped out of her room.

A moment later, she stepped onto the front porch. Brandon rose from a seat off to her right. His eyes widened slightly as he took in her appearance. He took a step closer.

"You're...lovely."

Her pulse quickened, and her face warmed. No one had ever said anything like that before. Not even Jed. No, he had never been one to speak such kind words toward her. Had he ever truly cared?

"I didn't mean to upset you," Brandon said.

Amanda met Brandon's eyes. His brows furrowed, concern on his face.

"No, it's not you. Your words are so…" Her eyes fell to the ground. What should she say?

Brandon closed the distance between them, taking her hand in his. "What?" His voice was low.

She looked up and caught his eyes. "You're too kind."

He reached up and grazed the side of her face with his fingers. "Am I?"

As much as she wanted to stay in that moment, she was all too aware of their surroundings. Their moment was not private here. What if Dan or Slim saw? Or Samuel?

She pulled back and smiled. "If we don't get started on this picnic, I'm afraid it's not going to happen."

He nodded. "Shall we?"

Stepping out of the way, Brandon gestured toward the cart. After they were both settled in the wagon, he urged the horse forward.

The ride was pleasant and only somewhat awkward. How was it that she could be so comfortable in his presence and yet still feel unsure of herself?

As they rode, they talked about the ranch, and he even inquired after Samuel.

"He seems to enjoy living at the ranch."

"Oh?" Brandon seemed rather shocked to hear it.

Amanda looked at him. Why the surprise? Did he not expect Samuel to become accustomed to life there? "Yes, I think Uncle Owen and Cook have helped him feel at home."

Brandon became quiet. After some moments, he met Amanda's eyes and smiled. "Speaking of Uncle Owen and Cook…"

Amanda quirked a brow. "Yes, now *that* is another story entirely." She laughed.

Brandon's laughter joined hers. It was a pleasant sound, warm and full.

It wasn't long after that Brandon slowed the horse. "Here we are."

Amanda glanced around. It was a wonderful location for a picnic—a lush meadow of sorts. They stopped near a large tree. It would offer shade from the hot noonday sun. The grass laid out a soft blanket all around the roots, and there were sounds of a stream nearby. "It's beautiful."

"I like it," Brandon commented before hopping down. He came around and helped Amanda out of the cart.

Then he laid out a blanket and went back for the basket while Amanda sat on the covered ground.

Settling himself on the picnic blanket, Brandon sat on his knees and began pulling out the foodstuffs. And it was as if he'd never stop. How much did he pack? Did he think she needed all this?

Reaching over, she laid a hand on his arm. "I think that's plenty."

His deep brown eyes caught hers; an eyebrow quirked.

She smiled broadly. Did he think her critical?

He let out a sigh, and sank deeper onto his knees. "I guess I just wanted to be prepared."

Amanda nodded. "You are that."

Slapping his hands on his thighs, he then waved a hand over the smorgasbord. "What'll you have?"

She looked over the plethora of food. How could she tell him she wasn't hungry? Could she eat with her nerves such as they were? Then she spotted Cook's blueberry muffins. Biting at her lip, she pointed at those.

"Ah. You'll start with something sweet, I see." He grabbed the muffins and handed them over.

Unwrapping the small basket, she inhaled. Cook's muffins. Divine. Her stomach growled. Perhaps she would be able to eat after all.

Raising one of the soft, fluffy pastries to her lips, she closed her eyes and bit into it.

When she opened her eyes, she found Brandon staring at her. And smiling.

"What?"

He shook his head and took a bite of the sandwich in his hand. "It's nothing."

"No, tell me." Her face heated.

"Just the way you enjoy the simple things. I like that about you."

She continued chewing. Was that true? Did she find pleasure in the small things in life?

Brandon looked at his sandwich. "I think I take too much for granted. Especially the simple things."

Amanda swallowed her last bite of muffin and watched him. What did he mean? She wouldn't describe him as being discontent with life. "How so?"

His eyes sought hers. They seemed to peer into her. She wanted to shrink away, but there was nowhere to go. So, she held his searching gaze.

Brandon took another bite of sandwich and broke eye contact, looking off toward the horizon. "Do you know what it's like to have everything you want the moment you want it?"

Amanda shook her head slowly. What would that be like? Imagine! Life at your fingertips. Did anyone truly live that way?

"I do."

Though she attempted to maintain a neutral expression, she feared her widening eyes gave her away.

"Wharton City is not where I grew up. But you knew that."

Amanda quirked a brow. He wasn't from this small town?

"I didn't come out west until I was twenty."

"Oh?" Out west? He was from the east? His speech alone had told her that he'd been more formally educated, but she hadn't given it much thought.

Taking a bite of sandwich, he shifted so that he sat on his rear, his legs bent in front of him. "I assumed you knew. Aren't you from a town in this area?"

"You didn't know then…" How could she say it? How did he not remember?

"Know what?"

"I came to Wharton City when Jed answered my ad." She turned her face down, but peered up at him, hoping to gauge his reaction.

Brandon slowed his chewing. So, he didn't know.

Looking off to the side, Amanda picked at the blanket. "Yes, I placed an ad. I, um, was looking…hoping really, to move further west. And, here I am."

She met Brandon's eyes then. They were soft, kind. What had she expected? Disgust?

"What brought you to Wharton City?" She strengthened her tone and reached for another muffin.

"Uncle Owen. And a love of ranching." He popped the rest of the sandwich in his mouth.

"So, Uncle Owen ran the ranch before you?"

"No, he was a ranch hand. I spent a summer out here on the ranch helping him. The ranch owner at that time was a man named Blanchard. Jim Blanchard." Brandon looked off to the horizon, almost toward the sky, when recalling these details.

"Blanchard was a hard man. But fair. He worked his men, but they knew what was expected of them. That man knew ranching. I learned a lot that summer. And I fell in love with it. I felt at home out here, you know? But in the end, I had to go back to Richmond. This life and what I experienced here never left me."

Amanda took in everything he said. Was there more to this story?

Brandon ducked his head before turning toward her.

Yes. There, under the surface, in his eyes, she could see it. There was longing. What was it? Should she prompt him to go on? Or just remain as she was and wait for him to continue?

He snatched an apple. "You don't want to hear all of this."

Amanda scooted closer to him. They were inches apart now. "I do." She searched his eyes.

His eyes fell on her lips. Was he going to kiss her?

She held her breath.

Leaning over, he raised a hand to cup her face. He pressed his lips to hers. At first, the contact was gentle, then seeking something more than that. Her lips parted, and he deepened the kiss.

The core of her being turned molten. The sensation shot out from her center and spread throughout, stretching to the far reaches of her limbs.

Then he pulled back. When he broke contact, she remained in a haze for some moments before opening her eyes.

His were still closed as he took in a breath and let it out. When he opened them, it was a few seconds before he met her gaze.

Then he continued, "My father is a lot like Jim Blanchard. He is a hard man, but fair." Brandon set his knees in front of him again, intertwining his hands on top of them.

Amanda's head swam, but she attempted to follow what he said.

"He's a lawyer in Richmond. His father was a lawyer. And his father was a lawyer. They held one of the most prominent law practices in the area for many generations."

Brandon looked at his hands. "It was his dream that I would carry on the family name and the practice."

Only he didn't.

"But I couldn't." He met Amanda's eyes. "I hate everything about it." Brandon managed a slight laugh. "Truly. I would have made a terrible lawyer. I probably would have ruined the practice."

Amanda wanted to contradict him, but thought better of it.

"My father wouldn't listen. He didn't understand. This," Brandon waved an arm, "Is where I belong. This is where my heart is."

He looked off to the side opposite her and fell silent for several moments.

Amanda put a hand on his arm. "I'm sure you did everything you could…"

Brandon nodded. "He just wouldn't listen. He said that ranching was no life at all. That my Uncle Owen had ruined his life coming out here and I was throwing away my life, too." His voice became raised as he spoke. Were these things so painful?

"I'm sorry." Amanda rubbed her hand along his arm.

"He told me I would never succeed. And I guess he was right. I'm about to lose the ranch."

"No." The word shot out of Amanda's mouth. "You won't. We're going to save the ranch." Her other hand was on his.

He looked over at her. "Are we? Let's be honest. Half of the money I had left from what my mother gave me is gone thanks to Kid Antrim. I needed that money."

"When auction time comes, you'll see. We have a strong herd. We'll make it."

His eyes on hers became intense.

She warmed. Those pleasant feelings began to spark in her anew.

Then his gaze drifted over her head. What was he looking at? She turned. The sky had become dark. A storm was coming. And it moved quickly.

Brandon stood, reaching a hand down for Amanda.

"We need to get back!" she gasped as he pulled her to her feet.

Brandon shook his head. "There isn't time."

What were they going to do?

"But I know a place."

She looked over at him.

"Jed's ranch."

Raindrops pelted Brandon's face. As they neared Jed's ranch he spotted the homestead on the horizon. Snapping the reins, he urged more speed out of the horse.

Amanda huddled closer to his side.

They would be wet by the time they arrived, but at least they would be out of the worst of it soon enough.

Moments later, he stopped the horse and jumped down out of the wagon. Amanda scooted over to his side of the bench. He reached for her as she all but fell into his arms. There was little time to relish the feel of her warm body against his.

Tugging her hand, he directed her toward the house while he began unhitching the horse.

Instead of taking immediate shelter, Amanda moved to the other side of the horse and assisted.

Brandon wanted to argue with her, to tell her to go into the house, but his words and time would be wasted.

Together they freed the animal from the wagon and secured her in a barn stall.

"Should we just stay here and wait for the storm to pass?" Amanda looked at him after they latched the stall door.

Here? In the barn? They weren't quite drenched, but he was uncomfortably wet. "I don't know how long the storm will last. And I would rather wait it out by a warm fire."

She nodded.

Brandon took her hand, and they raced to the house. In short order, they were inside. He released her and moved to the fireplace.

There was a small stack of firewood in the corner. He thanked God for that. Anything outside would be soaked through soon. Crouching in front of the stone hearth, he made short work of stoking a decent fire.

Only then did he turn toward Amanda. She stood in the center of the room, looking about as if she'd seen a ghost. Was something the matter?

Then it struck him. To him, this had simply been the best place for shelter. He had not truly considered what it would mean for her to be here. She had come back at least once seeking solace since they married. But was each time just as strange for her?

Crossing the room, he put his hands on her arms. "Come over by the fire."

She seemed to look through him when she turned to face him. But she allowed him to lead her to the heat source.

Grabbing a blanket off a nearby trunk, he shook it off and placed it on the floor. She needed to be as close to the warming flames as possible. He brought her over and settled her in front of the hearth. Then he sat beside her and rubbed her arms.

Amanda stared at the fire. It was eerie.

Brandon became concerned. What was the matter? Was she simply caught in her memories? Were they painful? Should they not have come here? He raised a hand and touched her face.

She jerked away. But then looked at him. This time, she truly looked at him.

Then she leaned forward again. "I'm sorry. I don't know why I did that."

Amanda slid a hand into his then he wrapped his fingers around hers and squeezed.

She looked toward the fire.

Brandon watched the flickering lights play across her features. So sad. Why?

As if he had said these things out loud, she spoke.

"This is the first time I've been back since…"

He waited. Would she say more?

Her mouth closed and she sniffled twice.

"Since what?" He spoke in soft tones.

She looked at him. Was she deciding whether or not to trust him? A tear escaped. "Jed and I had a different kind of marriage."

What had the man done to her? Brandon's chest constricted. But he bit his tongue and let her continue, as she was ready.

She turned back toward the fire and wiped at her face. More tears? "I should have expected no different with how it began."

Brandon used his thumb to rub the back of her hand, hoping the simple gesture would soothe her.

"And I never did have big dreams about love and marriage. How can you, when you post an ad?" She let out a little laugh. "But he needed me."

Brandon looked away. He couldn't keep his face neutral on this subject. Jed didn't need Amanda. He had used her. Why couldn't she see that?

"Or so I thought."

Brandon's eyes jerked to her face to find her looking at him. For how long?

"I thought he was well pleased to have a wife that could help out around the ranch. I didn't know that I was just another ranch hand who shared his bed."

Brandon had to concentrate to keep his hands from tightening into fists. Especially since he still held her hand in one of his.

Her gaze returned to the fire, and she fell silent.

"Did he…" Brandon struggled to even his tone. "Did he hurt you?"

Amanda's eyes closed and she nodded, almost imperceptibly.

Brandon's chest tightened even more. His throat burned.

"It wasn't often. And he was always sorry." Her voice was just a whisper.

He couldn't speak, the anger so consumed him.

"He was always so loving for days, weeks afterward. And he needed me so much."

That's what she wanted. So badly. To be needed. And what was the one thing Brandon had refused to give her? A place to be useful.

He closed his eyes and searched for words. The right words, to express how sorry he was. For not being a good neighbor and stopping the abuse…no matter how difficult it would have been, for not being a good husband and giving her a suitable place to belong in her new home.

She pulled her hand out of his.

Brandon looked at her.

Amanda laid her head in her hands. Was she crying? She pulled her hands down over her mouth, exposing her eyes and nose, and took in a ragged breath.

"I can't do it. I can't be here anymore." The words were muffled against her hands, but he was able to make them out.

Then she was on her feet.

He reached out to stop her, but she spun around and ran toward the front door. "Amanda, no!"

She ran out into the downpour.

***

Openness. At last. She could breathe again. And she did, drawing in air until her lungs couldn't hold any more. Rain poured down on her, but she didn't care.

Her feet carried her off the porch and out into the yard. Moving away from Jed's house, she tried to create distance between herself and the memories.

And then the water pump was in front of her.

Was Jed's blood still on it?

She stepped closer, her hand trembling as she reached for the handle.

There was no mark on it. Nature had removed every sign of Jed. Why couldn't it have done the same for her?

Hands grabbed her from behind and spun her around. Then she faced Brandon.

"Come back inside!"

Her hands pressed against his chest. "Leave me be."

"I won't." He pulled her in the direction of the house.

"Please…I'm not good for you. For anyone." Her eyes burned, but the rain washed her tears away as they fell.

"That's not true."

Why wouldn't he let her go?

"Jed may not have needed you, but I do."

Amanda shook her head and pushed against him. He needed her to keep the ranch alive. She couldn't do that anymore.

"Don't you understand? I love you!"

He what? Amanda's eyes widened as she stared at him. Did he just say what she thought she heard? That he loved her? Heart soaring, her eyes met his.

Brandon pulled her to himself and kissed her. It was not like the gentle kiss on the picnic blanket. This kiss was meant to slake a hunger. She had never been kissed like this before.

Amanda melted to him, clinging to his shoulders to remain upright.

He leaned her over to allow himself better access. And she welcomed it, wrapping her arms around his shoulders, her knees now weak and useless.

When he broke off, she gasped for breath. How long could one go without air?

Leaning over, he put an arm behind her knees and lifted her.

Amanda pressed her face to his shoulder and hugged him closer as he carried her back into the house.

Once inside, he brought her back to the fire and set her on the blanket. She was loathed to release him, but she did.

Brandon moved over to the fireplace and stoked the dying flames. Now that the fire roared once again, he returned to her side. Settling close, he wrapped an arm around her and drew her to himself.

Silence fell between them for several moments.

"I didn't mean to frighten you." His words came softly.

Amanda moved a hand to his chest. What was this awkwardness? Why couldn't she just return his words? She turned her face into his shoulder again.

He kissed the top of her head.

"I lost your ring." Her words surprised her. But she needed to tell him.

"I know."

He knew? How? She sighed. It was no matter. "I'm so sorry."

Brandon pressed a kiss to her forehead. "It's all right."

Leaning her head back, she looked up at him. "Why? Why are you being so good to me?"

"Because," he said, grazing her chin with the tip of his finger, "Love is patient." He kissed her forehead again. "Love is kind." He kissed her the tip of her nose. "Love keeps no record of wrongs." He kissed the side of her face. "Love endures all things." He kissed the other side of her face. "Love conquers all." At last, he pressed a kiss to her lips.

This kiss was neither gentle nor demanding. But somewhere in between. His lips were firm, but searching.

She opened herself up to his kisses.

And he explored her lips. And then continued to press kisses to her face, then her neck.

Amanda groaned and would have surely lost her ability to sit up were he not holding onto her.

Brandon's trail of kisses stopped where her skin met the collar of her dress. His lips nuzzled that spot.

She didn't want it to end.

But he began to pull away.

Amanda gripped his shoulders.

He met her eyes, a question in his.

"Please."

"Are you ready to be my wife? Only mine?" he whispered.

She nodded.

He sat her up straight, pulling back from her.

What was he doing? This was not how this was supposed to go. Shouldn't he be kissing her again?

Brandon reached into his pocket and pulled out a small object that he quickly covered with his other hand. His eyes met hers.

Amanda's stomach became uneasy. What was it? What were his intentions? She pushed those thoughts to the side. And trusted him.

"May I have you hand?" His voice was smooth and deep.

She put her hand forth.

He held his out and opened it.

Her ring sat in the center of his palm.

"Where did you find it?" Her eyes went wide.

"By the stream. Near where I caught you bathing." He smiled. Then he became serious. "Would you like it back?"

She nodded. "More than anything."

Brandon took her left hand in his and slid the ring on her finger. Then he lifted her hand and pressed a kiss to it.

Amanda then brought their joined hands to her lips, her eyes on his as she pressed a kiss to his knuckles.

Then Amanda rose on her knees as their bodies came together. They sought each other's lips, hungry for connection. When they broke apart, Amanda drew Brandon's hand to the buttons at her collar.

His eyes flickered to hers. Was he uncertain?

She reached up and brushed his hair back off his forehead then used that hand to graze the side of his face. Only then did she notice that his features had colored. And she understood.

He had never been with a woman.

Amanda moved her fingers over his and slipped the top button through its hole. And then the second.

Then she pressed his fingers to the revealed skin.

His breathing quickened.

She worked her way a little closer to him and began unbuttoning his shirt as well, touching his skin. His racing heart was evident under her hand.

Now closer, she leaned forward and pressed a kiss to the skin at his shirt opening.

He sucked in a breath. And moved his arms to surround her, pulling her tightly against himself.

There, they would take this one step at a time. And it would be perfect.

CHAPTER TWELVE

Newness

BRANDON PRESSED SOFT kisses to Amanda's shoulder. His arms were wrapped tightly around her, and his chest warmed her back.

She turned her head so that he might kiss the side of her face.

Never. Never had she been loved so tenderly or so completely. And she was safe to let her heart feel what it desired.

Amanda pulled Brandon's hand, intertwined with hers, toward her lips and closed her eyes.

"I love you," she murmured before she kissed the back of his fingers.

He pulled her impossibly tighter, burying his face in her neck.

Warmth pervaded her being. It filled her in sweeping, swirling movements that reached the farthest stretches of her body. What was this…this pleasant sensation? It was as if she would explode, she was so happy. Her body could surely not contain it. But because Brandon held her, she would remain whole.

He wanted her. He needed her.

Deep words rumbled against her skin.

"Hmm?" she turned her head toward him again.

"I said, 'You are good for me.'"

She looked away.

"How did I walk around all these years half a person and not know it?"

His words tugged at Amanda's heart, but his earlier statement had caught her. Was she good for him? Or would he come to find out, as everyone else had, that she would be a source of resentment? Could she bear that?

Her eyes stung.

Brandon leaned up on one elbow and traced a line down her arm. Then his lips were on her neck. It was divine.

But she couldn't respond. How could she encourage more? When it would only lead to greater hurt. She shouldn't have let it get this far.

He pulled back.

Silence.

Did he sense her hesitation?

"What is it?" His voice was low, husky.

She swallowed past the forming tears and worked to steady her voice. "Perhaps we should start heading back."

His breathing remained even, but she felt his eyes boring in to her. Could he read her thoughts?

"Look at me."

Amanda closed her eyes. She could do this. Opening them, she turned to face him. His eyes were soft, alight with the flickering flame from the fire.

"I only think of the others. They will worry after us."

He shifted so that she was on her back and he placed a hand on the side of her face. "What is this?"

Tears threatened to spill, but she fought them. She furrowed her brows. "I don't understand."

"Tell me. Why are you so afraid of this? Of me?" He took her hand and held it over his heart. It beat strong and sure, perhaps a bit rapidly.

She held his eyes. "I am not afraid."

"No?"

He leaned down and pressed a kiss to her lips.

The now familiar fire within her stirred. It lit and licked its way from her belly to her extremities. But she fought to quiet it. She would not lose control again.

Brandon pulled back. "That is not fear?"

She turned her head so he couldn't see her eyes. "I would like to go now."

"Don't do this." His voice was gentle. "We've come so far."

Amanda sniffled. So it was happening now. He would resent her. Her eyes watered. The tears were coming.

Brandon wrapped her in his arms and turned her onto her side. They now faced each other, and she could not turn away.

She looked down at his chest.

"Talk to me."

Her vision blurred.

His hand cupped her face, and the pads of his thumbs wiped at her tears.

She peered up toward his eyes.

There was concern there. And kindness. Was there hope for them? Could she trust in that hope?

"I've always been a burden." There, she'd said it. Now he knew.

"That can't be true." His words were kind, but hollow.

She closed her eyes. More tears came. "All my life."

"Don't let what Jed did—"

"I'm not talking about Jed!" Her eyes flashed as she opened them. "Jed saved me."

Brandon appeared stricken. She hadn't meant to do that. Once again, she had hurt someone she loved.

Placing a hand on Brandon's face, she wanted to connect with him again. How could she explain? Where to begin?

"You have to understand. My life wasn't like yours. My parents were poor."

He watched her and remained silent.

"They didn't have anything. My father made enough money to keep him and my mom comfortable." She shifted, looking at his chest again. "Then my mom got pregnant."

Amanda bit her lip. "My father had such hopes for a son, but I came." Her voice caught. "And my mom was never quite well after that. It became harder and harder for my father's income to stretch to cover the doctor bills and our livelihood." Her eyes flickered to Brandon's.

His eyes glistened, but he still said nothing.

"If I had been a boy, I could have found some way to help. As a newsboy, or a grocery boy. Or something. But no one wanted to hire a girl. Even as I got older."

If only she could have helped. Maybe then her father would have cared more. Seen her value. She was willing.

"My father resented that he had no help. I was a burden to him. So, as soon as I was old enough, I placed an ad to come out west as a bride. Jed saved me from that life."

Story told, she looked to gauge Brandon's reaction. Surely he would pity her. As well he should. She was a pitiable creature. From the day she was brought into the world.

Brandon gathered her close to himself, wrapping his arms tighter around her and drawing her to his chest.

Did he think she would cry? Her heart ached as if it could explode, but no tears came. She had cried enough over her childhood.

Still, she closed her eyes and soaked in what he offered: love and acceptance. No, he did not pity her. He truly loved her.

And that was the most she could hope for.

***

The sun had begun its descent in the sky when Brandon spotted his ranch on the horizon. It did not thrill him the same as it always had. Truth told, he had been loath to leave Jed's homestead and the spell that had been cast on him and Amanda there.

Would they return to the awkwardness they knew before? Or would their newfound relationship prevail? After the interchange before they left the smaller ranch, he was unsure.

Reaching a hand toward Amanda, she slid her smaller one into his and interlaced their fingers. A good sign. It caused his heart to do a flip-flop. She leaned closer, brushing his arm with a part of her that he had become all too familiar with.

His face heated. The urge to pull her fully to himself and kiss her almost overwhelmed him.

She had always seemed a bit timid around the ranch hands and Cook. It would be best to take things slowly where their interactions were concerned here at the ranch.

That meant he would not be able to sleep with her in his arms tonight. He did not particularly like that thought. But it was necessary.

Pulling alongside the porch, Brandon hopped down and then helped Amanda out of the wagon. Their bodies once again connected.

The front door opened and Amanda stepped back.

"We were so worried!" Cook raced across the porch and down the stairs. "What a storm!"

Amanda's eyes met Brandon's. "Indeed, it was."

"I hope y'all found shelter." Cook stopped just short of Amanda, taking her hands.

"We did," Brandon interjected. "As you see, we are both well and safe."

"And hungry I'm sure." Cook eyed him. "Come right inside. I'll fix y'all a plate of something."

Cook took hold of Amanda's arm and led her toward the porch.

Amanda glanced over her shoulder at Brandon and shrugged.

He smiled. "I'll be along after I settle Candy."

As he walked the horse and cart to the barn, he began to ache for the closeness he had come to know with Amanda, but he could not deny that he welcomed the solitude all the same. Some time to himself. To his thoughts.

Brandon went through the motions of putting the wagon and horse away, but maneuvered his body as if the task did not need his full attention. Indeed it did not.

What would this new intimacy mean for him and Amanda? For the ranch? Could he continue to allow her to work? Or would he be as bad as Jed? Could he afford not to?

When would he be able to share her bed? How would they make that happen? Would they tell the others or simply move him into her room and let everyone figure it out?

What did Amanda think?

Amanda.

Even then he could almost feel her hair threaded in his fingers, her soft skin against his, and the curves of her body molded to his stronger frame. How did one think clearly after such an encounter?

And she returned his affections. His heart leapt forth in his chest.

Had he responded well to her? She shared some rather difficult things with him. As much as he would like to be able to chase away the hurt, he was not able. But could he point her toward healing?

Father, Amanda is Your daughter. Nothing has happened in her life apart from Your knowing. You have held her in Your hand. Would You draw her to Yourself now?

Having placed her in God's care, he was prepared to face her again.

A small voice calling out broke into his thoughts. Where did it come from? He moved to the barn door. The voice became louder.

It was a younger voice. Samuel? As Brandon continued to move toward the pasture, he could make out the words.

"Daisy! Here, girl!"

Was he looking for the dog? Didn't he know they had tied her up by the ranch hands' quarters?

Brandon lengthened his stride and searched for the boy. As he came around the barn, he spotted the boy's mop of brown hair.

Samuel wandered in the yard to the south side of the barn, calling for the animal, stopping to look behind crates and trees along the way.

"Samuel." Brandon picked up his pace, hoping to close the distance between himself and the child.

The boy turned. His expression fell. Who did he expect? Did he not like Brandon?

Now directly in front of the child, Brandon crouched to meet his eyes. "I'm sorry, Samuel. We had to tie Daisy over by the bunks."

Samuel's brow furrowed. "I know what you did." His voice was harsh, even in its smallness.

Never mind his anger. "Then why are you calling for her?"

"She's not tied up where you left her."

Brandon blinked. "What?"

"Daisy ran away." Samuel's lower lip trembled slightly. Brandon almost missed it.

The dog must have been scared of the storm. She often was.

"Don't worry about old Daisy." Brandon put a hand on Samuel's shoulder.

Samuel jerked away.

Should Brandon be offended? He hadn't much experience with children. The boy was upset about the dog. Perhaps that was the whole of it.

"She'll be back. Sometimes she gets scared and runs off to find someplace to hide."

Samuel studied Brandon's face. Was he gauging whether or not to trust the older man?

"She's never been gone more than a couple of days. I promise."

The boy looked off toward the horizon. "What if she's hurt?"

"Daisy can take care of herself. She's a good dog. Smart."

Samuel did not appear assuaged. But that was all Brandon could offer him.

The two stared at each other for several moments. Several uncomfortable moments.

"May I go now?" Samuel broke the silence.

Brandon nodded.

Samuel ran off in the opposite direction. Where to, Brandon did not know, perhaps on some wild adventure. Brandon had other things to think on. He stood and turned his attention to the homestead. Amanda awaited him.

Moments later, he stepped into the house and into the dining room. Amanda looked over from her seat at the dining table. A smile graced her lips.

His whole being lit up. Could he walk over and press his lips to hers? Just briefly?

"Did I hear the front door?" Cook called from the kitchen.

"Yes, ma'am." The opportunity was lost. So, he moved toward his seat, adjacent to the one Amanda had taken. He did allow a hand to graze her arm and across her shoulders.

He broke contact just as Cook kicked the door open. "Got some biscuits and bacon here for ya."

Setting a hand on Cook's shoulder, he nodded. "Thanks."

Pulling his seat out, he then sat in the chair. But his eyes were on Amanda's face as Cook placed the warm plate in front of him.

"I'll leave you two be. But I want to see clean plates."

"Yes, ma'am." Brandon mocked a salute in Cook's direction as she stepped back toward the kitchen.

His gaze fell on Amanda again. Her eyes quickly turned toward her plate. But she didn't eat, just moved the food around.

"Not hungry?"

She shook her head.

He took a bite of bacon. How could Amanda not be famished? Brandon felt as if he could eat two meals.

Amanda peered up at him, but distracted herself with her napkin soon after.

Brandon watched her. What could he do? He refused to return to this awkwardness between them. Not after what they had shared.

Extending a hand between them on the table, palm up, he waited.

She slid her fingers onto his hand.

"We don't have to rush into anything." Brandon lowered his voice.

Amanda let out a breath and her shoulders relaxed.

He squeezed her hand. "I don't want to push. I love you."

She smiled. "I love you, too." Amanda's lips drew his attention. But he pulled his eyes upward to connect with hers. They were bright and hopeful.

And that soothed his fears. Everything was going to be all right.

What was that sound? Amanda was fully awake in a moment. When had she fallen asleep? Many hours had she lain awake wishing, wanting for Brandon's arms.

Silly. Such adolescent notions. But she wanted for him all the same. Ached for him. Her bed was cold and empty. Not even the extra quilt could provide the warmth that seemed to elude her.

Should she just go to him? It wasn't possible. Even if it was, would it be wise? Was she prepared for everyone, Samuel included, to know that their relationship had...progressed?

Turning to her side, she shoved a fist into her pillow and closed her eyes. She would find sleep. No matter how it frustrated her.

Tap, tap, tap. A gentle knock on her door gave her pause. Who would disturb her at this hour? Samuel? Did he have a bad dream? He wouldn't knock.

Could it be...Brandon? Did he miss her as much as she missed him?

Sliding from beneath the covers, she padded across the floor, not bothering with a robe. Her heart pounded. It had to be.

Working the latch, her fingers fumbled. Why must these things frustrate her so? At length, she managed to work it and pulled the door open.

In the dimness, she could not make out the details of the figure in the hall, but the scent, the silhouette...all of it spoke of her beloved.

His breathing was ragged. Stepping into the room, he took her face in his hands and kissed her thoroughly.

The way she needed to be kissed. Every day. For the rest of her life.

Amanda welcomed him into her arms, placing her hands on his shoulders.

When he broke contact, he pressed his forehead to hers. "I couldn't. I couldn't be without you. I know what we said. And I don't know how we're going to do this. Or even if we can. Or even if you miss me half as much as I do you. So, send me away if you must, but I had to be with you, if only for a moment."

"Don't," she choked out the word. "Don't go."

174

He wrapped his arms around her and nothing further was spoken between them for quite some time.

How life had changed. Here Brandon lay, with his wife beside him, huddled against him, dozing. And she loved him. His heart was full. More so than he ever thought possible.

He ran a hand over her golden tresses. Was God so good? Closing his eyes, he sent up a prayer of thanksgiving.

If only he could remain in this dream created by him and Amanda. This world where all was well and nothing existed but the two of them.

But it would be dawn soon. And the others would begin to rise.

Could he disentangle himself from her? Go back to his own room and behave as if none of this ever happened?

But that was how she wanted it.

For how long?

How long could they keep up such a show?

Brandon did not relish the idea of the deceit they would work upon his closest friends. Could he justify it? Should he?

She needed space and time to let Samuel get used to the idea. He understood that. But perhaps the boy could handle more than she gave him credit for.

Was this an excuse for her to ease into the idea?

His gaze drifted over her face as she slumbered. So peaceful. He had not seen her so since coming to the ranch. Always she had been conflicted, sad, distressed. But now, in his arms, she was at peace.

Could he ask her to give that up?

Or would he simply be asking her to embrace it?

Brandon ran a hand down his face. He'd had far too little sleep for such deep thoughts.

One thing was certain—it was time for him to depart, if they didn't want to risk being found out. Could he slip out without waking her?

Easing away from her, he worked his arm out from underneath her. As he pulled it free, she shifted in her sleep.

He held his breath.

She resettled.

Standing, he pulled on his clothes and made his way to the door.

"You would leave without so much as a farewell?"

He turned.

Amanda, propped up on an arm, pursed her lips and gave him a hurt look.

"I didn't want to wake you."

She met his gaze, eyes still wide.

He moved back to the bed and sat on the mattress. "If we don't want the others to know, I need to return to my pallet."

Amanda looked toward the window. Did she regret this as much as he?

He placed a hand on top of hers.

She turned back to look at him and nodded. "It is best."

His heart dropped. He moved to stand.

Amanda placed a hand on his shoulder. "It won't be long."

Brandon's eyes found hers again. An eyebrow quirked.

"I'll talk with Samuel. Soon."

He leaned over her and caught her lips with his. A promise was sealed between them.

Amanda pulled back first, smiling and rubbing the side of his face with her hand. "I'll see you at breakfast."

"Breakfast, then." How could a couple of hours seem like days away?

With great reluctance in his heart, Brandon rose and made his way to the door. He longed to look back at her, to connect with her once more in that way, but he feared that would only make it more difficult to leave. So, he opened the door and stepped into the dark hallway.

As he stepped into his room and lay down on his pallet, he let the loud snores of Uncle Owen ground him to reality. Even at that, he could not help that his mind escaped into the dream that was Amanda. His Amanda.

***

Why did the men have to go? It wasn't all that long ago Amanda would have looked forward to a reprieve from Brandon's presence. Now, she dreaded his absence.

Some days it seemed she lived for the moment he would knock on her door in the middle of the night. Their late-night rendezvous may have detracted from her sleep, but she had never felt so energized, so alive.

And now, the time had come for the men to go to auction.

Tomorrow. They would leave tomorrow. And they would be gone for a solid two weeks.

She would miss Brandon terribly. But a lot depended on this auction. Brandon had been rather distracted by it.

Stepping onto the front porch, she watched for signs of Brandon amongst the cattle. He, Slim, and Dan had been busy making final arrangements for their drive.

She couldn't pick out any sign of the men in the pasture, but she did spot an incoming carriage. A black carriage, somewhat ornate. It would be at the homestead in a few moments.

Should she get Cook? Or run after Brandon? How would she do that with no knowledge of where he was? Would it serve everyone better for her to intercept their guest?

Perhaps that would be best. As well, it may be her only option. So, she stood her ground and watched the rather fancy carriage coming in. As it did so, the figure of a man could be made out in the driver's seat. He seemed to be the sole occupant. Had she seen this man somewhere before?

The carriage came to a halt near the porch. And the man, in a full suit, took his hat off and waved at her.

"Mrs. Miller, I presume?"

"You are correct. I am afraid I am at a disadvantage."

"Mr. Perkins. George C. Perkins. I own the town bank."

Like pieces of a puzzle, things fell into place for Amanda. The man had been out to Jed's ranch before.

Mr. Perkins struggled to get out of his carriage. It seemed as if he wasn't in full command of his own limbs. There were a few moments in which Amanda was certain he would topple to the ground. But, with much effort, he made it down under the command of his own two feet.

Then he turned and smiled as if Amanda should be proud of him. She was not.

"What can I do for you, Mr. Perkins?"

He moved toward the steps as if he intended to ascend to the porch.

Amanda met him at the bottom stair, barring his way up, arms crossed.

"Mr. Miller at home?"

"He…is." Amanda thought it better to not let on that she had no idea where Brandon was.

Mr. Perkins eyed her. He seemed skeptical.

"But he is rather busy. As you may know, he and the ranch hands are off to auction soon. Is there something I can help you with?"

"Actually, yes." He smiled, flashing some of his teeth at her. "I hoped you would say that."

Amanda's stomach turned.

"I made a very reasonable offer to your husband a few weeks back and I never heard anything from him."

"Perhaps, then, sir, he is not interested." Amanda prayed Brandon wouldn't make a deal with a man such as this.

Mr. Perkins took a step up, a step closer to Amanda.

She fought to hold her ground, to keep from stepping back.

"I had thought that you might be able to speak some sense to him. That is, if you care at all about your future livelihood. And that of your boy. What's his name? Samuel?"

Amanda's eyes widened. "Are you threatening me, sir?"

"No." Mr. Perkins waved a hand. "I wouldn't dream of it. I am simply saying that Mr. Miller has big dreams that have no basis in reality. But you seem like a reasonable woman, Mrs. Miller. Surely you must see that putting all your hopes in one auction is risky. Sell the land to me. Go buy a farm somewhere. Or go back east."

"I'll thank you to take your fine carriage and leave our property." Amanda kept her tone even, though she seethed underneath.

"Come now, Mrs. Miller," Mr. Perkins stepped forward again; he was directly in front of Amanda now. He placed a hand on her arm. "Let's think about—"

She jerked her arm away and opened her mouth as another voice boomed from behind Mr. Perkins.

"I think you heard my wife."

Brandon strode from the direction of the barn, hands clenched in fists, pace rapid, steps lengthened, and eyes narrowed.

Perkins lifted his hand. "Mr. Miller! I was, uh, just having a conversation here with your—"

"You were just leaving." Brandon stopped just short of where Mr. Perkins stood. "Would you like some assistance?"

Mr. Perkins held up his hands as he scrambled around Brandon and toward his carriage. "This won't be the end, Mr. Miller. I'll be seeing you. Sooner than you think."

Amanda watched the muscles in Brandon's jaw work, but he did not respond. Did he not trust himself?

They looked on as Mr. Perkins tripped over his own feet several times trying to get up and into his carriage. And he was off.

Only then did Brandon turn toward Amanda.

"I'm fine." She answered his unspoken question. "Just a little upset."

"Aren't we all?" Brandon sighed.

"You're so tired." She longed to reach out and stroke his hair, but this was not the place.

He smiled. "Wonder whose fault that is."

She swatted at his arm. "Would you rather I let you sleep?"

Brandon grabbed her wrist, holding it gently, tugging her toward himself.

Amanda allowed it.

"Not on your life." He grinned, pulling her dangerously close.

What was this spell he wove around her? Dizzied by sensation, she drew up on her toes and kissed him.

All too soon she became aware of where they were.

She pulled back.

His eyes, a bit hazy from their passion, held a question.

Amanda's head jerked around as she searched for onlookers. No one appeared to have seen. She took a deep breath. That was close.

He groaned. Had he realized what she was concerned about?

"When?" That was all he said. But that was all that he needed to say.

"Before you return from auction. I promise."

He nodded and leaned forward for another kiss.

She laughed and swatted him away. "Back to work with you!"

CHAPTER THIRTEEN

Challenges

EVERYTHING WAS SET. Brandon had checked and double-checked everything. They couldn't be more ready. The days ahead would bring to fruition the realty of his fears or an end to them. How he prayed for the latter.

And all the more with his blossoming relationship with Amanda. The urge to provide a comfortable life for her, and for Samuel, was stronger than ever. Would he succeed? Or would his father's words come to pass?

He approached the ranch hands' bunkhouse. It had been at least a week since he had checked in on Cutie's progress. Between the extra work and his recent distraction, he just hadn't the time.

As he neared, the door swung open and Amanda stepped out. What was she doing here? Had she been in there alone with Cutie? For what reason?

His eyes met hers.

She stared back at him, face coloring. "I just, um, came to drop off some dinner for Cutie."

Brandon quirked an eyebrow.

"Cook was…ah…busy finishing something."

He continued to watch her. How often did this happen? Her finding herself in the bunkhouse unsupervised?

This is nonsense. Of course, there wouldn't be anything going on between Amanda and Cutie. Why, then, did Amanda act so oddly?

Brandon forced a breath out and a smile onto his face. "How is he?"

"Good. He's doing quite well." She continued to fumble with her words.

Perhaps he had just caught her off guard? He took a step toward her.

She sidestepped him and moved toward the house. "I'd best get back and help Cook."

Brandon frowned as she turned and walked away, leaving him to ponder—and worry—after the strangeness of their encounter. He eyed the door to the bunkhouse. Should he go in and question Cutie? Would his ranch hand give him honest answers? It was doubtful the man would be any more forthcoming.

What was happening? And right under his nose? Was he this naïve? This trusting? Brandon turned from the structure and moved toward the south pasture, toward his place of solitude.

As he reached the edge of the pasture, he settled himself next to a tree by the stream. The same tree Amanda had huddled against when he had caught her bathing. Pushing that to the side, he moved to clear his head. This was his place. Here, he could think. Here, he could pray with a clear mind.

Only, as he sat and began to quiet his thoughts, his heart remained clouded. Could he commune with God when his heart was thusly distracted? He could but try.

Father, I don't know what to do. My very heart is divided. You know I love her. Can I survive if what I fear is true? Give me a discerning spirit. And eyes to see what is real and what is false.

Brandon opened his eyes. The clouds shifted overhead as the wind blew. That same wind soothed him. He was certain God heard him. A sense of peace settled in his core.

He stood. Would there be time to speak with Amanda? There would have to be.

The jangle of the dinner bell sounded across the field. Conversation or not, he would have to face her across the dinner table. Sucking in a breath, he prayed for strength, and then moved toward the homestead.

When he entered the house, he was greeted by six sets of eyes. His quiet moment with the Lord had made him the last to arrive. The others were already seated and passing the food around.

"We started to wonder if you were coming," Cook said, plopping a pile of green beans on the empty plate at his seat.

Brandon smiled. "Just needed a few moments to myself." He couldn't stop his gaze from wandering toward Amanda.

She seemed all too interested in the squash she had just served herself.

What did that mean? Brandon's mouth became a thin line. But he recovered, turning back to Cook. "It's been a long day."

There was a chorus of agreement from Dan and Slim as they dug into their food.

Cook slapped the table.

Everyone halted.

"Boys, has that sun made you sick in the head? Made you forget yourselves and your manners? Grace first." Cook stared them down.

Dan and Slim looked at each other, swallowed, and then set their forks down.

"Mr. Brandon, if you're ready…" Cook waved a hand toward his chair.

Brandon nodded, relieved to not be on the receiving end of Cook's ire. He stepped to his seat, but remained standing. "Let us return thanks."

He watched as everyone bowed their heads.

Amanda chanced a glance at him, but quickly bowed her head when he caught her eyes. Did she expect him to not be looking?

Brandon cleared his throat. "Dear Lord, we thank You for this meal of which we are about to partake. Bless it, Lord, as you bless us. And I pray especially for the light of Your truth. May it shine in our lives always. Amen."

As he concluded the prayer, he sat.

Amanda's eyes were on him. He felt it—her gaze boring into him. Why had he said that? Did he intend to stir up trouble? If that's what it cost to get the truth, he supposed he did.

Brandon spent much of the meal in silence; concentrating on his food and listening to Uncle Owen tell tales of the cattle drives he had been on. He would go on this one if Brandon would let him. But Brandon and Uncle Owen both knew his body wouldn't make it. A sad truth, but truth all the same.

By the time Cook took the dinner plates, the men were yawning. They had put in several long days. Brandon found himself opening his mouth and stretching. Was a good night's sleep in his future?

"It think it's time we retired," Brandon spoke up, pushing his chair back from the table. "Cook, as always, thank you for a wonderful meal. But you best get going before it gets dark."

Cook nodded.

As Dan and Slim stood, Cook gathered her things. The men walked her out.

"That leaves you." Brandon turned to Uncle Owen. "What will you do with your evening? Whittle?"

"I want to whittle!" Samuel spoke up.

"It's your bedtime, young man." Amanda's soft voice spilled into the space.

Samuel's face fell, but he obediently headed to his room.

Uncle Owen's gaze shifted from Brandon to Amanda and back. "I think I'll turn in early."

Brandon's eyes widened. "You all right?"

Uncle Owen nodded. "Just want to be up bright and early to see you boys off." Then the older man made a move to stand.

On his feet in a moment, Brandon was soon by Uncle Owen's side, arm under his shoulder. "Take it easy."

As Brandon assisted Uncle Owen to his feet, he glanced at Amanda. She met his eyes.

How could he communicate that he wanted to speak with her? Or should he just visit her later as always? That seemed a bit disingenuous.

Still, as they locked eyes, she nodded slightly, almost imperceptibly.

A plan was formed.

Brandon refocused on Uncle Owen and supported the man's frame as he hobbled out of the room.

The older man made only grunts and groans as they progressed toward their shared room. However, once he was settled on the side of his bed, he grabbed for Brandon's arm.

Brandon crouched in front of him.

"You have to make things right." Uncle Owen rasped, his breathing a bit heavy from the effort of the trip across the house.

"Pardon?"

"Between you and Amanda. Whatever has gone wrong, you must see it put right before you leave tomorrow."

Brandon's face warmed. How much could Uncle Owen know? Surely he referred to Brandon and Amanda's amiable relationship. The older man couldn't know about…

"You haven't been sleeping in here," Uncle Owen said. "You got to be sleeping somewhere."

Brandon's face heated and his pulse raced. "I…it's not…" Did he want to tell an outright lie? After he'd just prayed for the truth? He dropped his head.

"It's all right." Uncle Owen put a hand on his shoulder. "Your secret is safe."

Brandon met his uncle's gaze. "I'm just so confused. Things seem so complicated."

"Do you love her?"

"Yes."

"Does she love you?"

"She says she does."

"Then uncomplicate it."

Brandon fell silent for several seconds. Could he just untangle everything that easily? "How am I supposed to…?"

Uncle Owen held up a hand. "That is something you have to work out in your own way."

If only he could.

"Now let this old bachelor be." Uncle Owen smiled. "And go talk to your wife."

Amanda drew Samuel's covers to his chin. Just the way he liked them. Sitting on the edge of his bed, she then drew a hand across his forehead, brushing his hair out of his face. She had neglected his haircut long enough. Tomorrow. After the men left.

Had she too often neglected Samuel altogether? He had been rather taken with Uncle Owen. Perhaps she had relied on their companionship too much of late. Her son needed her.

"What's wrong, Mama?" His voice was small, but caring. So caring.

"Nothing, sweetheart. I'm just thinking." She continued to stroke his hair.

"About what?" He scrunched his nose. Could he get any cuter?

She leaned toward him. "About how handsome you've become."

He waved her off, swatting at her hand still in his hair.

She pulled it into her lap. He'd never fought her affections before. What was this about?

He leaned up on his elbows. "Want to see what I made today?"

Amanda choked back her confusion over his earlier dismissal. "Of course!"

Samuel hopped out of bed and moved over to his trunk. The lid creaked as he opened it. She wasn't surprised. That trunk had belonged to Jed's mother. It was rather old and in need of repair. But it didn't seem to bother Samuel. He pulled out an object made of a light-colored wood and closed the lid, paying no mind as the rusty hinges protested once more.

Then he jumped back into bed, this time remaining on his knees as he faced his mother. He held out the piece of woodwork as if it were made of glass.

But there, in his hands, lay the crudest, but sweetest bird Amanda had ever seen. Truly, the workmanship was quite rough. Still it thrilled her to know that her son's hands created it. That made the chunk of wood beautiful to her eyes.

"Oh, Samuel, you made this?" She put her hands under his.

He nodded, his hair once again falling into his face. "All by myself."

"Truly?" Amanda laced a shocked tone into her reply, though she had no doubts.

"Uncle Owen watched and talked to me a little, but I did all the work."

"That's wonderful!"

"Here." He angled his hands and transferred the bird into her palms.

Holding it as if it were a priceless jewel, Amanda drew it to her chest. Then up to her face to more closely inspect it. Up close, the flaws were rather evident.

The figure was grossly lopsided—one wing was rather large while the other was quite small. There were no legs or feet, yet where they should connect, there were signs of damage. As if they'd been carved too delicately and had broken off. And the face was grooved heavily with marks from the knife. Yet all of this did nothing to detract from the preciousness of the object.

"Do you want to keep it?" Samuel's eyes were bright.

"Oh, I couldn't. It's your first by yourself." Amanda held it out to him.

But Samuel made no move to take it back. Why was his face so suddenly downcast?

"What is it?" Had she upset him?

"I made it for you," Samuel said, shifting to pull the covers over his lap, eyes still not meeting hers, but looking downward. "Cause you've been so lonely. I wanted to make you smile again."

Her heart shrank back at his words. Had she seemed lonely to him? It had only been a few days since she and Brandon had come to this newfound part of their relationship. Had she been lonely before? Or was Samuel lonely?

Reaching toward him, she gathered him to herself. "I'll never be lonely when I have you. We've got each other, remember?" She kissed the top of his head.

He sniffled.

"Do you miss Pa?" Difficult words to speak, but she needed to know. Samuel remained quiet.

"If you do, that's okay." She rubbed his back.

"Is it okay, too, if I miss someone else more?"

As confused as Amanda became, she couldn't help the relief that flooded through her. "Of course."

Samuel pulled back far enough to look up into his mother's face. "It's not that I don't miss Pa."

She pushed that errant hair out of his face again. "I know you do."

"It's just that..."

Amanda gave him a few moments to continue. When he didn't, she prompted him, "What? You can tell me anything. I promise."

"I'm worried about Daisy. Mr. Miller said she's never been gone more than a couple of days, but I don't know. Did you know he tied her up?" Samuel's eyes were wide.

Amanda chose her words carefully. "Yes, I did. And I'm sure Mr. Miller didn't want to. But he felt as if he needed to after she growled at us like—"

"At you!"

"At me like she did."

That did not seem to soothe Samuel in the slightest.

"Mr. Miller just doesn't care."

"That's not true, Samuel."

He fell silent.

"I know you are worried about your friend. But Mr. Miller has known —and cared for—Daisy for a long time. He doesn't want anything bad to happen to her."

Samuel opened his mouth, but Amanda held up a hand to halt him.

"Let's just give him a chance. If she's not back tomorrow, we'll go looking for her day after. All right?"

The frown was still set on Samuel's face, but he nodded.

"Good. Now let me tuck you in."

He lay down, and Amanda pulled the covers to his chin once more.

"Now what story shall we have tonight? Red Riding Hood? Pirates? Gulliver?"

"I'm too old for bedtime stories." He stared up at her.

It was as if he'd flung a dagger straight through her heart. Surely she was bleeding all over the place. But when she looked down, she was not. As she collected herself, she spoke in a soft voice. "You didn't seem too old last night."

"I'm too old tonight." Then he turned onto his side, his back to her.

"I see." Amanda was stricken. "Then good night."

She stood, her stomach dropping as she did so. Moving gingerly, she stepped over to the lantern and blew it out. Thankful that the room was now in darkness, she turned back toward her son, knowing he couldn't see the tears forming in her eyes. Amanda made her way to the door, pausing there to look over at her son's silhouetted form. She clutched the bird in her hand.

"Thank you for my bird. I will cherish it."

No response.

So she stepped out into the hall and closed the door before she lost control of her tears.

<hr/>

What could be keeping her? Brandon had been standing outside Amanda's room, waiting, for quite some time. Was she in the room with Samuel? Had she gone somewhere else? Should he just go to bed?

No. He wanted, no, needed to talk to her. Tonight.

The door down the hall opened. Could he see inside? Darkness within. But his lantern illuminated the hallway, casting a light on the figure that emerged. Amanda.

And she was crying.

He set his lantern down and went to her. "Are you well?"

She nodded, putting a hand on his arm, drawing him away from the room.

Did she still fear Samuel finding out? A pang of hurt coursed through him. How could she not trust in them by now?

Still, her tears moved him. And once they neared the door to her room, he stopped her. He would go no further, could go no further until he had some answers.

"What is it?" He softened his tone, though in his desire for satisfaction for the uneasiness churning within him, he wanted to be anything but soft.

She waved a hand. "Nothing." Biting at her lip, her eyes cut toward Samuel's door.

"It's not 'nothing.' I can see something is bothering you. Tell me." He reached out to cup her face.

She closed her eyes. "I'm sorry. It's just hard for me. Samuel isn't happy with me right now."

"And you feel alone in that?" he guessed.

She looked up at him, nodding.

Was it not natural that her relationship with her son would be separate from their relationship? At least for a while? Still, it stung. Why did it feel that they should be together on this? How he wished the boy felt more comfortable with him.

Every time he'd tried to reach out, Samuel turned away, ran off, or shot him down. Had Brandon truly tried? Or had he been all too thankful for Uncle Owen and Cook's connection with the youngster and left it alone? Why? Was he not ready to be a father to Jed's son? Or did it have more to do with his up and down relationship with Amanda? Had that been a distraction? Or had he simply not cared?

"I don't want you to be alone."

Amanda quirked an eyebrow.

"If we intend to be a family, I'm going to need to step up as the boy's father. I need to start acting like it."

Her eyes widened and her lips parted, but she remained silent. Why wouldn't she speak?

His hand on her face fell. "That is if you intend for us to be a family."

Amanda's brows jerked upward. "What is that supposed to mean?"

Why had he said that? Surely it came from a place a hurt and pride. That pride of his again! But he had yet to sort through his thoughts without visiting his anger upon her.

"I just…don't know how to feel about what happened earlier."

"What happened earlier?" she repeated, her brows now furrowed, a frown marring her features.

Was she going to play a game with him? Surely they were beyond this. "It's late. I'm going to bed." He turned.

She gripped his arm. "No. Not until you tell me what you mean."

He glanced at her hands on his arm then at the floor. A part of him wanted to shake her off. But the bigger part of him knew better. This is not who he was. He may have pride issues, but he had never been the jealous type.

Drawing in a deep breath, he faced her. "Earlier today…when I saw you come out of the bunkhouse. Alone."

Her hands fell. "Oh."

"It is not appropriate for you to be alone with one of my ranch hands. It's just not proper."

She gazed at him. Her eyes seemed glassy and sad. But he would not be swayed.

"And then when I caught you on your way out, you were elusive and acted rather oddly."

As he spoke, she crossed her arms in front of her chest. "Is that all? Have you said your peace on the matter?"

Brandon eyed her. Why was she acting so defensively now? He was the one in the right, and she had every appearance of wrong. Still, he could think of nothing more to say, so he nodded.

"If you must know, I do not visit Cutie in the bunk house on my own. Neither today nor any other."

"But…" Brandon started, confusion filled him. He wracked his brain. He had seen no other with her. Of that, he was certain.

Amanda held up a hand to halt his speech. "Samuel goes with me on that errand. And while I check on Cutie, he and Samuel usually engage in a game of checkers. Today, they happened to not be finished when I needed to leave. So, I said Samuel could stay and finish. If I was elusive toward you, it was because you were being forward and I feared Samuel may step outside at any moment."

The pieces, all there. And they fit nicely into place. Brandon felt like a jealous fool. He had once again let his pride take hold of him.

He closed his eyes. "Amanda, I'm sorry. I was so wrong." Opening his eyes, he wanted to reach for her. But could he? Would she spurn his advances? "I—"

She touched his face. "I know."

He fell silent and just enjoyed the simple comfort of her hands on his skin.

Amanda sighed and closed the distance between them, snuggling up to his chest. She pulled him closer, putting her arms around his waist.

Brandon's arms surrounded her.

"I don't want to fight. Not tonight," she mumbled into his shirt.

He kissed the top of her head. And his body relaxed. She was right. Tomorrow, he, Dan, and Slim would ride off for a couple weeks. How was he to survive being away from her for so long? And how much more so the torture, should they not have this night together, should they not part amiably?

"Hmm," she muttered.

"What is it?" His curiosity piqued.

"Your heart. It's thumping quite loudly." She picked her head up off his chest to look at his face.

He smiled. "I'm not surprised."

"No?" She raised a brow.

"With you so near, it's a miracle it doesn't beat right out of my chest."

Her eyes widened, and she placed a hand over his heart as if to stop it from exploding out of his chest.

He lifted that hand and slowly, deliberately kissed each finger in turn, starting with the smallest and then one by one, working his way to her thumb.

Amanda's breath caught.

His eyes were on hers the entire time.

When he reached her thumb, he kissed and nipped at the pad.

Her pupils seemed to darken as they became larger.

When she, and he, could stand it no longer, he intertwined their fingers, shifted their hands to the side, and pressed his lips to hers.

She drew her body even closer to his. How was that possible? Amanda responded to his search with her own. The kiss held a hope and a promise on both sides.

One kiss became several, and Brandon fumbled for the door's latch.

But something threatened to break the spell they had cast. A word that floated into the edge of his consciousness.

Amanda started to pull away.

Only then did he understand the entreaty.

"Mama, what's going on?"

"Samuel!" Amanda's heart dropped as she looked into her small son's wide-eyed face. The hurt was evident. The accusation was clear.

She stepped toward him.

He ran back into his room and shut the door.

Amanda rushed to his door, slamming her open hand on the wooden surface. "Samuel!"

No response.

"Samuel, let me in or I'm coming in," she warned, reaching for the latch.

Brandon's hand fell on hers.

She looked at him. What was he doing?

"You don't want to do that."

"What?" Was he now going to give her parenting advice?

"What good will come from you forcing your way into his room?"

She thought for a moment, envisioning just that—her opening the door and barging into his room uninvited. Samuel would be mad, yes. Perhaps he would feel his privacy was violated. But he would have to speak with her.

"He will have to talk to me."

Brandon raised a brow. "Will he?"

"At least he'll have to listen."

A skeptical expression met her gaze.

Was Brandon right? Would Samuel just shut her out if she pushed her way in?

She looked over at the latch. How would she feel? What would she do if someone did that to her? Probably ignore them.

Amanda allowed Brandon to remove her hand. "But he needs me," she protested.

"That may be true. And he knows where to find you when he's ready."

Amanda looked up at Brandon.

"We need to let him do this in his time. This is a lot for him to take in."

Her gaze shifted back to the door. "But he's my baby."

Brandon's hands were on her arms. "Not anymore. He's growing up."

Amanda sniffled. That wasn't true. It couldn't be true. He was still the same young boy that needed his mother to tuck him in at night and help him get dressed in the morning.

Except...

Except she hadn't dressed him in months. And he seemed to fare just fine when she wasn't here to tuck him in. Was he allowing her to continue for her benefit? To appease her?

Her chest tightened and her breaths came in gasps.

Brandon shook her gently. "What's the matter?"

Amanda wiped a hand across her brow. "He doesn't need me anymore."

"Now, I didn't say that." Brandon turned her to face him. "You're his mother. He'll always—"

She shook her head. "I've ruined it all. He hates me." Samuel had voiced his anger toward Brandon about the dog. She should have taken better care. What he must think of her!

"Amanda, you're not thinking straight. Samuel doesn't hate you. He may be hurt, upset, even angry. But he doesn't hate you. You must know that beyond all of this, he loves you."

Her vision blurred as she sought his eyes. "I don't know where to go from here."

Brandon gathered her in his arms, stroking her hair. It soothed her, but she wanted him to speak, to offer some magical wisdom. But he remained silent, simply comforting her.

"How? How do I fix this?"

There was silence for several moments more. He pressed a kiss to the top of her head. Would he just say something?

"I don't know. But I do know that there is guidance readily available whenever you need it."

She sighed. "Yes. Uncle Owen is very understanding—"

"He is that. But I'm not talking about Uncle Owen."

Amanda drew back so she could look at him. "No? Who then?"

His gaze softened, and he opened his mouth.

She spoke before he could. "You don't mean God, do you?" Amanda's heart beat harder. They had never talked about the Bible or prayer. Not really. Though she was aware that Brandon put stock in that sort of thing.

"Of course, I do." Brandon's voice was even, his face remained expressionless.

She shook her head. "I know you believe in all that. But I'll be honest, God has never done anything but punish me. So, I'm not interested in praying to Him or reading about Him." The aches from old wounds in her heart opened and began to throb.

Brandon's eyes glistened.

Moved by his concern, she laid a hand on the side of his face. "These things are quite deep for such a late night."

He watched her. Was he trying to decide whether or not to continue the conversation? Eventually, he closed his eyes and turned his lips into her palm. And then nuzzled her there.

"I think it's time we got some sleep," he said into her hand. Then, taking it in his, he tugged her toward the door to her room. Once there, he pulled her toward him for a gentle kiss. "This, I fear, is where I must leave you."

"No," she mumbled against his lips. Why would he want to be away from her on this, their last night for so long?

"It is best," he said as he pulled away.

"Please," she said, not releasing him. "Just lie next to me. I need to feel you near me."

His eyes searched hers.

"I promise I'll be good." A smile tugged at the corner of her mouth.

"How can I resist?" Though his words seemed teasing, there was no hint of a smile on his features.

Amanda worked the latch and opened the door easily. Then, taking Brandon's hands in hers, led him into the dark room.

CHAPTER FOURTEEN

Gone

BRANDON FIT HIS saddle on Candy. It was far too early in the morning for anyone to be awake. Candy seemed to agree. She snorted at him as he buckled the leather straps around her midsection. Apparently, she wasn't ready to be disturbed.

Neither had he been. He had doubted the wisdom of going to bed with Amanda just to lie with her, but that was indeed all that happened. However, the feel of her in his arms had blessed him with the deepest, most comfortable sleep he knew. It had been pure torture to remove himself from her an hour ago when he heard Uncle Owen shuffling in the hall.

Pulling away from her sleeping form, knowing he would not see her for so many days to come…that he would lie awake at night, longing for her caresses…it was almost more than he could stand. The desire to press a last kiss to her full lips was overwhelming. But he resisted. Waking her would only make things more difficult.

Brandon had been grateful for Uncle Owen's sympathy when he made his way into the kitchen. The older man greeted him with a mug of steaming coffee and a quiet smile. And his relative neither pried nor pushed, but let him be as they sipped their warm brew together.

Did he know that Brandon was falling apart inside? Did he know what lay beneath the surface of Brandon's barely contained calm? Perhaps there were secrets to Uncle Owen's youth that Brandon did not know.

Still, naught was spoken between them as Brandon finished his coffee and then moved toward the door.

But as he passed Uncle Owen, the older man's arm reached out and grabbed for Brandon's shoulder.

Brandon stopped and glanced at his friend and mentor.

Uncle Owen gave his shoulder a hearty squeeze and offered Brandon a kind smile.

Was this Uncle Owen's way of connecting with his sadness? Of wishing him well on his journey? Brandon didn't know. Perhaps it was both. Perhaps something else altogether.

Brandon's hand came up and rested on Uncle Owen's arm, patting the man's weaker muscles.

Then Uncle Owen's arm released its hold and slid down to his side. And Brandon moved out of the house and toward the barn. There were many preparations to be made.

Even now, he looked over at Dan and Slim, readying their own horses. They appeared tired as well. Their coffee may not have had time to wake their bodies yet.

A horse and cart sounded nearby. Cook. She had promised to come early and make them breakfast. Brandon told her it wasn't necessary. Still, she insisted. It would delay them a bit, but he appreciated it all the same.

Brandon drew his attention back to his horse. Now that she was saddled, he wanted to double check the chuck wagon. He walked over to it, hauled himself up inside the wagon, and began rummaging through the provisions.

"Ain't you been through that stuff already?"

Brandon poked his head out.

Dan smiled up at him, stifling a yawn.

"Yes, but one more check can't hurt anything, can it?"

Dan raised his hands. "No, sir."

"When them other fellas supposed to be here?" Slim walked over.

Brandon frowned. The other three men he had hired for the drive should have arrived. He pulled out his pocket watch. Perhaps they would be here by the time breakfast was finished.

"We'll give them another half hour." He tried to sound more

confident than he felt. "Meanwhile, I think Cook has some vittles for us."

Brandon jumped out of the wagon and led the men back to the homestead.

The men were either famished or readying themselves for a long stretch of nothing but beans and bacon because they ate everything Cook put on the table like they'd never seen food before.

Brandon, too, found it difficult to pace himself. Why was that? But his thoughts soon drifted to Amanda. He prayed she still slept peacefully down the hall. What he wouldn't give to hold her once more. What would these next two weeks be like if he was already aching for her?

Tearing his mind from thoughts of her, he looked across the table at Dan and Slim. They appeared to be rather uncomfortably full. The grimaces on their faces betrayed their discomfort. Surely, they had the best cook this side of the Rio Grande.

"Thanks, Cook. No better way to start a long journey." Brandon glanced over at her.

Her eyes seemed to glisten. But just for a moment. Then she came forward and started collecting dishes. "Just doing my job."

Was she upset? Worried for them?

Brandon touched her arm. "It's more than that."

She looked over her shoulder at him. Her eyes were glassy. But she blinked back any tears that might be forming and refocused on her task. "Y'all best get on your way. Don't want to get a late start."

Glancing at Dan and Slim, Brandon nodded.

The men stood and moved toward the door.

As they stepped onto the porch, Brandon saw the dust stirred on the horizon. It must be his hired help. Finally. He'd have to keep his eye on them if they couldn't be trusted to show up on time.

Brandon and his ranch hands moved toward the barn. He kept watch on the approaching men as he did so. As they came nearer, he was more and more certain he could only count two horses bearing riders. This could not be good.

They all met at the entrance to the barn. Indeed there were only two riders, the men he had hired as extra drovers. Where was the cook?

"Where is your friend? The one who cooks?" Brandon did what he could to maintain his veneer of calm. It would do no good to get upset. Not yet anyway.

The men looked at each other. Who would speak to him? One of them better open his mouth and tell him the truth.

The red-haired cowboy eventually turned back to Brandon. "He is unwell, sir."

"Unwell?"

The other drover, a man with sandy-blond hair and freckles made a motion of someone upending a bottle.

"I see." How was he to contain his anger? The man had been out drinking himself into a stupor the night before a cattle drive?

Perhaps it was better the man did not end up on the drive after all. A blessing. But what were they to do without a cook?

How could they proceed down one man?

Dawn streamed in through Amanda's window. Light coming into her room roused Amanda from her rest. She turned toward Brandon, seeking the comfort of his arms. But he wasn't there.

Why wasn't he there?

Oh, yes, it was dawn. He would have gone back to his room.

She fought the emptiness that filled her. This was how it had to be for now.

Then the memories from the night before crept into her consciousness. Samuel's face. Brandon's words.

After all that, surely he would not see the need to keep up the charade. Then why?

The cattle drive. Today was the day they departed for the cattle drive.

She sat up. Had she already missed him? Missed saying good-bye? Why hadn't he wakened her?

Anger threatened on the edge of her mind. He had to know she would have wanted to say farewell. How could he have been so selfish? She pounded the bed with her fists and then crossed her arms in front of her chest.

There was nothing for it. What was done, was done. And she could either harbor this resentment for the next two weeks and let it fester, or release him of it and forgive. That was what she truly wanted—to think on him with fondness, even if it ached.

She slipped out of bed, splashed water on her face, dressed herself, and pinned her hair up. Then she ventured out into the house. All was quiet except for movement in the kitchen. So that was where she headed.

As she neared the door, she heard voices. She almost turned around, but found herself caught by the conversation.

"It will be all right."

It sounded like Uncle Owen. In the kitchen? Wasn't it breakfast time? Shouldn't he be gathering the men for the meal? But then, they had left already. Was he helping Cook clean up?

"I wish I could believe ya." Cook's voice. It broke as she spoke. Was she crying?

"Brandon has a good head on his shoulders. He knows what he's doing." Uncle Owen's voice was strong, confident.

"But he's so young. Part of me wishes you could go with him. Only…"

There was silence. Amanda should leave. Eavesdropping was beneath her. It was rude.

"Only what?" Uncle Owen's voice sounded oddly like Brandon's when he stood close to her, when he spoke tenderly to her.

"I fear I would worry all the more."

"Truly?" That soft, husky Miller voice.

"Of course, I would, you old goat!"

Amanda couldn't help but smile at Cook's response. The room fell silent. Were they embracing? Kissing? Amanda's face warmed. She slinked off, back toward her own room.

So, Cook and Uncle Owen at last? It shouldn't come as a surprise. There had been moments when Amanda thought she witnessed a look, a gesture, a smile. But nothing so great that she truly suspected anything had happened. Still, it warmed her heart to think that they might find such happiness with each other.

As she walked down the hall, she passed Samuel's door. The memories from last night filled her mind. Brandon's hand on hers, telling her not to invade his privacy. Did that hold true for today? Should she wait for him to come out? It was rather late for him to still be sleeping. Would he respond to her attempts to talk to him? She'd just have to try.

Knock, knock, knock. She tapped her knuckles on his door.

No response.

She did it again. "Samuel? It's Mama."

Nothing.

"Samuel, I'm so sorry about what happened last night. Please, let me in."

No answer.

"I just want to talk."

Stillness.

"Samuel, I'm getting a little worried. Can you please let me know that you're all right?"

She put her ear to the door. Still nothing.

Whether or not Brandon was right last night became irrelevant. This was a new day. And this was a different issue entirely. She had to make sure he was all right.

"Samuel, I'm coming in." Amanda released the latch and pushed on the door.

It budged.

A little.

Something was in the way.

Her heartbeat quickened and something sped through her body, a sensation that made her feel more than a little on edge.

She pushed harder against the door.

It budged again. A little more this time.

The door was now opened a crack. She saw into the room. Samuel's bed appeared to be empty, but messy.

Slamming into the door with all she had made the door move more. Enough that she could shove her way into the room.

His trunk had been pushed up against the door. That had been her obstacle. But not her main focus.

Her eyes swept the room. It was empty but for the furniture and smattering of things. Samuel wasn't there.

She couldn't breathe.

Moving about the small room, she tore the covers off the bed. He wasn't there.

Dragging in air, she fought for every breath she took in.

The window!

Amanda rushed for it, flinging it open and sucking in the fresh air. She seemed only a little more able to take in air here.

She paused. The window had not been latched. Why was it open? Then it came together — the trunk in front of the door, the window being unlatched. Samuel had slipped out through the open window at some point during the night or early morning. But when? How long ago?

Dread filled her. What if something happened to him? She was supposed to protect her little boy. Not cause him to run off.

Enough of that. She had to find him! But she would need help.

Where would she find such help? Uncle Owen? Cook? Amanda

couldn't imagine either riding out with her. Cutie? Was he in any condition to assist her? She would find out.

Slipping back out through the narrow crack in the doorway, she rushed toward the front door.

Cook and Uncle Owen were in the dining room, sitting rather close to each other, talking in low tones. They separated when Amanda came into the room.

"Amanda! We didn't realize you were up. Can I get you some breakfast?" Cook rose, her chair scraping the floor.

"No, I can't talk now. Samuel's gone."

"Gone?" Uncle Owen was on his feet faster than Amanda thought possible. But she didn't stay long to watch. She rushed out the door.

Once she was on the porch, she spotted the men gathered around the entrance to the barn. And her heart leaped. Brandon was not gone! Perhaps all was not lost!

Lifting her skirt, she ran toward him, paying no heed to how she appeared or how she may seem to the other men, though their eyes were surely on her.

Brandon's were no exception. His wide eyes leveled on her. He was concerned. What did he think of her? That she had gone mad? That she wanted to wish him farewell? What a state she must be in!

He stepped out of the group and caught her in his arms.

Amanda was thankful for his embrace. And glad that he cared not for what the others might think.

"Are you well, my love?"

She thrilled at those two words he had not spoken to her before. They sounded wonderful sliding off his lips and into her ear. Amanda clung to his shirt. And resisted the urge to let loose her emotions and cry.

"It's Samuel." She was surprised how breathless her response came out.

"Samuel?" He pulled back.

She couldn't stop the tears that filled her eyes. "He's gone."

Brandon's brows furrowed.

"His room is empty, and his window was open. I fear he ran off during the night."

He drew her to his chest again. "We'll find him. It will be all right."

"How can you say that? What if something's happened already?"

"Sh…" Brandon stroked her hair. "We'll do everything we can. We're a team, remember?"

She nodded against him.

But as he pulled back, his gaze drifted over to the men waiting to depart for the drive. What was he thinking? Would he delay the drive to search for Samuel? Could they? Or would he put someone else in charge of the search for Samuel? Would he put the cattle drive first?

What was Brandon to do? He couldn't leave Amanda in such a state. Would she allow him to delegate this to Uncle Owen or even the town's sheriff? One look in her pleading eyes told him all he needed to know. It had to be him. But could he abandon the cattle drive and sacrifice their future, their livelihood?

He rubbed her arm, hoping to reassure her. Then he stepped away from her, toward the men that continued to watch him.

"Ready the horses." He spoke in soft tones.

"For what, sir?" Slim's brows were near his hairline.

"For the drive." Brandon's words were resolute. He then turned and walked back toward Amanda. "Can you saddle one of the remaining mares for yourself?"

She nodded. "What about you? What are you going to do?" Amanda reached for his arm.

Brandon slipped from her grasp and moved toward the house as if he hadn't heard her. He did not look back. What he needed was a moment to think. Just one moment. Or two.

Though he felt her eyes on him the entirety of his walk, he continued to move as if unfazed into the house.

Wringing his hands, he stepped into the great room. Jerking off his gloves and throwing his hat down, he began to pace.

Dearest Lord...

What was the answer? The drive was already down one man. How could they proceed without yet another? And the Trail Boss no less. Besides, he needed to be there at auction. That was a task he couldn't trust to his ranch hands. It was too big.

Help me, God...

Perhaps they could delay? No, he couldn't pay for the hired hands one more day than allotted. And it was already well into the spring. Any longer and they'd risk trouble on the drive.

"Thought I heard someone in here." A voice boomed behind him.

Brandon startled, turning to face whomever invaded his private moment. He spun around, prepared to deliver a tongue-lashing, however, he found himself face to face with Uncle Owen. He let out a deep breath and relaxed.

"My you are tense." Uncle Owen hobbled to one of the chairs nearby. "I thought you would have been gone by now."

Brandon leaned against the fireplace mantel, rubbing a hand along the wooden frame. "I would be. Should be. But there is a complication."

"Samuel."

Looking over at Uncle Owen, eyes widening, he wondered after the man. How did he seem to know everything before it happened? It was no matter. "Yes."

"Well?"

"Amanda has asked me to help search for him."

"Seems like the right thing to do."

"But that could take hours, all day even. And if he's…it could prevent me from meeting up with the drive if I sent them ahead."

Uncle Owen rubbed his chin. "That's true. Maybe you should go on with the drive then."

Brandon let out another breath. "That makes the most sense. We're already down a cook. They can't be down another man as well."

He stepped over to where he had discarded his gloves and hat. Sliding his gloves back on with ease, he looked at his hat, fingering the brim, not quite able to put it on.

"What's the matter?" Uncle Owen's voice cut through the stillness between them.

"I just…" he couldn't finish that sentence. Couldn't put his thoughts into words. What would happen to Samuel? To Amanda? How would she react when he told her he had to leave on the drive instead of search for Samuel?

"I have a crazy thought. Maybe my craziest yet." Uncle Owen broke into Brandon's thoughts.

Brandon looked up at him. Was there a solution he wasn't seeing? *Dear Lord, may it be so!*

"What if I went along as the cook?"

The fire that had begun to stir in Brandon was doused. He shook his head. "No, that's just not possible."

"And just why not?" Uncle Owen stood on shaky legs. "I'll dare say I've been on more cattle drives than all those young men out there put together."

Brandon eyed him. He couldn't be serious. "But you're in no condition to—"

"And I wouldn't have to ride a horse with my bum hip. I'd be in the chuck wagon."

That was true. But it was more than that. "What if Dan and Slim don't help you? What if they abandon you? You could be injured out there. Or worse."

"You have to trust someone. Either way you choose. Do you trust Dan and Slim with the drive or do you trust men you don't know to help your wife in her time of greatest need?"

Uncle Owen had a way of making it all seem so simple.

"What about the Trail Boss? How can I trust Dan or Slim at auction?"

Uncle Owen hobbled over to Brandon and took his hand. "You have to trust that Dan and Slim and I will be a team."

Brandon was vaguely aware of the door opening behind him. Was Slim or Dan coming to retrieve him?

"What about the amount of cattle? You'll still be down one drover?"

"Not if I go."

Brandon's head turned toward the voice he had not heard in quite some time.

Cutie stood in the door. He leaned on the frame, but he was there, on his own two feet. And he appeared much improved.

"That's not possible," Brandon asserted. "You aren't well enough—"

"I am." Cutie's eyes were set, his jaw firm. "And I remember what you told me after I was injured. We are family. And family sticks together. Family tells the truth, too." Cutie looked off to the right.

Something about the way Cutie's eyes became downcast caused Brandon's heart to sink. "What are you saying, Cutie?"

Cutie closed his eyes and let out a long breath. "I got something to confess, Boss."

Brandon swallowed, could his heart take any more? Still, he held his tongue and listened.

Meeting his eyes at last, Cutie spoke, "I got a problem. And I know that now."

Nodding, Brandon remained silent.

"See, the thing is I used to feel awful strong jealous of ya, Boss. I thought mean thoughts."

Brandon couldn't be more shocked. Cutie? Jealous of him?

"And, I got to drinking one night and mouthed off about your money." Cutie's head dropped.

As did Brandon's heart. So that was how Kid Antrim knew about his nest egg. All this time. Cutie—a snake in the grass.

"And if you want to turn me out I understand."

Brandon let out a long breath. He wanted to be angry. That slip had cost them dearly. Had almost cost Amanda her life. But God had not held him accountable for his sins. No, He had bestowed grace again and again.

Walking over to Cutie, Brandon stopped just short of the man.

Cutie grimaced, looking away from Brandon's gaze.

Brandon laid a hand on Cutie's shoulder. "I meant what I said about family."

Cutie looked into Brandon's eyes at last. There was moisture welling in Cutie's green orbs. "Then what kind of family would this be if I didn't step in?"

Brandon nodded. He glanced at Uncle Owen.

"What'll it be, son?"

Son. Uncle Owen had never called him that. But it suited him. It suited their relationship just well. In so many ways Uncle Owen had become a father to him.

"I can't leave her. Not when she needs me."

Uncle Owen smiled. "Then God speed. My prayers are with you." The older man's arms came around Brandon's shoulders and drew him in.

Had Brandon made the right decision? He made the one his heart told him to. But as much as he worried after Samuel, he knew he would fret over the cattle drive. Trust was not one of his strong suits.

And here he was placing Uncle Owen's life and the future of them all in the hands of Dan, Slim, and Cutie. Would they prove true?

<hr />

Tears created a haze in her vision as Amanda worked to saddle a painted mare. Her heart weighed heavy in her chest. Brandon wasn't going to help her.

And she understood. The auction was too important to all their futures. Would he leave someone behind to help her search for Samuel?

Or would he send for the lawman?

As much as it hurt, she couldn't blame him. He had to think of everyone, not just her. And certainly not just Samuel. Jed's son. Sobs shook her body, and she hurt so deeply she fell to her knees.

What a fool she had been. To think she loved Jed, to defend him and his actions. But regardless of who Samuel's father was, he was her son, too. And she loved him. He was the most precious thing in her life. The thought that he could be hurting or lost made her ache with worry. It was as if the pain would never stop.

What if they never found him? She couldn't think like that. Wouldn't think like that. But without Brandon, she was alone. No matter who came alongside her in his stead, she would be alone.

Clutching her stomach, she leaned over her knees and sobbed. For Samuel. For herself. For her lost hope.

After some moments, hands, strong and comforting, fell on her back. Her crying subsided as those hands pulled her to her feet.

Then she was against a warm chest. And a familiar scent filled her nose as arms surrounded her.

She clung to his shirt. "When will you leave?"

"Leave?" His voice rumbled under her ear.

Amanda sniffled.

"I'm not going anywhere." Hands stroked her hair.

"You're not?"

"I couldn't. We're a team, remember?"

She nodded against him. Her heart felt as if it would explode. Was this man possible? That he cared for her this much? "But what about the cattle drive? The auction?"

"Others will go. My place is here."

Amanda pulled back to look into his eyes.

He wiped the tears from her cheeks. "We'd best not waste another moment."

She nodded.

Brandon released her and moved to the painted mare, checking the straps on the saddle. "What are the chances he's gone back to Jed's property?"

Amanda frowned. She had not considered where he might go. It seemed like as good a place to start as any. "He wouldn't know many places. But he would know that one."

"Go and search there first." Brandon hoisted Amanda into the saddle. "Then go to town and ask around. Perhaps someone has seen him."

Were they not to go together?

"I'll search out some of the area around here. We'll cover more ground that way."

She nodded.

"God be with you," he said, laying a hand on hers.

This time, she didn't mind his reference to God. She did hope that He was with them in their search. If ever she needed Him to be watching over her and caring about what happened, it was now.

CHAPTER FIFTEEN

Searching

BRANDON WATCHED THE drovers lead his cattle off into the horizon. It was done. There was the chance that if Samuel were found quickly and well enough that he could catch up to them, but he dared not count on it.

As he watched them disappear, he couldn't deny that his heart still felt torn. Not that he questioned whether or not he had done the right thing. He still questioned how much he could trust his ranch hands. They were paid workers. And auction was one big payday. What would keep them from taking the jackpot and running off? Uncle Owen certainly couldn't stop them.

He had nothing left but to trust them. And to trust God that his future was secure.

A wind blew across the plain and over him. He closed his eyes. As was the case so often, he imagined it was the Spirit of God passing over him, assuring him of God's presence and guidance. It soothed Brandon's soul.

Opening his eyes again, he urged his horse forward. Samuel could not have gotten far.

Brandon spent the next hour searching the pastures and the area surrounding them to no avail. There was no sign of the boy. He hoped

Amanda was having better luck, although that would have been a great distance for Samuel to have traveled on foot. An almost unrealistic distance without some assistance. But Brandon himself was evidence that when you put your mind to something, you find a way to make it happen.

This ranch would never had made it into his hands if it weren't for his sheer determination. And his mother's kindness. It was because of the money she had kept to the side and from his father that any of it had been possible. It still touched him that she was willing to risk defying his father to give him the money to go after his dream.

Especially since she hadn't wanted him to head west any more than his father did. But she believed in him. And wanted him to succeed. Perhaps she had a different definition of success? He certainly did. How he would like to one day repay her for the generous gift, but he doubted he would ever be able to. Not that she expected repayment. Mothers were like that. Good mothers. They gave of themselves.

He'd never taken much time to observe Amanda as a mother. But the pain in her eyes as she told him about Samuel's disappearance was rather telling in and of itself. What would it be like to watch her mother a child? A baby? His baby?

Scanning the area, he refocused his attention on his search. This was no time for daydreaming. Had he unturned every stone? Could Samuel have wandered this far away in the allotted time? Would he have gone this direction or made straight for Jed's ranch? Did he even know which direction to go? Or was he wandering aimlessly out here? If so, their chances of finding him went down drastically.

Dear Lord, I am asking not for myself, but for this innocent child. You know where he is. You see him, Elohim. Keep watch over him. Please guide my steps. Guide Amanda's. Help us find him.

Brandon was struck with a thought—Uncle Owen. Where would Uncle Owen have taken the boy on the property? Perhaps Samuel would have gone somewhere familiar. Where did Uncle Owen take Brandon when he was younger? They did so many things together.

Uncle Owen taught him to ride a horse and race through the dusty open plains. They often fished together in a nearby stream. When he was especially good, they went to the town cafe for a sarsaparilla. And then there were the shooting games down in the gully.

It wasn't likely Uncle Owen was giving horseback lessons anymore. And Amanda would be checking out things around town. That left the nearby stream and the gully.

Urging his horse into a trot, Brandon directed the animal toward Uncle Owen's favorite fishing stream.

❧

The overgrown property came into view. Amanda did not relish the idea of being at this homestead again. Why would they not just sell it? What was Brandon waiting for? Her blessing? He could have it!

But not until they found Samuel.

Pulling her horse to a halt near the front porch, she jumped off and made sure to secure the horse to the post. No need to have a repeat of what happened before.

"Samuel!" She rushed toward the door to the homestead.

It gave way easily under her hand.

"Samuel!" Amanda stepped inside.

The house remained as she had left it when she and Brandon had… when they had last been here. Pushing those thoughts to the side, she rushed through the few rooms of the house, calling for her son, tears forming in her eyes as it became more apparent he wasn't there.

She paused in his room, now little more than a straw mattress on a frame. Still, she sat upon the edge of his bed, laying her head in her hands.

Where could he be? If not here, where? Where would he seek solace?

He had been so angry at her. Did he think she no longer loved his father? That she was betraying Jed's memory? While it was true to some extent that the feelings she had for Jed no longer existed, she would always love him. Jed had given her Samuel. And she would always love him for that. But how do you explain to a five-year-old boy that life doesn't end when someone dies?

How hardheaded had she been when learning that lesson? Perhaps Samuel's flight was not that different from her own earlier escapes. Except she was a grown woman who should have known better.

Enough. Enough of this. She had to find her son.

Forcing herself to stand, she made her way outside. The horse still stood where Amanda had left her. Amanda thanked the God she wasn't sure she believed in.

Pulling herself back up into the saddle, she pushed the horse into a trot and toward Jed's pastures. Over the next hour, she scanned and searched the land Jed had maintained, the area Samuel had known as home.

All the while, her heart continued to sink in her chest. What could have happened to her boy? Was this a bad sign? The fact that she hadn't found him already? Could he have made his way into town? Should she abandon hope here and search there?

Maybe her father had been right. She had hurt the person who meant the most to her in the world. The one person she was determined would never question her love. Perhaps she wasn't good for anybody after all. A disease.

She didn't know what to do. At a loss. Without direction. Without hope.

❧❧❧

Brandon pulled back on his horse's reins as he arrived at the stream. But he was alone. Yet again. Hanging his head, a sadness settled into his chest. If Amanda had not found him by now, the chances of them ever finding him dwindled.

And he had not truly expected her to find Samuel. It may have been wrong of him, but he hadn't wanted her to come across Samuel in case he had met with a terrible fate. No, it was better that Brandon searched the area surrounding the homestead himself.

He'd best take his chances over at the gully then. As he turned to go, however, something whispered on the edge of his consciousness.

Lift your eyes up to the mountains. Where does your help come from?

Brandon shifted his gaze back across the stream. There was a smallish sort of mountain across the stream. Would Samuel have tried to cross the stream? The waters were fairly calm. But he was so young. The water must have gone up to his chest. Wasn't he afraid?

Still, whatever it was in the corner of his mind urged him toward that mountain. How to cross the stream? He maneuvered the horse further south until he found a shallower crossing point. The water still came up to the horse's belly, but they made it to the other side with little effort.

From there, it was a short ride to the base of the mountain. As they ascended the gentle slope, Brandon began to question the wisdom of distracting himself. But decided this was as good as any place to search.

Several more minutes up the slope, the journey became difficult and Brandon wondered whether or not the horse would be able to make it. And whether or not that meant he should continue. He could spend hours hiking this mountain on foot and find nothing. Wouldn't he be better off on horseback searching more widespread areas?

As he brought Candy to a stop and all was still, something, a voice, perhaps carried on the wind, but rather faint reached his ears.

Was this some trick of his mind? Or was it truly a voice? Could it be Samuel?

He strained his ears.

Nothing.

It was probably all in his head. Wishful thinking.

Brandon turned the horse.

And there it was again. So faint. But undeniable.

He held his breath, praying for another confirmation.

Nothing.

And then crying. Barely audible.

Turning the horse around, Brandon leaned over the pommel. Where did it come from? It was so faint; he had a difficult time discerning its location. Now that the crying was more constant, he was more assured it was real.

There. Up ahead and to the right. He was sure of it.

Brandon slid off the horse and led her forward, keeping her steps slow to ensure he would not lose the voice. As he neared, he was more and more certain it belonged to a child. His heart started to race, and he prayed it was Samuel. Turning right, he found himself on the edge of a shallow ravine that dropped about thirty feet. And there, at the bottom, with his leg twisted at an odd angle, was Samuel.

What could she do? Stay or go? Or run away? Her heart cried out at that thought. She couldn't leave not knowing what happened to her son. Brandon would find him. He wouldn't stop until he did.

But if she stayed, she would eventually ruin Brandon like she'd ruined her father, her mother, Jed, and now Samuel.

Hunching forward, she broke into sobs. She was useless. After all she'd been through. After all her striving, the truth had found her.

She had nothing left. Nothing to give. Nothing worthwhile.

Turning her face toward the heavens, she cried out. "Why?"

Silence.

Of course. What did she expect? But she would not accept that. He would answer her. She deserved that much.

"Why go on with this? I'm done, I tell you. Done."

Nothing.

"Aren't you supposed to love everyone? Why do you hate me so? Why do you delight in watching me suffer?"

She looked down at her hands holding the reins. Just as she thought, no God to answer her.

Then she felt the strangest sensation. Like tingles on her skin, as if her limbs were being moved after a long time of resting. And the sensation went deeper until it filled her whole being.

Memories flooded her mind. Her father, smiling at her, holding her, telling her she was precious. She did not recall these things. Were they real? They seemed real. Then she saw in her mind's eye that awful day when he came home upset. Amanda had heard him come in the door and she started to rush downstairs to show him her English paper, but then heard those words that had wounded her—"this is too much."

It had been so hard for him to care for her and her mother. She was only a burden to him. He was overworked. Amanda had run back up the stairs.

But in her mind's eye, she saw the rest of the conversation. "I was forced to fire someone today. Someone who needed this paycheck. He has children Amanda's age."

She never knew.

And then she saw Jed. Flashes of him. In her memories, she saw him for what he really was—a lonely man who never felt loved and didn't know how to show love. Her heart broke for him.

As the memories faded, she slid off her horse and onto her knees.

"God, I…I never knew."

How could she have been so blind? Blind to the pain of others? To their stories?

"Why…?" was all she could manage. Her heart broke. For Jed. For her father.

Beloved.

Where had that come from? She looked around. Had someone spoken to her?

Beloved.

Was it in her head? Closing her eyes, she listened for the whisper.

Beloved.

It was in her heart. And it was for her. She was beloved. A wall came down. The floodgates opened. In the stillness of that moment, God met with her.

~୧ଓ୫ଡ଼ ୨ଋଡ଼ୗ~

Brandon looked down at the crying boy. What had drawn the boy to this place? Up this mountain?

Crouching on his knees and leaning over on his hands, he called down. "Samuel!"

The young boy looked up. His crying stilled for a moment. "Pa? Is that you?"

Was the boy not able to see Brandon with the sun behind him, silhouetting his figure? Or was he in shock?

"No, it's Mr. Mil—Brandon. It's Brandon."

"Mr. Miller?" The disappointment was evident in the young voice, but there was hope there, too.

"Yes, Samuel. I'm here. And I'm going to help you."

The boy sniffled. "I'm hurt real bad."

"I know. I need you to be brave, though. We'll get through this. Together."

Brandon watched Samuel's head shake in some semblance of a nod.

Then Brandon scanned the area, taking in his surroundings, figuring his options. The ravine was not too deep. He could reach Samuel with the length of rope he had attached to Candy's saddle. But how would he secure the rope? And what would he do to ensure Samuel was not injured further as he pulled him back up? Was there a way to splint his leg?

Brandon spotted an outcropping that seemed large enough to secure the rope for him to climb down. Moving in that direction, he tried to block out Samuel's cries. The boy was no doubt in terrible pain. But Brandon had to focus if he was going to get them both out of here.

He tested the rock face at the place where it jutted out. It appeared to be solid, but he wouldn't truly know until he put his full weight on it. But that would be the point of no return, for him and for Samuel. It was a risk he'd have to take.

Walking back to Candy, he loosened the rope and made his way over to the ledge again. Now for the next part: the splint. A dead tree nearby provided a couple of nice sized branches. And his knife would strip cloth for him. He was as ready as he could be.

Tying the rope up top with a couple of hitches, he lifted a prayer for safety and dropped the rope off into the chasm. Just as he hoped, it reached the bottom.

Then he began his descent. He rappelled down the mountain, using his body for friction and bracing the rope against his back. Several leaps backward brought him to the bottom. The outcropping held. Now on solid ground again, he let out a breath. But getting down was the easy part.

Then he turned his attention to Samuel. The young boy was in a state by this point. His face was pale, and his features contorted in pain. Brandon took off his gloves and touched Samuel's forehead—cold, wet, and clammy.

The leg was twisted and at and odd angle. Was bone coming through the skin?

God, help me.

How was he going to do this? Should he bother to look and see if it had broken the skin? There would be no benefit to that. He needed to splint it as best he could and get Samuel to the doctor.

Brandon had only seen Uncle Owen splint a fellow ranch hand one time when he was a younger man. And then he had seen the doctor work on Cutie's broken limb, nauseating as it was. There had been much too much blood for his comfort. But he had to do this.

"I'm going to check out your leg, Samuel."

Samuel nodded slowly.

Brandon took hold of Samuel's leg and began to move it.

Samuel screamed.

Brandon wanted to stop, but he couldn't. He had to keep going.

"What, ah, you thinking about whittling next?" He maneuvered the leg a tad more.

Tears streamed down Samuel's face. "What?"

"I heard you carved a right nice bird. Got plans for any more animals maybe? A horse? Or a dog?"

Samuel whined. "M-m-maybe a d-d-dog."

"Like Daisy?" Brandon was relieved there didn't appear to be any blood in the area. Chances were the bone had not come through the skin. He almost had the leg in place.

"Yeah."

"You and Daisy are good friends, huh?"

Samuel sniffled.

Brandon looked at him.

Samuel grimaced and moaned.

"I'm sorry, pal." Brandon put a hand on Samuel's chest. "This is going to hurt real bad. You go ahead and scream as loud as you want, okay?"

Samuel nodded.

Brandon clenched his teeth, held his breath, and jerked the leg into place.

The boy wailed, but did not pass out, much to Brandon's surprise.

Laying the small branches on either side of Samuel's leg, Brandon ripped at the shoulder of his own shirt. Once it came free, he pulled out his knife and began cutting strips.

"Samuel!"

The boy's head rolled back and forth as he cried.

"Stay with me."

Samuel made a sputtering sound.

"Tell me about Daisy."

Mumbling.

"What was that?"

"Off…she ran off." He seemed to be delirious.

"Daisy? Oh. Because of the storm."

"No. She…mad…I have…find her." Between his cries and grunts, it was becoming harder and harder to discern what he said.

"You have to find her?" What was he saying? Was he even coherent? Brandon halted his work for a moment and leaned closer to Samuel's face.

"She ran off."

"No, Samuel. She was scared of the storm. She'll be back."

"I have to find her."

"Is that why you came out here? To find Daisy?"

Samuel nodded. "She's over here. I heard howling."

Brandon frowned. Coyotes. "It's all right, Samuel. I'll find Daisy and make sure she gets home safely."

Samuel's eyes opened and he looked at Brandon. What was that in his face? Gratitude? Acceptance? It was there one minute and then his eyes rolled back in his head.

"Samuel!" Brandon grasped his shoulders, shaking him ever so slightly. "Samuel, stay with me!"

And bad just got worse.

CHAPTER SIXTEEN

Finally

AMANDA SATISFIED HERSELF that Samuel was not at Jed's. She needed help. This was the time to reach out to the townsfolk. Would they receive her well? It was her last hope.

God, may they be open to my plight. Help me communicate my need, my heart. Help them hear me.

The town appeared before her. She pulled on the horse's reins to slow the animal. Within moments, she was on the main streets of town. Should she yell for help? That seemed drastic. So were her circumstances.

Sliding from the horse, she rushed in front of the animal and toward the people gathered in front of the General Store.

"Help! Help me! My son is missing!"

The women stared at her. How could she expect anything different? She must seem mad to them.

"Please. His name is Samuel." She turned to a couple passing to her other side. "He's only five."

There were tears in her eyes, but she didn't care. Why wouldn't these people help her?

She remained there, in the middle of the street, continuing to call for help.

A hand touched her arm. She whirled around and came face to face with Reverend Mason.

"Mrs. Miller, you say your son is missing?"

Amanda wiped at her face. "Yes, sir. Since sometime last night."

He took her arm and led her out of the street and off toward the side, in front of the telegraph office. "We must search for him, of course."

Amanda let out a breath. At last, help.

The Reverend directed her to a nearby bench.

She sat.

"Give me an hour to round up a few men to go looking for him."

"An hour?" The words shot out of her mouth before she could stop them.

"These things take time."

She looked down at her hands. "Yes, of course. Perhaps I can ask around. Maybe someone has seen him." Amanda started to rise.

The preacher placed a hand on her shoulder and pressed her to sit again. "I think it's best we not make any more spectacles."

Spectacles? Is that what he thought was important? That she not make a spectacle? Her son was lost, perhaps injured or worse, and he was talking to her about spectacles?

Brushing his hand off her shoulder, she stood. "Reverend, I will do what I must, so help me God, to find my son safe and sound. Whatever it takes."

Reverend Mason's eyes widened. He opened his mouth, but no sound came forth.

A man stepped up from behind the preacher. Where had he come from?

"Are you the lady looking for a little boy?

Amanda stepped around the Reverend. "Yes. Yes, I am."

"That rancher, Mr. Miller, brought an injured boy in to see the doctor might near a half hour ago."

Her heart lurched. It had to be Samuel! Brandon had found him. And he was injured? But alive. He was alive!

She lifted her skirt and ran toward the clinic, stopping briefly to thank the man who had brought her the news.

The clinic sat on the opposite side of the main stretch from where she was, and it seemed an eternity until she stood at the door that would lead to her son.

Drawing in a breath, she stilled herself. What kind of injuries would she see? What state would he be in? Was she truly prepared to see what was behind this door?

Whatever it would be, was better than not knowing. Yet she closed her eyes, hoping to draw strength from her newfound source.

Father, You made Samuel. You love Samuel. You hold his future. Still my heart. Help me to trust.

Placing a hand on the door's latch she released it and stepped in.

The examination table was across the room. Samuel lay on it, but all she could see was his bushy hair. Brandon stood to one side, holding Samuel's hand. The doctor was on the other side, leaning over Samuel's lower limbs. Both men looked over at the intrusion.

Brandon recovered the quickest. He held his free hand out to her, curving his fingers. Was he inviting her toward himself?

She couldn't. Why wasn't Samuel moving? Was he all right? Was he…?

Her eyes met Brandon's. There was warmth there. If Samuel was in a dire situation, he would not be so calm. With tentative steps, she closed the distance between them. Reaching out her hand, she slid it into Brandon's waiting one. He drew her to his side.

Amanda pressed her face to his shoulder as she clung to his shirt. Dare she look at her son? Confirm once and for all his state of being? For once it was known, it could not be unknown.

Brandon's lips were near her ear. "It is well."

She looked up at him. His eyes were deep, honest. And his face showed no sign of tension.

Turning her head, she gazed upon her son's body. He was still. No sign of life came from him. His eyes were closed and he was laid out as if in death. Gripping Brandon's arm even tighter, she drew in a sharp breath.

"He is only sleeping." The doctor caught her eyes. "I had him breathe something to help him rest while I set his leg."

Only then did Amanda's gaze travel to Samuel's lower extremities. The leg the doctor held was oddly off-angle. And, as she watched, the doctor maneuvered it this way and that, in an unnatural way.

She opened her mouth to entreat him to stop. But Brandon's hand fell heavy on her shoulder.

"It must be done," was all he said.

She glanced down at Brandon's other hand, still holding Samuel's.

Why? Her son was not aware of this gesture. Why then would Brandon bother? Amanda looked up into Brandon's face.

"He asked me to." The words were not much more than a whisper. "And I told him I wouldn't leave his side."

A tear fell down the side of Amanda's face at the tenderness of Brandon's words toward her son. Had they truly had such an interaction? Did Brandon care so much for Samuel and his feelings?

She saw only truth in his eyes.

Perhaps there was hope for the three of them after all.

⁂

Brandon looked back in the wagon at Amanda, cradling Samuel's torso in her lap. How he wished he could hurry the horse along, make it to the ranch before Samuel might awaken. But he dared not risk damaging the recently set bones in his leg. They would get there. All in good time.

He faced forward again, eyeing the path ahead, looking for bumps and ruts along the way. It would be impossible to avoid them all. Thank God Samuel was still out. *Please keep him that way, Lord.*

It seemed to take forever before he spotted his homestead in the distance. And even longer still until it was close enough for him to make out Cook on the porch.

She rushed out to meet the borrowed wagon as it came to a halt. "Mr. Brandon, I have been so terribly worried! I wish you could have sent word sooner. And then it's been so long since I heard anything. I feared the worst…"

Cook's voice droned on as Brandon jumped down and circled around the wagon to the back. She remained close behind.

Brandon met Amanda's gaze.

Her glassy eyes stared back at him. Was she not handling this well? Could he blame her?

Holding his arms out, he reached for Samuel's small form.

Amanda pressed a kiss to her son's brow before lifting him and scooting across the bed of the short wagon toward Brandon. Then she laid Samuel in his arms.

If it were possible, Brandon would have taken her in his arms as well, bear her burdens as well. It wasn't possible. Some things she had to do on her own.

She slid off the back of the wagon and followed close behind as he moved toward the house.

Cook continued to chatter on, and he all but ignored her. He didn't have it in him to cater to her questions and emotions. There were too many within him.

Amanda maneuvered around him to open doors as need be on the short walk to Samuel's room.

"Please," she spoke up. "Put him in my room."

He caught her eyes.

"There is the issue of the trunk still blocking his door."

Brandon hadn't considered that. He nodded. And stepped further down the hall, allowing her to open the door to her bedroom.

Amanda moved in first, pulling the quilt and sheet down. Brandon set Samuel in the prepared space, making sure to stretch out his splinted leg, giving it proper space. Then, stepping between him and the bed, Amanda drew the covers up over Samuel's small body. She took a moment to run a hand across his forehead, brushing the hair out of his face.

"That hair. I should have cut it long before now." Her voice caught.

He put a hand on her shoulder. "It's all right."

"But he needed me. And I pushed him away." It was evident from her voice that she was crying.

Brandon gently took her arm and led her out into the hall. Then turned her to look at him.

She kept her face angled to the side.

"You know that's not true."

Amanda bit at her lip.

He took her chin with his fingers and turned her features toward his. "This is not your fault."

She closed her eyes. "I just can't seem to make myself believe that." Then her eyes were on his again. Piercing, seeking, hoping.

He searched those hazel orbs, wanting to reassure her with his love. So very much. "Then trust me."

Her eyes widened slightly but for a moment.

"Trust that God has a plan." Why had he said that? Surely it would cause her to pull back now.

Instead, she swallowed and whispered, "I do. I know He does."

His brows went up.

"He has shown me things. Things I never knew. Things that have changed me." Her face seemed to light up as she spoke, despite her sorrow, despite her doubts, despite her circumstances. It had to be God's hand in her life.

He raised a hand to cup her face. "And what are you left with?"

"Light. And love. For me. For you. For us."

Truly his heart would explode. Had God reached down and done this thing in her life?

Amanda reached forth and touch his cheek. Was there moisture on his face?

His lips found hers.

Her arms wrapped around his neck as his encircled her, pulling her to his chest. This was bliss.

Amanda snuggled closer to Samuel. She opened her eyes and placed a hand on his chest, once more reassuring herself that he was indeed alive. How long would he sleep?

"I'm keeping watch." Brandon's voice sounded from across the bed. He sat in a chair on the opposite side of Samuel. "You rest. I'll wake you if anything changes."

"You must be exhausted." She laid her head back on the pillow, but did not close her eyes, keeping them on Brandon.

He shook his head and smiled. "It's nothing I wouldn't be doing out on the trail."

The trail. The drive he would be on, if it weren't for Samuel.

She rolled onto her back, staring up at the ceiling. What would he do when Samuel awoke? Could she expect him to stay? That would be selfish. He needed to join his men. Their futures depended on it. An ache settled in her chest. Just the thought of being without him left an emptiness in her.

"You don't look like you're sleeping. Looks like you're thinking," Brandon whispered. "And that can only mean trouble."

She offered him a smile. He was so handsome in the flickering light of the lantern, his fine, crafted features highlighted. It was as if she could reach out and draw his features with her finger, painting with shadows and hues the way the flame did.

"Will you leave when Samuel wakes?"

Brandon's face fell. "What?" His hurt was almost palpable. Did he presume she thought he would abandon her and escape responsibility?

"When we know all is well, will you ride after your team? Try to join them on the drive?" Did he understand now? She did not mean to insult him, but simply to prepare herself for the inevitable.

His features remained set. He stared at her blankly.

What was he thinking? Did she offend him?

Brandon leaned on the side of the bed, propping himself up on his elbows. "How can you think that? I wouldn't leave you. We're a team in this. And we'll make it through this. The three of us. Together." He took Samuel's hand in his and reached for hers.

Her heart did a flip-flop. She lifted her hand to join his.

And Samuel stirred.

Amanda's eyes were on her son. She leaned up in the bed, on her knees in a moment.

Samuel shifted for several moments, grunting and groaning before his eyes opened. He blinked several times. Was he not certain of his surroundings?

"Mama? Where are you? Where am I?"

Amanda let out a little cry. "Samuel, you are home. With me. I'm here."

Samuel grimaced. The doctor had said he would be in a great deal of pain. Then he opened his mouth, but Amanda cut him off.

"Don't try to talk too much. Rest yourself."

"But, where is—" He continued to blink as if his vision was still clearing.

"Uncle Owen is on the cattle drive. I'm sorry. He won't be back for a couple of weeks."

"No," he insisted. "Where is Mr. Brandon?"

Amanda looked over at Brandon.

He pulled Samuel's hand closer to his chest. "I'm here, too. I told you I would be. The whole time."

Samuel smiled.

"You did it. And you were so brave."

Amanda found herself tearing up again. Only these were not sad tears or angry tears or frustrated tears or hurt tears or any of the other kinds of tears she had cried in this house. These were tears of joy. Pure joy.

Brandon sat on the porch. It had become his routine. Or his obsession. Three weeks had come and gone since the group headed out on the trail. And there had been no sign of them. No word.

What was there for Brandon but to fear the worst? One of many scenarios played out in his mind. The ranch hands and the hired hands decided together to split the money and left Uncle Owen for dead somewhere along the way.

Or, giving his ranch hands the benefit of the doubt, perhaps they were overpowered in the night and the hired hands ran off with the money, leaving his men with no horses.

Either way, all was forfeit. The only thing to be determined was whether or not Uncle Owen was lost to him. That hurt more than the lost money and the loss of the ranch.

Since about the two-and-a-half week mark, Cook had become fairly insufferable to live with. She ranted and raved about how they could have let Uncle Owen go. As if Brandon didn't feel the full force of that all on his own.

The only comfort he felt was that Amanda was by his side. And would be, come what may. They would be able to start a new life perhaps. Even if they had to do it from nothing. And without Uncle Owen.

A wet nose rubbed his hand. He looked down. Daisy. That dog had caused her share of trouble. She showed up a few days after everything calmed down. Her coat was mangled in places like she'd tangled with a wild animal, but she recovered just fine.

Brandon stood; his heavy heart weighed on him as he moved toward the door to the house. As he reached for the latch, it moved and the door opened.

Amanda stepped outside.

He moved, giving her room.

"I was looking for you." She smiled at him.

"I thought I might head inside for another cup of coffee."

"You and your coffee," she grunted. Sliding a hand over his arm, she led him back to the nearby bench.

He sat and pulled her to his side, pressing a kiss to her hair.

They sat in silence for a moment, watching the horizon.

She broke the silence. "Do you think it will be today?"

Brandon felt her eyes on him, but he kept his trained on the road. "Could be."

He didn't believe they would truly come. Not after all this time. No need to tell her that.

Another silence befell them.

Then she took his hand and shifted her body to angle toward him. "I have something wonderful to tell you."

"Good news?" He set his cup down and turned to face her as well. "Please, do share."

She gazed into his eyes. What was she looking for? Her demeanor dropped. Brows furrowed.

"What? What is it?"

"I don't know." Amanda looked off into the yard. "All of a sudden, I'm not so sure."

He took her other hand in his. "Sweetheart, you can tell me anything."

She licked her lips. "It's just..."

Brandon touched her face. "What?"

"When my mom had me, it was such a hardship on my father. He struggled just for us to survive. And I don't want this baby to be a source of sadness—"

He held up a hand. "Wait. What? This baby?"

Amanda put a hand over her mouth. A bit too late.

"Are you...?"

She nodded.

Brandon's body filled with such happiness, he was certain he could not contain it. He pulled her to himself. "That's...that is wonderful news! We're going to have a baby."

But Amanda didn't respond. Was he holding her too tightly? He pulled back.

"Are you...are you all right? Did I hurt you? Or the baby?"

She shook her head. But the smile on her face was small. A token.

"Sweetheart, you have made me so happy. You cannot know how much. Can I...?" He tentatively reached for her abdomen, which didn't look any different to him.

"It is early yet, but you can if you'd like." She moved her arms out of the way.

He pressed his hands to the lower portion of her stomach. Nothing. But it did not take away one bit of his happiness.

When he met her eyes again, however, she seemed even more bothered.

"Am I...is this not all right?"

"It's fine," she insisted.

"Then what is it?"

Amanda drew in a breath. "I don't want this child to be a burden. Here we are, about to lose the ranch. Don't think I don't know it. I see the way you look at those hills. They're not coming."

Brandon pulled her closer. "Do not think that way. This child is a gift."

"You say that now. I have seen struggle. I know what it looks like. The pain it brings."

"We can start anew. I have the money left from my nest egg. And I am not friendless. I have a mother and a sister who could help us. And do not forget that God will provide all that we need."

Amanda let out a ragged breath. "There's a lot I need to learn about faith."

Brandon smiled and kissed her forehead as he pulled her to rest her head on his chest. "As long as we're together and God is sustaining us, we have nothing to fear."

As he held his wife, Brandon gazed out at the horizon once more. The future never looked more uncertain. Or more bright.

Just then, on the edge most parts of his ability to see in the distance. A group of horses, a wagon, and a whole lot of dust was headed straight toward them.

EPILOGUE

Amanda watched as Samuel ran ahead into the churchyard. He had the slightest limp in his right leg. Would she even notice if she hadn't been looking for it?

Brandon moved behind her as she chased the growing boy toward the side of the church. They had come here for Samuel's benefit, after all. It had been Brandon's idea, but Samuel was the one who truly needed the trip. Perhaps it was partly for her, too.

She hadn't been to this spot since that day so long ago. Had it truly been two years? Much had happened. Growing pains, blessings, healing…there were many names for it. But on this side of it, she knew it had been God's hand.

God had blessed them richly. The ranch had been saved. That sly Mr. Perkins had been caught defrauding his customers and was locked away. And they had indeed never heard from Kid Antrim, now better known as Billy the Kid, ever again.

"Careful of the posts!" Amanda called out.

It was unnecessary. Samuel knew quite well how to scale a fence. Especially one so short.

"Would you wait for us?" She let out a frustrated sigh. But it was mostly put on.

Samuel did pause. Turning around, he waved an arm. Were they not coming fast enough for him?

Amanda picked up her pace and took Samuel's hand as he picked up step again.

"Which one is it, Ma?"

At some point in this last year, he became too old to call her 'Mama.' Now it was just 'Ma.' Just one more sign he was growing up.

"Over here." She tugged at his hand and directed him toward the far end of the fenced-in area, farthest away from the church.

They came to a halt in front of a carved stone. Samuel got on his knees in front of it. "Jedidiah Marcus Haynes." He read.

Amanda stayed back, but near. She folded her arms across her chest. This was where it had all started. The wind whipped as if whispering reminders of the day. Were there voices on the wind as she imagined?

"Pa, I came to ask you something." Samuel took his hat off. "And 'cause there's someone I want you to meet."

Brandon came alongside Amanda, shifting Louise to his opposite hip and putting his arm closest to Amanda around her.

"That's my new sister," Samuel said. "But that's not who I wanted you to meet." He looked at Amanda and then leaned in close to the stone and said in a lower tone. "She's a lot of trouble."

"I wanted you to meet Mr. Miller." Samuel indicated Brandon behind him.

Brandon's eyebrows shot up then he pulled his hand out from behind Amanda and did a little wave.

When Samuel turned back to the stone, Amanda shook her head. What boys she had!

"And I wanted to ask, Pa…" Samuel paused. "If you had a problem if I call him 'Pa' now."

Brandon's eyes widened and he looked at Amanda. He turned toward Samuel and opened his mouth, but Amanda put a hand on his arm and shook her head.

Samuel sat for a while. Then he spun and looked at Brandon and

Amanda.

"What is it?" Amanda found her voice.

A smile broke out on Samuel's face. "He doesn't seem to mind." Samuel stood and walked over to Brandon. "What do you think? Would it be all right if I called you 'Pa'?"

Brandon passed Louise to Amanda and crouched down until he was eye level with Samuel. "I think I'd like that very much."

Amanda hugged her wriggling baby girl to herself to keep the tears from coming. God was so good to her. After all this time, He had knit her family together. The best was surely yet to come.

AUTHOR'S NOTE

Hey! I love writing clean Historical Romance, though as much as it can be fun, it has it's moments of challenge. I love finding a marriage between a fictional story woven with an acutal, historical event. That, I feel, makes my stories feel authentic in a way. Gives the sense of a real place and time in history. For me as much as for my reader friends.

For *A Convenient Risk*, I wanted a historical event in southeastern Arizona. And I had a feeling I wanted to connect it to an American outlaw. Billy the Kid seemed to fit the bill and I was thrilled when my research proved it to be so.

Born Henry McCarty, he was only 14 when he was orphaned. Early in his life, before his "career" as a gunslinger and criminal, he worked at well known Henry Hooker's ranch in southeast Arizona Territory. There he met some "not so great" characters that lived in the area. Horse theivery earned him the name "Kid Antrim" (due to his youthful looks).

The incident referred to in the novel occurred in the village of Bonita. Antrim and a blacksmith got into an argument that ended in a physical struggle. In the end, Antrim shot the blacksmith (and the man died the next day). After fleeing, and being caught by the local justice of the peace, he was detained at Camp Grant. But, as mentioned in the story, he escaped.

What is known after his slip from justice is that he rode toward New Mexico Territory, had his horse taken by Apache, and walked many miles to the nearest sign of civilization. So, while the version of the events following his escape in this novel are not founded in fact and, in truth, were not likely to have happened, they make for good fiction.

He went on to later be known better as "Billy the Kid," kill more men, evade capture, and give lawmen the slip in escape yet again. The real stories surrounding this historical figure are truly wild.

CHAPTER ONE

It's In The Air

AMANDA MILLER TIED another red ribbon into a bow on the fireplace mantle. Hopefully she was nearing the end. As much as she loved decorating, it could become tedious.

Hands slid around her waist, and she was pulled against a strong chest. Her husband's masculine scent filled her nostrils, and she leaned into him. How had she become so blessed?

He planted a kiss to the side of her face. "Any chance we can slip away?"

She turned her head to peer at him. Was he serious?

A playful gleam in his eye answered her unspoken question.

Her lips tugged upward. How she loved this man! Laying hands atop his on her stomach, she relished the feel of him. His strong arms and secure hands were well known to her. Worked by ranch life, they were capable and calloused. Yet gentle as well.

"Momma," a little voice called from across the room.

Pulled from her reverie, Amanda's attention fixed on the small girl toddling toward them.

Reluctantly, she pulled free of Brandon's embrace and, squatting, put arms out to receive the girl. "That's it, come to Momma."

"Momma."

It didn't matter that Louise said the word a million times a day; it was glorious.

A grin broke out across the child's face, creating dimples in her chubby cheeks.

The wriggling bundle, teetering with every step, somehow made it to Amanda's outstretched hands before falling.

She lifted her daughter, swinging her into the air and kissing the baby-fine skin. When she stopped, she caught Brandon's eye.

"I see you've forgiven her for saying 'Daddy' first." He reached forth a hand for Louise to capture it.

She did, pulling at his fingers.

"I don't know what you're talking about." Amanda spoke to Brandon, but she looked at Louise and spoke in a sing-song voice. "Do we, Louise Ann? We don't know what Daddy is saying."

"Oh, Louise knows good and well."

The child grinned and pulled two of Brandon's fingers into her mouth.

He jerked them back with a catch in his breath.

"Oh, no!" Amanda became instantly concerned. "Did she bite you?"

Brandon looked at his hand and nodded. "It's not so bad."

"I'm sorry. I think she has teeth coming in. She's been biting everything."

His brows furrowed, and he let out a concerned grunt.

"Yesterday, Samuel brought Daisy closer so Louise could pet her. And what we thought was going to be a kiss from Louise turned out to be an attempt to bite the poor dog's ear."

A chuckle escaped Brandon. Was it something to laugh about?

"It wasn't funny." She widened her eyes. "The dog could have been hurt."

He cleared his throat and tightened his mouth. "No, of course."

Amanda shifted Louise to her other hip. "I don't want her to become a biter."

Brandon furrowed his brows and let out a long breath.

Amanda fingered the curls in the child's soft hair.

"Let's not jump to that while she is still teething. But we *can* watch out and make sure she doesn't hurt anyone."

Was that truly all they could do? What more would she suggest?

Perhaps Brandon was right.

"After all, she comes by that feistiness pretty honest. It's one of her mother's more…intriguing qualities." His voice was husky as he put an arm around her, drawing her near.

Amanda's head cleared of all but him. She was helpless when he spoke to her like this.

He pressed a kiss to her forehead, his breath lingering on her skin.

The door opened, and Louise wriggled for freedom, but Amanda didn't let her escape.

"Aw, Ma, do ya have to?"

Amanda spun toward Samuel. Where had he been? Shouldn't he have been helping her with the decorations? She opened her mouth.

"Did you finish with the horses?" Brandon's chest vibrated as he spoke.

The horses? What did Brandon have Samuel doing with the horses?

"Sure did." Samuel grinned.

Amanda clamped her mouth shut. She would not disrespect Brandon in front of her son, but this was not over.

"Good. I think Cutie and Slim are going fishing."

Samuel's eyes lit up. His gaze shifted toward Amanda.

"Go on." She pulled away from Brandon and set Louise on the floor with her blocks. "You don't want to miss them."

A clapping of the door on its hinges was his only response.

Standing, she eyed Brandon, brow raised.

He tilted his head. "What?"

"You have him working with the horses?"

"It's good for him."

"That's what you said about mucking stalls."

"Was I wrong?"

Amanda crossed her arms. Dare she concede? Could she not? Why did she want to keep her boy close to her skirts? Why must Brandon constantly be pushing him further away?

Reaching out, he pulled her toward his chest. "You know I'm right."

She looked away and bit at her lip. "Maybe."

He hooked her chin with a finger. "Probably."

Her lips twinged at the edges. She fought the smile. "Don't push it."

His mouth curved upward, but his brown eyes rested on her lips. "I might just take the risk." Leaning forward, he pressed his lips to hers.

Would she ever become numb to this feeling? This excitement, this heat coursing through her? Or would his kisses thrill her for as long as they both should live?

She hoped so.

His arms wrapped around her back, and he tilted his head to deepen the contact.

But after a few moments of bliss, she pulled back.

Brandon traced a finger down the side of her face. "Is it time for Louise's nap?"

If only...

No, she couldn't get distracted.

"I'm afraid not. And I need to talk to you." She drew farther back.

"Oh?" He watched her every movement.

She glanced at Louise. Had she caught hold of something dangerous? There was no end to the child's mischief.

The small girl sat where Amanda had set her. For once.

Amanda reached for the box of ornaments, picking it up and, moving toward the dining space, placing it on the table.

"Everything all right?" Brandon called from where he had remained.

She pushed her hair back and sighed. How to broach the subject? Why was she so nervous? Couldn't she tell Brandon anything?

She turned toward him and leaned against the table.

"I know that look." His brows furrowed.

What look? How did she look? Did her features display her worry? Her trepidation? It would be best to just be out with it.

Drawing in a deep breath, she closed her eyes briefly and then met his gaze. "Cook and Uncle Owen won't be coming for Christmas."

"Oh." He set his hands on his hips. "That's not at all what I expected. But it is their first Christmas as man and wife."

Amanda nodded.

"But that can't be what has you so worried." He crossed the room, closing the distance between them.

She chewed on her lip.

"What is it?" His eyes were caring. Concerned.

Guilt filled her. She had to tell him.

"Are you nervous about making the big meal alone?"

Her eyes widened. That had not occurred to her.

"Oh, no." He gently clasped her arms. "Forget I said that. I'll help. Anyway I can."

She waved a hand between them. It wouldn't be easy, but she would manage. "It's not that."

"Then what is it?" He rubbed his larger hands along her upper arms.

"A letter came."

"A letter?"

She reached into the pocket of her apron and pulled out the lightly crinkled envelope. "From your parents."

Brandon's jaw clamped shut. She watched as the muscles twitched.

How long had it been since he had heard from his parents? Years? Decades? And all of a sudden a letter comes? Why now?

"When?"

"About two hours ago. While you were…"

He nodded. "Out with the cattle."

She searched his face, holding the envelope between them, ready for him to take it.

But he just stared at it.

"Did you read it?" His eyes met hers, and there was a darkness to their depths she had not seen in a long time.

"No." She pushed the word out.

His hands on her arms had grown limp.

Should she insist he take the letter? Or offer to read it for him? Was this something *he* needed to do?

Louise let out a cry.

Amanda looked in her direction. There was a block in her hand that was well wet.

Louise broke out in fierce tears.

Had she been chewing on the block and hurt her gums? Or bitten her finger by accident?

Amanda glanced at Brandon, pushing the letter toward him. She could no longer give him time to think.

Brandon stood, holding out his hand with the envelope.

She rushed to Louise and picked her up. The child immediately snuggled into Amanda's chest, her cries now muffled by Amanda's shoulder.

Amanda rubbed her back. "It's all right, sweet girl."

As the crying let up, she shifted the child to her hip and examined her fingers.

"What happened? Did you bite your finger?"

Sure enough, there was a reddened place on the forefinger of her right hand.

"Oh, my baby!" Amanda put a light kiss on the tiny finger. "There. All better."

Louise looked at her finger and then at Amanda. Her cries waned as if she wasn't sure what to do. But they soon vanished as the small girl stuck her finger toward Amanda's mouth again.

"Momma kiss."

Amanda grabbed her little hand and pressed several kisses to the finger. "Yes, Momma kiss it. Make it all better."

Louise giggled.

Then Louise stuck her hand in the direction of the dining room. "Daddy kiss!"

Amanda spun toward Brandon.

He stood just as she had left him, staring at the unopened letter.

She moved toward him. Drawing close, she put a hand on his shoulder. "Do you need some time alone?"

Shaking his head, he met her gaze. "No, I need you."

What could she do? What could she offer him? She stopped herself. That was the old Amanda. He needed her support. Her love.

"And I am right here with you."

He nodded.

She reached for a dining chair and pulled it out.

Brandon all but fell into it.

Grabbing for the chair next to him, she sat with Louise on her lap. His eyes met hers, and she nodded.

He slid a finger under the flap and tore through the seal.

Freeing a hand, she squeezed his arm in reassurance.

Pulling the papers free, he unfolded them. His eyes drifted over the writing.

He let out a long breath.

"It's not possible."

⁂

Brandon pulled back on the reins, causing Candy to slow.

He watched the cattle shift into the northern pasture. But his thoughts were not on the animals. Not truly.

They were on that letter.

His parents had never written him. He had not heard a word from them since he left Richmond. And he had never looked back. Well, not often.

Now. They chose now.

Why?

His life was good. Truly good.

He had a thriving ranch, a wonderful family, and an amazing marriage that he never would have anticipated being so good.

Now this.

And it was only the beginning.

For they would be here in a week.

It had been many years since Brandon had reconciled himself to the fact that he quite possibly would never see his mother and father again. He had mourned that loss.

Having to revisit it was…uncomfortable at the very least.

But there was nothing for it. They were coming, and he could do nothing to prevent it.

Had they arranged it this way?

He wagered so.

Their letter arrived one day too late to send a telegram to stop them from starting their journey.

Would he have stopped them?

He didn't know.

Perhaps he should be thankful he didn't have that decision to make. Yet he wasn't.

"Boss?" a loud voice called to him.

Brandon jerked his head in the direction of the sound.

Cutie rode toward him.

"Yeah?"

The ranch hand slowed his own horse as he approached. "Did you want us to move the second herd to the back pasture?"

"Sure."

Cutie shifted. Almost as if he were uncertain about his next move.

Brandon didn't have time for this. "You need something?"

The ranch hand frowned.

Perhaps he was harsher than he'd intended.

"Sorry, Cutie. I'm just…my thoughts are elsewhere today."

Cutie nodded.

"Was there something you wanted to ask?"

"It's just that…well, me and the boys were kind of hoping that…the thing is…"

"Saints alive, spit it out!"

Cutie's face colored, and Brandon regretted snapping again.

"There's a Christmas dance in town next week. And we were hoping you might see fit to let us go."

A dance? Was that all? Brandon let out a laugh. "That's it? You fellas all want the evening off?"

Cutie shrugged, his color deepening. "Yeah."

Brandon slapped his thigh. "Go ahead. Just don't have too much fun." He gave his ranch hand a wink.

"'Course not." One side of Cutie's mouth quirked upward. With that, he turned his mount, steering the painted mare toward the far pasture.

A Christmas dance. Brandon gazed toward the house.

Amanda was in the yard chasing Louise. They both laughed. Not only could he see it, Louise's shrieks were audible, even at this distance.

Should he take Amanda to that dance? It had been a while since he'd made such an overture.

Perhaps Cook and Uncle Owen could mind Louise and Samuel.

But then, his parents would be here.

How might that change things?

Oh, but how…

The sounds of Louise's giggles entranced Amanda. She would never tire of that music. And to know that it was her big brother who brought out such delight…such joy to a momma's heart.

Even though her children were in another room, separated by a wall, nothing could disguise their playful engagement.

"Children truly are a gift from the Lord."

Amanda faced the older woman kneading dough. "Yes. They are."

"When will we hear more little feet around here?"

Her face warmed. She reached toward her bowl of beans for the next one. Gripping it firmly, she snapped it.

Cook's stifled laughter shook her frame.

Amanda threw a bean at her.

"You best not make a mess in my kitchen." Cook's face became stern.

Had she upset the woman? She looked more closely into the features she had come to know so well.

There was a glint in Cook's eye that was impossible to miss.

Amanda grinned.

Cook winked and focused on her work, and began humming.

There were so many things Amanda had come to enjoy about her life. These times with Cook, whether they were confiding in each other, in lively conversation, or companionable silence at work, were definitely one of them.

A few minutes passed as they continued on task, preparing food for the evening meal.

Amanda snuck a peek at Cook. What did she know of Brandon's past? Of his parents? Dare Amanda ask? How to broach the subject?

Cook smiled and looked at Amanda. "I think Louise is going to nap well today."

"Hope so." A yawn escaped.

Cook quirked an eyebrow. "Something keeping you up at night?"

Amanda furrowed her brows. "Not what you think."

"Oh?"

Tossing another bean in the pot, Amanda leaned forward and thrust out her response. "No."

"Is Louise getting up at night again?" Cooks features rearranged into something akin to sympathy.

Amanda shook her head.

"Well, don't keep me guessing, child!"

Looking at her for a moment, Amanda gauged the older woman's reaction.

Cook paused and set her full attention on Amanda.

"Has Brandon not told you?" She narrowed her eyes.

"Told me what?"

Amanda quirked a brow. Brandon told Uncle Owen and Cook everything. How had they not heard about the letter?

"I don't like that look," the older woman warned, rising. "You best tell me now, or I'll march out to that field and drag that husband of yours in here."

Amanda stuck an arm out. Was Cook not speaking in jest? Did she truly not know? "I'll tell you."

Cook sat, mumbling. Something about yanking teeth. She crossed her arms and leveled her gaze on Amanda. Would she not return to her work?

Amanda swallowed. She certainly did not intend to put so much pressure on the moment. Sucking in a breath, she pressed on. "Brandon received a letter."

Cook's expression did not change.

"From his parents."

Still no visible reaction.

"And they are coming for Christmas. They'll be here in four days."

"Is that all?" Cook uncrossed her arms and set her hands back to forming the bread.

"All? You speak as though they correspond regularly."

Cook's hazel eyes were on hers again. She opened her mouth and then closed it. Did she have something to add?

Amanda wiped her hands on her apron. "What? Do you know something?"

"No." Cook stood, taking the loaf pan to the oven.

Then Amanda was presented with the woman's back as she opened and closed the small door.

Curious. Very curious.

When she didn't turn again, Amanda pursed her lips. Something wasn't right here.

"What do you know?"

Cook spun, wringing her hands in a cloth. "Nothing."

"Cook…" Were they not better friends than this?

The woman scanned the kitchen, looking everywhere but at Amanda.

"All right, all right! I can't do it." She stepped back to where she and Amanda had been settled. Flopping into the chair, she pointed a finger in Amanda's face. "But you best not breathe a word of this."

Amanda nodded.

"We got a letter about a month ago."

"You…!"

Cook put her hands up. "Shhh!"

Amanda lowered her voice. "A month ago?"

"Yes."

"Do you know why now? After all this time?"

Cook shrugged, sitting back. "Mrs. Miller didn't say. Maybe it's time. People change as they age. The things that once seemed so important aren't so important anymore."

Amanda nodded. This had occurred to her, too. And she prayed it would be so. That his father was prepared to reconcile.

"Lord knows, it's about time those stubborn men put their wills to the side."

"What do you mean?" Amanda rose and set the beans on the counter.

"Brandon's father has his part in this, that's for sure. But you didn't think it was all him, did you?"

What was she saying? That there was more to Brandon's role in the falling out than he had shared? "I suppose I didn't think too much about it," she lied.

Cook shot her a look.

"All I know is what Brandon has told me."

"There are two sides to every story, you know."

"I suppose." What had Brandon left out? Dare she ask him? But she had promised Cook she wouldn't share. How else would she bring it up?

Cook slapped her knees. "I'd best get started on the ham."

Amanda nodded. "I need to check on Louise. No doubt it's time for that nap."

Sweeping past Amanda, Cook began her routine dance around the kitchen. That was Amanda's cue to get out of her way. She slipped from the room and stepped into the great room to find both Samuel and Louise asleep on the floor.

She folded her arms in front of her. If only life could always be so simple.

<hr />

Brandon scuffed the bottoms of his boots against the wooden planks that made up the walkway. And he continued to wait. He stared down the main stretch into town and watched.

The town was decked out in greenery, highlighted here and there by red ribbons. They had done their part to make everything festive. Still, the spirit of the season must have missed him as it made its way further west.

He had yet to come across anything special enough to give Amanda. And he needed to find something fantastic. There was little doubt she would find the perfect gift for him. That must be her hidden talent—giving gifts.

Letting out a deep breath, he folded his arms in front of his chest and paced toward the telegraph office. There was a myriad of postings hung there.

His heart skipped a beat when he saw the wanted poster of Kid

Antrim. What was he calling himself now? Billy something… Oh yes, Billy the Kid. Brandon frowned at the drawing of the man whose visage still visited his darkest dreams.

Tearing his eyes away, he scanned the other writings. The most recent copy of the town gazette had an article about the upcoming Christmas dance, the event of the season. He had not yet spoken with Cook about minding Louise and Samuel that evening. What of his parents? Would they go to the dance? Or would they be insulted that Brandon had planned an evening away for him and Amanda?

He grumbled. There was no easy answer. His parents were fairly unknown to him now.

Moving back to the road, he glanced at the sun's position in the sky. Why had he arrived with so much time to spare? Had he been concerned the stage would come early? It never was. Perhaps, had he not come, it would have been today.

That was nonsense.

Still, he was left waiting.

Wasn't that all he had done these past five days since the letter arrived —wait?

None of the answers he sought would be forthcoming in the meantime. No, his parents, more likely, his father, was the key to all of it.

The tell-tale thundering piqued his senses. He turned his head to gaze down the strip of buildings, in the direction the coach would appear. How long would it be now? His heart beat wildly in his chest. Was he so nervous?

Moments later, the coach appeared, right on schedule, rounding the corner at the end of Main Street. The coachman pulled hard at the reins, and the horses slowed.

Brandon closed his eyes. *Lord, I don't know what to say. I don't know what to do. But here I am. May I be responsible with my words, with my actions. Give me strength.*

The coach stopped, surrounded by a cloud of dust.

Still, Brandon did not move. Could he?

Jumping down, the coachman reached for the latch. "Wharton City!" he yelled into the compartment before jerking the small door open.

A tall man with broad shoulders, a slender frame, and gray hair looked out. He was well-dressed in fine traveling clothes. Though he scanned the area, bushy brows furrowed, he soon descended the small step and reached in to assist the other passengers.

A young woman stepped out. And the next to appear was a face Brandon would never forget as long as he lived. Though age had salted her dark hair and caused her frame to sag slightly, her features were as kind as ever, her eyes as bright as he remembered—Mother.

Brandon let out a breath.

Once her feet touched the boards, she set her hand on the older man's arm. Was that?

The years had not been good to Father. His hair had grayed, but so had his features. They were set and grim. But just as Brandon remembered, he appeared generally displeased with everything around him.

They spoke to one another briefly, and Father motioned to the driver as the man pulled their things from the top of the coach.

Shouldn't Brandon help? To do that, he would need to step forward, make himself known. And his feet just wouldn't work.

Mother scanned the area, her mouth moving. What was she saying?

At last, her eyes landed on him, and she smiled. She reached for Father's arm and pulled at him, pointing in Brandon's direction.

Father's gaze leveled on Brandon. He scowled, but something passed in his eyes. Something Brandon wasn't sure he could identify.

Brandon wasn't quite certain how he got there, but he soon found himself standing in front of his parents.

"Brandon," Mother said, taking him in. "My, look at you." She opened her arms.

It was both awkward and easy to embrace her.

As he pulled back, he did not miss the unsteady half-smile on her face.

"You have changed." Father's voice was deep. His words did not sound like a compliment.

Brandon nodded. "We all have." His voice came out tight. Amanda wouldn't like that. It might very well be up to him to set the right tone.

Father's mouth became a thin line.

Silence fell between them. A tense silence.

Mother looked from Brandon to Father then back to Brandon. "Where shall we have them put our things?"

"I'll pull my cart around."

"I won't hear of it," Father said. His features were hard. "Did you not read the letter? We will stay at your town's hotel." His gaze drifted down the main stretch.

"Wharton City doesn't have a hotel."

Father's brows met. "Surely you must have something."

"There is a boarding house that serves as a sort of hotel."

"Then we shall inquire after—"

"But I insist that you stay in my home."

"Absolutely not. There cannot be enough room for—"

Heat flashed through Brandon. "Though I may not have a grand house, there is plenty of space for you both to stay there comfortably."

Father lowered his brows. Was he preparing another argument? He opened his mouth to speak.

Mother laid a hand on Father's arm and met Brandon's gaze. "We would be happy to stay at your home if you are certain we won't be a bother."

Brandon swallowed the words he wanted to speak. And instead said, "No, it won't be any trouble at all."

"But—" Father started.

Mother turned toward him.

Brandon could not see her face, as she now had her back to him. They spoke in hushed tones. He watched with wide eyes for a moment. Mother had never spoken against Father before. What was this new dynamic? Was he intruding?

He stepped to where the coachman had stacked the bags and trunks. "Which of these belong to Mr. and Mrs. Miller?"

The man quirked a brow at him. "All of it."

"All of it?" Brandon searched for the other passengers. "But what of the young lady who…and the…"

The driver shook his head.

"All of it."

A nod was his only answer.

Brandon pushed out a breath. "All right."

He looked back toward his parents.

They seemed to be having tense words. Father spoke less and less. Finally, he nodded.

Mother put a hand in the crook of Father's elbow and he led her to where Brandon stood with their things.

"We would be…honored to stay at your home," Father bit out.

Brandon attempted to disguise his surprise, but was perhaps unable to. His eyes widened, but he kept his mouth clamped shut. "Very well. I'll get my wagon."

He turned and moved off.

What kind of visit was he in for?

To read more of Amanda and Brandon's Christmas adventure, pick up a copy of

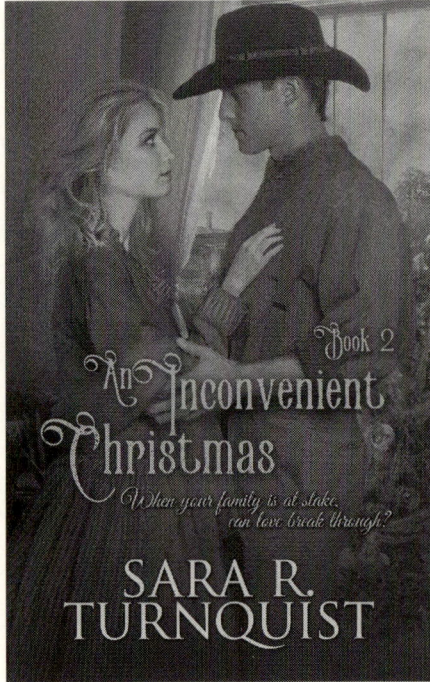

ACKNOWLEDGMENTS

There are so many things I am grateful for and so many people in my life who contribute in so many ways. It is just not possible to thank everyone who touches my life in a real way. But I want to take a moment and acknowledge the people whose contributions had a more direct impact on this book.

My editor, Julie Sherwood, you keep me honest. And make my work stronger. And my irreplaceable beta readers Christina Horton, Hillary Harvey, and Stacy Schoenwetter—without you three, I wouldn't be the writer I am today. Your encouragement and feedback are priceless to me. Hannah Conway, my writing mentor, pours not only craft into me, but time, attention, and friendship. Thank you. This book would not be as crisp and well-read if not for my critique group, whose thoughts are so valuable to me.

Cora Graphics, my cover artist, is just phenomenal. There is no other word to describe her. I am impressed by both her talent and how easy she is to work with.

My photographer, Rachel Bull, who makes this crazy hair look stylish, is also one of the most talented people I know.

For my sister, you make me want to be better. For my parents, you make me feel so good to have achieved this dream of writing. And for my husband and kids, you give me every reason to smile.

Last, but certainly not least, my readers, you give me a reason to keep writing.

Check out what else is available from Sara R. Turnquist

A Convenient Risk
An Inconvenient Christmas
A Less Convenient Path
A Convenient Escape
An Inconvenient Acquaintance
These Golden Years
A Less Convenient Arrangment

The Lady Bornekova
The Lady and the Hussites
The Lady and Her Champion
COMING SOON – *The Lady and Her Secret*

Leaving Waverly, a prequel novella
Hope in Cripple Creek
Christmas in Cripple Creek

<u>Stand Alone Books:</u>
The General's Wife
Off to War
Trail of Fears
Among the Pages

Sara resides with her family in Middle Tennessee and though she has enjoyed her career as a Zoo Educator, Sara's great love of the written word has always drawn her to write. An avid reader, she has been, for many years, what she terms a "closet writer." Her travels and love of history have inspired her to write Historical Fiction. Sara's debut novel, *The Lady Bornekova*, was greatly influenced by her time spent in the Czech Republic.

Web: SaraTurnquist.com
Twitter: @sarat1701
Facebook: AuthorSaraTurnquist

Sign up at SaraTurnquist.com/list to keep with the latest.

21013647R00151